Praise for *Nine Years*

'A truly captivating story with multiple layers that create a very dynamic and evocative experience. Every character adds so many elements to the story that by the time you finish one chapter to get an update on one of them you want to read the next one because you wonder what the others are up to.'
John, Goodreads

'The author's writing style is fluid and extremely easy to read. Clear and concise description made one read every word with enthusiastic ease.'
Sarah-Jane, Goodreads

'Her emotive language is so stunning and draws you in to each character.'
Claire, Goodreads

'I love the raw nature of how the author delivers the story.'
Tess, Goodreads

'Yep...it's one of them !!! - those books you just can't put down and are itching to see the continuum of... even demand it! Certainly captivating.'
Oli, Goodreads

'The emotion that runs through the whole book is so raw.'
Deanne, Goodreads

'An emotional, well plotted and character driven narrative.'
Anthony, Amazon

'Jessica describes so well, getting into even the tiniest detail.'
Thabiso, Goodreads

'I am so impressed with the fluidity of her writing and it was an enthralling read that found me not wanting to put the book down.'
Alex, Goodreads

'I think what struck me the most about this novel is how relatable it is. Not all of us have been through the exact same struggles that Sienna faces in the novel but we can all relate, on some level, to the pain of holding onto something so dear to you, even when it starts to destroy you as an individual.'
Beatrice, Amazon

'A wonderfully entertaining novel that captivated me from page one. The author's construction of the characters was very well done.'
Jeanne, Goodreads

'A passionate captivating story filled with love, heartache and wonder that will take you on a relatable journey enriched with twists and turns that will keep you guessing and asking for more.'
Ashley, Goodreads

'This story of new beginnings and leaving the past behind is worth reading.'
Rosemarie, Goodreads

Here I Stand

Here I Stand

Beneath the Clouds Series

JESSICA LEED

Here I Stand

First edition, November 2020
⌀ Hillford Press
Melbourne, Australia

www.jessleed.com

Editing: Dominic Wakeford
Interior formatting: Glen Sarco
Cover photo: Max Rovensky
Cover design: Alina Lubina

ISBN: 978-0-6486797-5-2 (eBook)
ISBN: 978-0-6486797-4-5 (Paperback)
ISBN: 978-0-6486797-3-8 (Hardcover)

For all the light we cannot see, the sun is stable, the clouds will flee.

Jessica Leed

One

Everything was all over the place.

Nothing was marked. Not a single box. Maybe that was the reason why there was an avalanche of anxiety closing in around her chest. The woman she knew was extremely organised. She sighed heavily and wedged her knees between the small space of carpet in her new apartment that wasn't engulfed with brown, cardboard boxes.

Just focus on one. One at a time.

She smoothed her hand over the lid sealed with thick tape, completely unmotivated to tear it open. She knew herself better these days to know that her lack of OCD wasn't the reason for her heart's flightiness. It wasn't even the unmarked boxes. It was everything else that led her to the very moment she found herself in. She never thought she would be doing this alone. But true to her deepest fears, here she was.

Starting over.

She would approach this as a new chapter. Starting over didn't have to be a bad thing. There was much to look forward to! Wasn't there?

She placed her feet either side of the box like a monkey from Madagascar, and with both hands aggressively tugged on the tape. Success. The thing completely peeled open, exposing the many books she had inside. There would have had to be about eleven or twelve more boxes filled with them. She was an avid reader, after all. It didn't matter that she didn't have a bookshelf of any kind to store them. Minor details. She would work it all out later.

Kind of like the rest of her life.

Come on, Sienna. Stop it. She took a breath out and stood to her feet. There were honestly boxes everywhere. This was overwhelming, but she had to be positive. She found a beautiful place, just a stone's throw away from her new school. She wouldn't have to worry about traffic again. That was a relief! And really, her place was almost double the size for almost half the price as her shoebox in Melbourne. This was fine. In fact, it was great.

Ting.

She shifted her eyes uneasily to the side. Already she could see his name lighting the screen. She curled her foot over the edge of the phone and watched it fling across the carpet, stopping short somewhere under the couch her dad recently assembled for her. Who would have thought IKEA would have such decent stuff? She had scored a three-seat charcoal leather sofa for under $600. That was unheard of. But up until this year so had an IKEA being in Aringdale. The little town wasn't so little anymore.

She glanced at her watch. It was just past seven. She was getting peckish. She opened her fridge door and smiled as her eyes landed on the vegetable lasagna sitting in the plastic container (compliments to IKEA) her mum had packed for her. No, she wasn't one of those adults that relied on their parents to look after her. She more saw it as "making up for lost time". There was something about old childhood meals that bonded a family. She now understood the reference from *MasterChef* that food was comforting. If it wasn't for these Sunday "cook in bulk and pass on to your troubled daughter" meals, she might have crawled under that couch and given in to what would have to be over fifty messages from her cheating ex.

She glanced over at the couch just in time to hear her phone make that *ting* sound again. Honestly, she was an idiot for not having blocked his number but something about his persistence made her feel like she held the power. And as volatile as that was, she liked it.

Back to the lasagna. She opened the container slightly and popped it into the microwave. She reached high, opening the cupboard doors, trying to find where she had put the plates. She finally found them in the last one and groaned to see that she had just stuffed the cardboard box up there and hadn't taken the time to unpack them. She rose to her tippy toes to take it down. She managed to edge it close enough for her to take hold of it with two hands when her phone started to ring. For some reason the vibration it made under that couch was enough to give her a fright with its amplified boom.

SMASH.

Just like that, all of the porcelain plates were in pieces. The box exploded open on its landing because she was stupid enough to have removed the tape when she stuffed it up there. She lost her balance and placed her foot down onto one of the shards of glass. She let out a little scream as she clutched her foot and quickly assessed the damage. There was something stuck into the side of her little toe. She began to feel lightheaded even though blood was something her feet were accustomed to, seeing as she had been a ballerina for most of her life.

In that moment the microwave timer went off and her phone started ringing again.

'Oh, give it a break,' she whimpered and hopped over to the lounge room to try and find the brush and shovel (courtesy of IKEA once again). She knocked over a glass of water sitting on the edge of the counter as she passed. Like the plates, she helplessly watched it smash into tiny shards on the kitchen floor.

'You've got to be kidding me!' she said even louder, almost scaring herself at how quickly she has lost it. What was *wrong* with her?

There was a knock at her door. She froze, feeling the blood rush to her head which only made her feel even more dizzy. She grabbed a sock from the couch and opened the door.

'Are you okay?'

A man, maybe in his late thirties, stood before her with a suspicious, yet amused look on his face. His eyebrows were lifted in an unnatural arch. Well actually, his left one was lifted a lot higher than his right.

Sienna took hold of the door frame and curled her foot up under her in a pointed position behind her, already feeling the blood seep its way through. This cut was bad. She needed to have a look at it.

'Oh fine! Yes, thank you.' She smiled brightly at the man,

not being able to turn her attention away from such an unusual eyebrow. It bore an uncanny resemblance to a caterpillar. She breathed in, feeling a wave of nausea sweep through her. Her foot was throbbing, bad.

The man seemed to sense that something was wrong and manoeuvred his head to peak into the apartment, kind of like an emu. Conveniently, the kitchen faced towards him, revealing the abstract display of smashed porcelain. The reminder for the microwave went off again just as her phone decided to ring in perfect unison with it. It sounded quite musical, actually.

The man chuckled and took a step back. 'I'll grab a broom'.

'Oh, no. It's just a little … accident … I've got it!' she responded a little too enthusiastically.

He nodded and shifted his attention to her foot. 'I'll grab a bandage, too.'

Damn.

She watched him dash off around the corner as she clutched her foot into her chest and let out a little whimper. Of course, it had to be a white sock. It looked like something from a crime scene the way the blood was spreading like wildfire, changing its colour like some sort of science experiment. By the time she looked around for something else he was back with a broom in hand as promised, and something strapped around his waist. She couldn't help but chuckle at what looked identical to the first aid kit she would wear during her many lunch duties as a teacher.

This guy was quirky.

'Which one do we tackle first?' The guy smiled and looked at the broom then patted the white plastic pouch with the giant red cross on it.

'A name might be a nice start, maybe?' She let out an awkward chuckle, stubbing her foot against the door frame as she did so. 'I'm Sienna,' she said, taking the reins. The pain in her face was enough for the man to unclip the first aid kit and reach inside.

He smiled at her. 'How on earth did you manage to do that to your foot, Sienna?' He looked like he didn't know whether to laugh or look concerned as he passed her an antiseptic spray and a really thick fabric band aid. It all looked very serious and professional. He pulled out a metallic looking tool.

Were those tweezers?

'Hey. No way, put that little device back where it came from.' She laughed and took a step back into her apartment, freeing the entrance way.

'I'm sorry. But from what I can gather, you've got a nice big chunk of glass in your foot. What else has caused all of that blood? Come on, we need to get that thing out.'

Oh gosh, the blood. She suddenly felt faint all over again. Her foot really was pulsing with a sharp pain. He passed her the first aid kit, took the broom and made his way into the kitchen.

'Hang on a sec. I don't even know your name. You could be anyone.' She laughed as she said it, but part of her was cautious. He could be a psycho for all she knew.

'Daniel,' the man said, beginning to sweep the porcelain into the shovel. He scratched his dark brown hair. 'See? Now we aren't strangers anymore. I promise I'll stay in a tight vicinity just so you feel safe.' He manoeuvred his broom around the kitchen as if he was on a mission with just one job to do. Maybe that's all he was here for. To help. Too late now if he wasn't.

With her eyes still on him, she took a seat at the end of the couch and started to sort out her foot situation.

'I have to ask though,' Daniel said as he looked up and flashed a grin. 'What was going on in here? It sounded like you were beating yourself up?'

She dabbed her foot a couple of more times, screaming internally when she removed the shard. She took off the sticker from the band aid. 'Something like that. I mean, really, what else do people do for entertainment around here?'

'That's a fair question. I'm still figuring that one out myself.'

'Was I that loud?' she said, ignoring his comment.

He shrugged. 'Well, yeah.'

'Sorry.'

He already seemed to be focused on the next thing. 'Do you have a bin?'

She gritted her teeth together and shook her head. 'Nope. I mean, I do…. somewhere,' she said, looking around at all the unmarked boxes. Little details such as marking things as you go had cost her so much time.

'It's ok. I'll take this out for you.'

'Oh, thanks.' She stood to her feet and placed her hands on her hips. She stared awkwardly at Daniel. He was done now, right? She appreciated his help. She did, honestly. But something about a guy she didn't know being inside her house felt a little off.

'I'm guessing you've recently moved?' He was clearly up for a chat.

She wasn't.

She studied him closely. She hated that she was so suspicious of everyone and everything these days. Gone were the days she could have a light-hearted chat with someone without wondering if there was some hidden agenda behind every word and action. It was as though Daniel could read between her eyes as these exact thoughts plagued her mind.

He leaned the broom against the counter and muttered something softly to himself that she couldn't make out. 'I think we've got this situation all under control. If there's anything else you need don't be afraid to give me a yell. I'm just a couple of doors down. The one with the barrel shaped letter box.' He stood awkwardly, studying his shovel that was stacked full of her porcelain.

She took the first aid pack and handed it to him. 'Thanks, Daniel. I appreciate your help.' She realised she was still holding the tweezers in her hand. 'Hang on, let me just give these a quick wash.' She bolted for the sink in search for something sterile to clean them with.

Daniel waved his hand at her and shook his head. 'Nah, nah that's fine. I can do that. Easily done.' He gently took them from her hands and made his way to the front door. 'Are you sure you won't go bashing yourself up again?'

'Look, I can't make any promises with those beastly boxes in my vicinity.' She smoothed her hands over her frizzy blonde hair that had somehow escaped her once sleek ponytail.

Daniel let out a honk of a laugh and clipped the first aid bag back around his waist. 'Good luck with that.' He raised his predominant eyebrow once more. 'Have a nice night, Sienna. I'm sure I'll see you around.'

'Night, Daniel. Thanks again.'

He gave a little wave with the broom and disappeared around the corner.

She darted between the boxes back to the microwave and set the timer for another three minutes. She made a mental note to drop into IKEA tomorrow after work to buy some more plates. She poured herself a glass of water and stared out the window, as the sun exuded pink and orange tones. There was nothing quite like a sunset in the country. It truly lit the whole sky.

Her phone started to buzz again. She placed her cup down a little too abruptly and belly dived to the carpet, reaching her hand under the couch. She took her phone in her hand and without thinking, swiped to answer.

'Hello' she said vacantly.

'Hey . . .' his voice came slow on the other end of the line. She took a breath in and took a seat back at the counter. She didn't say anything for a while, noticing the orange hues blending with the pinks more with every passing minute.

'What do you want, Patrick? You need to stop calling me.' She could hear his drawn-out sigh on the other end but it had no pull on her. 'Look, I'm in the middle of dinner. I've got to go. Please, I would really appreciate it if you don't call me again.'

'Wait.' His voice sounded pained.

She bit down on her bottom lip and squeezed her eyes shut and waited. She wouldn't back down. Not now, not ever.

'You've left some of your things here . . .' his voice tailed off.

She remained quiet, reminding herself that she owes him nothing.

'Your journals, S. You left two behind and . . . umm, well . . . I kind of read them . . .'

She opened her eyes, feeling the blood in her veins skyrocket to her head.

The timer went off on the microwave. Again. Was there a rule on how many times you could reheat food?

'You read my journals? You read my *personal* journals? Why would you do that, Patrick?' She shouldn't have cared but something about him reading what held the depths of her heart made her feel exposed. Exposed in a way he no longer deserved to know.

'Yeah . . . I'm sorry.' There was a pause. 'But you know what? I'm glad I did. S, I wish I had known . . .' He was on the verge of tears. She could tell. She knew all of his sounds, all of his expressions. She knew every detail about him. Or at least, she thought she did.

She frowned and tried to slow her breathing down. Even though she knew these things, it didn't spark her curiosity in the slightest.

She honestly felt nothing.

'Ok, great. I hope it was a good read for you. Take care, Patrick.'

'S,' he cut in. 'I've got something else to tell you. Can we please talk in person? Just for a couple of minutes. It won't take long.'

It was a nice try but there was no way she was going to go back there. She vowed to never see him again after that night she caught him with the woman from the café. The one with the cropped blonde hair.

'S? It'll only take five minutes. I promise. We don't even have to meet at the apartment. It could be in a car park or outside a park for all I care. Please.'

'Five minutes now, hey?' She stood to her feet and wandered back over to the microwave and reset the timer again. The lasagna looked completely mutilated but she had no back up plan. This was as good as it was going to get tonight.

She plugged in another three minutes on the microwave.

'I don't think it's a wise idea. I have no plans on heading to Melbourne anytime soon, anyway.'

'I can drive to you. I don't mind,' his response came quick as though he had already formed a plan.

She pulled the phone back from her ear and pulled a face. She wished she recorded this conversation. This had to be the first time he had ever offered to drive to Aringdale in over five years. It was actually quite comical.

'Yeah, okay Patrick.'

'Really?' He actually sounded hopeful.

'No.' With that she hung up the phone and placed it on airplane mode so that she didn't have to deal with him anymore tonight.

She finally settled down with her plastic container and took a bite as she stared out at the sky some more. By now the sun was nearly completely hidden behind the trees that stretched wide across her little backyard. She loved it here. She really did. She may not have been here long but there was something about being back in Aringdale that felt . . . right.

It wouldn't be long until everything else would catch up with her and she would feel like herself again.

It was only a matter of time.

Two

S ienna grasped her lanyard around her neck and smiled as she inserted the key into the glass door to the Mason Grammar Performing Arts Building.

She flicked the switch, bringing light to the offices on the left and the dance studios on the right. She walked down the corridor passing two rooms before reaching her office. Her own office! She still couldn't help but smile every time she sat in her leather chair as she admired the view from the second level. She couldn't imagine the sight ever getting old.

She hung her bag on the hook along with her coat and lowered her eyes to view the immaculate school grounds through the glass window. There was the three-story Science and Technology Centre to the left and the Gymnasium down the carefully paved hill on the right. Already at 7:45 a.m. the maintenance men had the sprinklers going and were pruning the gardens and rose bushes.

She took out her laptop and refreshed her emails, reached for her thermo and walked to the amenities room down the corridor. She had always been one of the first to arrive at work. Even a week into her new job it still felt like she had been doing it for years.

As she prepared her coffee, she couldn't help but think about one little boy who still held her heart in a way that gave her no rest.

Nolan Livingston.

She poured the coffee into her thermo and secured the silicon lid down onto it.

'Miss Henderson, you drink too much of that stuff, you know?'

His big brown eyes always looked deep into hers whenever he was so sure of something. She would throw her head back and laugh every time. He was highly observant and had a maturity well beyond his years.

She would click into her next email and smile at his remarks that continued to amuse her. 'What would I do if I didn't have you keeping me in check every morning, Nolan?'

He would shrug his shoulders and wiggle his freckled nose in a way that exposed his dimples and pushed his glasses higher up his face.

'I think we would both be in trouble.'

She would turn from her laptop and look at him closely, but his innocent face would give nothing away. It was as though the comment was forgotten about as soon as it escaped his lips and there he would be, onto the next thing. Whether it was searching the bookcase for the few books he hadn't read or resetting the classroom for the day ahead, without ever needing to be prompted.

Maybe she was a sensitive soul but she swore that there wasn't anything Nolan said, no matter how young he was, that was spoken without thought. She believed every word he said had purpose, intent and was carefully constructed.

I think we would both be in trouble, to an outsider, would come across as banter, a joke between two people familiar with one another. But after every conversation, every encounter she had with Nolan and his alleged "family" over the course of the year, made her question otherwise. She may never know what happened to him. As far as she knew he finished off last term at Kings Cross College and was headed to L.A. to start a new school year this term like his "mother", Miranda had told her.

Sienna sat back down at her desk and continued to admire the view. More staff were arriving now, dressed in coats like herself as the mornings were cold here—even in October. But her thoughts still hadn't shifted off Nolan. She had to let him go. She knew that. It was common for teachers to form a bond with their students but it would be unhealthy for her to continue to hold on.

'Good morning, super star!'

She placed down her thermo and swiveled her chair towards the door to find Richard, the Head of Music, standing by her door. He was a big man, with a peculiar dark moustache that really stood out against his bald head. 'Good weekend?' he asked in his usual booming voice.

'It was!' she replied, not wanting to delve into the details of her evening, even though they had established a relationship where they had quickly become quite open with one another. She had never had that at a work place before. Ever. It was refreshing.

'How was yours? Did you make that prawn linguini for your wife as promised?'

Richard lifted his finger and gave it a little wiggle.

'I did actually.'

'Ohhhh, and how did it go?'

'It was a disaster.' He threw back his head and let out a honk of a laugh. 'I think I'll leave Helen in charge of the cooking for now. I'll just make music for her.'

Sienna smiled. 'I'm proud of you for trying.'

'I'm proud of me too. It took me three bloody hours to make!' He began to tuck his white shirt back in, his theatrical laugh exposing his hairy belly. 'They're working on renovations in there tomorrow. Does that affect your classes in any way at all?' He pointed towards the studio down the corridor behind him.

Sienna quickly clicked on the tab that brought up her timetable online.

'Nah. Tomorrow is all theory, no practical. Hang on, renovations? What are they renovating? The studios are perfect, seriously.' She was still blown away by the place—it already had state-of-the-art facilities, on par with those she trained in during her professional days.

'Target floors or something. And, you know . . .' he lifted his right foot twenty centimeters off the floor and curved his left arm over his head in the same direction like a teapot. He quickly grabbed the door frame with his spare hand to balance himself. 'New whatever those rods are called that you do those stretches on.'

Sienna burst out laughing. 'Tarkett flooring would be the term you're after.' She took another sip of her coffee. 'And those "rods" are called "barres."'

He danced his head from side to side and lifted his nose in the air.

'Fine, Miss know-it-all, putting me back in my place like that. I'm

just going to go now!' He pulled down the leg of his suit pant that had hitched up in his little balletic move and playfully dusted himself off.

'Have a lovely day, Richard!' she twinkled her fingers and winked at him. She could hear his hearty laugh echoing somewhere down the corridor as he made his way towards his office.

She spun back around and felt a twinge sensation somewhere in her chest. Something about the word "renovations" and being back in Aringdale made her wonder. Made her wonder if it was possible that the man behind this particular job was the man she hadn't heard from in months.

Ethan Kahler.

Of course it was possible. He was highly sought after in a small town like this. As far as she knew, he was never out of work. She released a long, steady breath. It didn't matter either way. She had come to accept that things were different now. Their relationship was forever changed. And she had slowly, but surely, adapted to this change. Sometimes the brain has a way of holding onto the past, manipulatively latching onto memories in a way that creates its own realities. Realities that may or may not be real. Realities that cling onto the idea of something we desire, but may never have the potential to transpire in the way we imagine them. She had always been a bit of a dreamer that way, determined to see promise in every encounter, in every situation. But sometimes there comes a point where you have to let go. To see things for what they are, and not how you hope them to be. To trust that if it is meant to be, it will be—the way she had been effortlessly swept into this new season. This is how she knew she was exactly where she was meant to be. This is why she felt a peace about where she was positioned.

This was her next chapter and she was ready to embrace it.

'Okay, we are going to do it again. This time I want you to think less about the steps and connect more with the music,' Sienna said, demonstrating the first eight counts. The girls watched, their eyes following her every line that she made with her eyes and body.

'If you don't give yourself permission to feel something, how can you expect to move the audience?' She widened her stance and tied her hair back into a ponytail, keeping her eyes fixed on the group of seventeen girls before her. She took a big breath in. She was puffed but she wasn't going to show them that.

'We are storytellers! Until we evoke emotion and let it ooze through every fibre of our being when we move, then we haven't done our job.' She clapped her hands together twice and signaled for the girls to move back to try it again.

'Worry less about your technique and this time, focus on bringing dynamics to this piece. I don't want to see a visible start and end point between your movements, girls, I want you all to be fluid, seamless.' She stretched her arm out towards the speaker with the remote. 'Again. Two groups.'

She scanned her eyes for one particular girl. There she was, lingering at the back again. 'Isabelle, I would like you at the front this time.' The girl's blue eyes grew wide and for a moment she looked as though she wasn't going to move. But reluctantly she took four or five steps forward and smoothed her blond hair back with the palms of her hands.

She wasn't deliberately picking on the girl, although it may have appeared that way. Sienna saw a lot of promise in her. There was something about her, maybe how timid she was, the way she danced, or the fact that she looked like a younger version of herself, that reminded her so much of herself at that age.

'This time I would like you to have a go on your own. And remember; if you forget something, just improvise!' There were a few confident nods, a few nervous eye exchanges and then there were the one or two girls that just stared with attitude. She had quickly picked them out. Any class was always a mixed bag! But Sienna was excited to break down some of the barriers that existed within these four walls, in a way she wished hers had been cracked into when she was a teen.

The music to *Hallelujah* began and the first group took their places. Those who were waiting on the side were actively going over the routine, keeping time with the group performing. Sienna smiled. They were such hard workers and were well trained. She couldn't have hoped for a smoother transition into her role. She was working with girls who had intention and knew what they wanted—to pursue a career in dance. They were little professionals.

Nothing could have been more fulfilling.

As a teacher it was her duty to give attention to all of her students, which she had been doing consistently—well, for the most part anyway. But today was different. She couldn't keep her eyes off Isabelle. The girl was a natural with a facility that any dancer would envy: high arches in her feet; good hip rotation meaning that she had excellent *turn out*, with legs for days. To any normal person, noticing these physical attributes might seem weird. But from her professional eye and experience in the industry, Sienna knew that this girl was a talent one would want to snap up.

She studied Isabelle more closely. It was clear that the girl had no self-confidence but holy hell, she could move. And exactly in the way Sienna instructed—with emotion and fluency. Already her movements connected in a way that Sienna couldn't keep her eyes off her. She was a quick learner. She might not say very much but the girl sure did pay attention to detail. But what stood out to Sienna the most was her vulnerability; the way four sets of eight counts left a lump in her throat came down to the fact that the girl was a storyteller. She was able to pick up every lyric and throw her body into it so freely. But as soon as the choreography had finished and the music stopped, so did Isabelle. The confident, captivating dancer she witnessed in that moment quickly retreated back into the timid girl who hid in the back row. The one whose mind was constantly ticking, the one who was always questioning herself.

It was like looking into a mirror.

Sienna smiled at the girl and gave a little nod of approval. She could tell that Isabelle knew she was pleased and held her eye for a moment, resisting the urge to smile back before she pulled on the strap of her leotard and looked away.

"Well done first group! That was much better! Okay group two, let's go.' She cued the music, took a chair out and sat down to study the next group of girls. In all honesty, her muscles were on fire. She felt like she was back dancing full time even though she only had one week of teaching behind her. It would take some time to physically adapt to the load, especially when her body had been so weak. But she was regaining strength now, eating better without the voice in her head tormenting her. Instead, it was replaced with a different voice. A voice that kept finding its way into her subconscious and wouldn't leave her alone.

Do you know what music and reading have in common, Miss Henderson?' he asked her one day after his music class. Nolan was the first one in, taking out his lunch the way they always did on a Wednesday, being the last class before the bell. He took off his thick rimmed glasses, folded them and placed them beside his lunch box. She would stand from her chair, take out his lens wipe from his case and give them a little clean. She didn't have to of course, but those who are teachers know that there are many extra little things you do for your students. This was one of them.

'Hmmm let me see if I can work this one out.' She sat down on the chair opposite him and looked out the window. There was no sign of the rest of the class on their way. He must have run ahead. 'They both have a way of taking you to a different world?'

Nolan nodded and placed down his sandwich. He wiped his mouth with the back of his hand. 'Do you wanna know the best part about that?'

She nodded, hearing the familiar voices of her students as they made their way up the block of stairs towards the classroom.

He placed his elbows down onto his desk and sunk his round, freckled face into his hands. 'Everything would be different.' He lowered his voice and slumped further in his chair. 'Everything. And just maybe, it would be a world where we would all be okay.'

Just like that, chills went down her spine and she knew.

She knew that as much as she had convinced herself that she had to let go, she couldn't.

Three

Done.

Sienna performed a little victory dance in her apartment and punched the air on her final move. All nineteen boxes were unpacked. Nineteen! It was quite ridiculous that a person could own so much stuff. But she was impressed with how she managed to find a place for all of it without causing too much clutter.

She took the last sip of her wine and laughed at the gigantic tower of cardboard boxes stacked inside each other that remained. It really wasn't that funny but somehow wine made it so. Rising to her feet, she took her glass to the sink just in time to witness that beautiful sunset again. Loneliness started to creep in. Not because she missed him, because she didn't. But she missed being able to share moments like these with someone who would appreciate them as much as she did. She placed her hands on either side of the sink and closed her eyes for a moment. She would never forget the memory; the way he used to appreciate the details and pay close attention to them, to her.

She sunk into his lap on one of the many sand dunes as they stared out together into the horizon at their favourite beach in the Morning Peninsula. With the sun warm on her face she glanced down to see the diamond on her finger sparkling as beautiful as the way the sun had lit the sky. Patrick kissed the side of her neck and wrapped his arms around her tighter.

'It looks perfect on you.' She placed one hand in the sand to anchor herself and turned her head to face him. He was looking up at the sky with a dreamy look on his face. She kissed his forehead and followed his gaze back to face the ocean.

'I see you in the colours of the sunset.' Her insides tickled with delight and she interlaced her hand with his. 'The pink reminds me of the shade your cheeks turn whenever I smile goofily at you, the orange of your fiery personality . . .'

'Fiery?' she interrupted.

'Shhh, yes. Fiery,' he said and nuzzled his nose into her hair line. 'The yellow because you are a ray of sunshine to anyone you cross paths with.' He planted two, then three kisses along her shoulders. 'Red because our love is a force that pulls us together, and blue because I would miss you more than you could ever imagine if I wasn't by your side every time there was a sunset like this one.'

Sienna opened her eyes, noticing that the sunset had well and truly bled out. It was gone. And so was he. One day soon she would get lost in the beauty of the colours seeping together without remembering the pain. But for now, it would serve as a painful reminder of the past.

The boxes.

That's what she would do next. She would finally get rid of them so she didn't have to be reminded that her whole life could easily be reduced down and squished into the shape of a block. She could feel the wine finally take effect, filling her veins with a cool sensation. She slipped on her pair of black Nike runners and wrapped her arms around the top tier of the tower, managing to hold down three or four boxes. This would take a few trips. After struggling out the door she arrived at the recycling bin to realise that the only way there would be a chance of them fitting was for her to pull them apart. She yanked on the tape, reliving the scene of her monkey grip in the lounge room all over again. This would take forever. She dropped the stack on the grass and with two feet jumped on top of them. It could work. She jumped up and down like a bunny until she was sure that they were flattened enough to fit inside. She stepped off, feeling content at her efforts. Yes, it would fit for sure. She opened the lid, folded them a little and slid them inside. Perfect. Now for the next lot.

As she spun on her heel to make her way back inside, she found her feet slowing to match the rhythm of the melody that filled the air. Through the fierce rustling of the leaves from the plane trees above her, the beat of the music from the building rose above all other sounds.

She turned left and obediently followed as though it was leading her solely on its own. After half a dozen steps she recognised the letter box. Not because she had seen it before, but because she had remembered him telling her that the unusual green barrel-shaped one belonged to him.

She leaned against one of the plane trees to the side of his property and listened in. She was grateful that the trees were thick enough so that she wouldn't be spotted. She was even more grateful the street was so quiet that she could get away with doing such thing without looking like a stalker. Which she wasn't. She was just a creative soul that had a magnetic pull towards music. She couldn't see him but could hear the sound of the piano, wondering how it was possible for him to play like that, in multiple octaves that one would surely need more than two hands to make such sound possible. He was talented, that was for sure. The way he could evoke emotion so easily. Even with physical distance between them he still had the ability to transfer emotion onto her, so thick that it hit her like a ton of bricks. They say music is the language of the heart and that was exactly the effect Daniel's piece had on her. By playing the piano so expressively he quite literally changed her emotional state from one of loneliness, to one filled with hope.

Who would have thought this could all take place behind a tree in the middle of Ronson Lane?

The atmosphere quickly turned when a pedestrian taking her dog for a walk came into view. She studied herself for a moment, realising how dodgy she probably looked in her daggiest pair of track pants and what she imagined was a thick outline of red wine smeared around her mouth. And here she was, looking suspicious, with her back pressed up behind a tree.

The little dog, a fox terrier maybe, must have thought the same thing as it pulled against the lead and started barking like a maniac in Sienna's direction. She didn't even need a mirror to know that her mouth resembled something close to the clown in *It*. This was the very reason why she could only get away with drinking a Shiraz in private.

The woman on the other end of the lead shot an apologetic look at Sienna, in between hissing some words at her dog who just wouldn't shut up. With the back of her grey gym jacket catching onto the bark of the tree, Sienna nervously darted her eyes back towards the house to notice the blinds from the living area of his house start to lift. She had to quickly improvise. She stuck her index fingers into her ears, pretending she was adjusting her AirPods and forced a little laugh.

'You're on point with that one! I couldn't have said it better myself.' She reached down and pretended to tie up the laces on her shoes. 'Anyway, love, I might give you a call back now that I've got my breath back and can give this running thing another go!'

She straightened back up and eyed her surroundings. The woman and her dog had passed on the other side but even then, it didn't stop the fox terrier from looking at her, giving the occasional growl. She pretended to end the call in her tracksuit pant pocket with a phone she didn't have, just in case he was watching. She didn't have the nerve to look back as she remained in character and wiped her brow with the back of her hand as though she had been on a strenuous run. She buoyantly jogged back around the corner, not stopping until she was well and truly inside.

It was an opportunity of a lifetime. She didn't know if she was more excited for the kids, or for herself. It had always been on her ever-growing bucket list to go to L.A. Especially back in the day when she had been close to leaving the country to audition for the many renowned companies over there. This job was seriously the gift that kept on giving.

She exited the staff meeting filled with adrenaline at what was shared this afternoon. November 17 wasn't far away. At all. She quickly did the math; just over six weeks. In just over six weeks' time she would be responsible for a group of sixteen-year-old girls at an exchange program at a prestigious performing arts-focused school, *Charlton*. The whole prospect sounded daunting when she let it sink in. Sure, she had done many excursions across her years of teaching. But a ten-day workshop at a place overseas, all within her first term at a new job? That was a little intimidating. Especially in term four when assessments and reports were due right about the time they would be jetting off.

This was huge.

The more she thought about it, the more she felt the weight press down on her like a sandbag. It was a familiar weight that made her feel short of breath. She didn't even know where to begin with planning for such a big thing like this. It was a huge responsibility, one she wasn't confident she was ready for. But the executive team at Mason Grammar clearly thought differently.

'We wouldn't usually consider something of this scale at such late notice but for our College to have been offered it has been quite an honour', announced Diane, the Head of Performing Arts, at the meeting. Sienna at this stage hadn't had any background information to know why this was such a privilege for the school. She shifted her eyes over at Richard to see that he was listening intently with a smile spread wide across his round face. He was nodding at every second word as though he was waiting to be told that he had won the lottery. Sienna focused her attention back to the front.

'There is an opportunity for some of our students in our Dance, Music and Drama program to win scholarships to complete a semester of their studies in 2021 for their senior year of schooling following the exchange.' She flicked the light switch and turned on the projector with the little remote. 'Here is a short clip highlighting the facilities the school has to offer, along with a taste of what workshops and masterclasses will be available to the students. It's just fabulous!'

The three-minute video caused a lot of excitement in the room, stirring discussion amongst the faculty.

Not every student would be going. Only a few from each division. Immediately, the faces of a few girls came to Sienna's mind. But even then, that could change as not all parents would be onboard for such a costly adventure coming at such short notice. Anyway, she would learn more about the details in the days to come.

Diane switched off the projector as the meeting concluded and smiled in Sienna's direction. 'I'm thrilled that you've joined us in a time like this. This is the first year we've been invited to participate in such an elite program. We came this close last year.' She pressed her thumb and index finger together to emphasise her words. She looked at Sienna for a moment, as though she could see that she was still processing. She smiled a warm, motherly smile. 'I have every confidence that you will do an excellent job in leading these young women, Sienna. There will be a team joining you of course, but I know you'll be such a wonderful support and help open their eyes to the industry and its expectations.' Sienna beamed internally and held her belongings close to her chest.

'Thank you, Diane. I appreciate that. It will be so good for the girls. An opportunity I wish I'd had when I was their age.'

'A lot has evolved since you were here, hasn't it? The College really is achieving some incredible things,' Diane said with a grin, setting the comment up for a compliment. Sienna chuckled on the inside. The woman had been her music teacher when she was a student and worshipped the soil the College was planted on. It was because of her that she got this job—that she had this chance.

Sienna flashed her biggest smile. 'It has! It's soaring from one great height to another. I'm grateful to be here at a time like this.' She could see that Diane was satisfied with her response, but she truly meant what she said. She couldn't remember the last time she had felt this enthusiastic about her work. Diane patted her shoulder and pursed her pink, fuchsia lips together.

'You're doing a great job. Keep it up.' She gave her a nod of approval and moved towards the door. 'Have a lovely evening, dear.' Sienna said goodbye to the kind woman and went to collect the last of her things before making the five-minute drive home. She loved how that felt. The way she could save so much time doing other things . . . like staring out at sunsets that made her heart heave with every emotion under the sun and its wide spanning rays. But tomorrow was Wednesday where she would take a break from the sunset thing.

She had plans to travel back to Melbourne to catch up with her best friend Jacqui and visit her old school with the hope of learning more about what happened to Nolan. As for Patrick, she had no plans to see him even though he was still persisting. He could have her journals for all she cared. She didn't need to carry her past around for any longer than she had to.

The meeting had finished late and just like the mornings, she was one of few people left roaming inside the school building. She took hold of the silver handle to Studio One and opened the heavy glass door. The lights were left on which wasn't unusual with the cleaners being around. They were often here until after eight, which she knew as she had been guilty of staying late. But because of her late nights she had begun to make friends with one of them; Nina was her name. She was an unusual woman, one that she struggled to read. She would waltz in singing some days, her eyes focused on every wipe action her hand made. She also consistently wore the same purple baseball cap where her long peroxide blonde ponytail hung low down her back. Maybe today she would attempt another conversation with the woman.

But as soon as she placed her feet on the polished floorboards, Sienna felt different.

Something was different.

The door closed behind her and she felt a gust of air follow her in. Maybe it wasn't the door at all but the prickling sensation that had quickly found its way up her legs. He was here.

Ethan was here.

His back was turned from her as he kneeled down to measure something on the floor. The same floor she was standing on, positioned at the other side of the studio. She studied his reflection in the mirror, wondering how long it would take until he sensed her presence. The way she had quickly sensed his. She released her breath, feeling the prickling sensation spread through her body. She had half-predicted this, that he would be the one completing the job. It wasn't really a surprise. Maybe she should leave, before he saw her. He wouldn't know any different if she did—he didn't even know she was here. At the College, back in Aringdale—any of it. They hadn't spoken since they attended the same wedding almost two months ago.

'Sienna?'

She blinked, realising that she was staring beyond the mirror as her thoughts led her astray. She lowered her gaze slightly to catch his eyes looking at her in the mirror. He turned his head to face her and stood to his feet. His uniform really did seem out of place at a posh school like this one—dressed in a blue polo top, dark brown "tradie" flexi cargo shorts with the pull-up boots to match. Then there was that curly brown hair and those hazel eyes that had a way of searching the uncomfortable places in her soul. She smoothed her lips over, ignoring the effect he had on her.

'You always said you would build a dance studio for me one day.' She looked down at her feet as soon as she said it, feeling her face flush with a warm glow. What was she thinking? She wasn't. That was the problem. She couldn't be this way around him anymore. Their relationship had changed. The dynamics had changed.

It had all changed.

With her head still down, she lifted her eyes to see that his expression hadn't. Even after that comment, he hadn't budged. He still looked confused as though he was waiting for an answer to a question he was yet to ask.

'Sorry,' she said, suddenly feeling awkward. She pointed to her charger that was left plugged into the wall and took several steps towards it, towards him. The distance between them narrowed but the silence only widened.

'You're back?' he finally blurted out. 'What are you doing here?'

She pulled out the charger and nodded. 'Yeah. Teaching dance.' She tucked her blonde strands behind her ears. 'Secondary. I never thought I could do high school kids but I'm really enjoying it. I love that I can bring dance back into—'

'How long?'

'Huh?'

He snapped the measuring tape shut and scratched his left bicep with his right hand.

Keep your eyes on his, Sienna thought.

Her brain always had a way of disobeying her when she was around him. She gave in and peered at his muscles that seemed to increase in size every time she saw him. He was probably hitting the gym pretty hard these days now that Amber, his new girlfriend, was in the picture.

'How long are you here for?' He shifted his weight and crossed his arms. 'Are you teaching a workshop or something?'

Something changed in his eyes and just like that, the light-hearted Ethan was back. The version that wasn't looking at her so intensely.

'Well, who knows. Hopefully it's ongoing, but for now, at least twelve months,' she said, matching his tone.

He looked taken aback. 'What about your job in Melbourne?'

'I resigned.'

'Huh?' he said again. He was back to looking at her all weird again. 'Why?'

'This is my passion.' She circled her arm around the space. 'I needed to find a way to bring dance back in my life and the opportunity kind of popped up.' She fixed her eyes back on him. 'I didn't have to think it through for long. Actually, it was probably the fastest decision I have ever made.' She laughed on the last part but Ethan was barely smiling.

'. . . *You* didn't have to think it through?'

He didn't mean to sound patronizing but he knew her. Knew that her mind was always working a million times an hour, that she was an overthinker. He knew that she thought through everything.

'Not this time.' Sienna knew she was being cryptic but she wasn't about to expand on the details. She could tell that he wanted to ask about Patrick but he also knew that such information wouldn't be extracted in such a brief conversation, no matter how well they knew each other.

He nodded slowly and released a breath. 'Well, this is a surprise!'

She nodded back. 'A lovely one at that!' She waved her hand at his work space. 'I'll let you get back to it. I'm sure I'll see you around here while you're on the job.'

He narrowed his eyes and smiled that crooked smile of his. 'Like old times.'

She forgot for a moment that they shared eleven years of schooling here together. It had looked so different back then.

She saw it. That crooked smile of his. The one that killed her. She wouldn't react. She wouldn't fold this time.

'Like old times,' she agreed.

She turned her back and fiddled with the cord, turning it over in her hands and walked back towards the door. She wondered if he noticed—noticed that she no longer wore a ring on her left hand. She squeezed her eyes shut for a second as she took hold of the handle, feeling Ethan's eyes secure on her the whole time.

With her back still turned, she pushed it open and walked out.

Four

Sienna felt weird driving to her old workplace when she felt like she should be at her current one.

Something about a four-day working week made her feel guilty, especially when she was just minutes away from her old life. The one she vowed she would never return to as she sped off along the freeway with the container of chicken satay thrown somewhere in the back of her car. That was the last time she had seen him. Well, the second last time. She eventually went back to pack up her belongings—all nineteen boxes full. She had demanded that he was to be out of the house when she did so. He did respect her request but from that day forward his messages kept on coming through.

'You need to block his number. He's harassing you!' her sister, Mia had said. Mia never liked Patrick, so it was an easy thing for her to say. She had nodded her head and agreed with her but something inside her didn't want to. Not yet. Not when she had seen hints of a more sensitive side to him. She wasn't planning on taking him back. No way, not even though there was over five years of history between them. That wasn't it. She wanted closure—somehow. She knew that it wouldn't come from an apology or by turning back the clock, pretending that nothing ever happened. It was too late for that—for both of them.

She wanted to see something *in him*. She wanted to see glimpses of the person she fell in love with all those years ago. Not because she wanted feelings to resurface between them, because she didn't. She wanted him to *feel* again. To find a depth that would get him through whatever seasons he faced next—without her.

And that was why she gave in and agreed to meet up today. It was okay, she had already arranged to visit the College at 1 p.m. and it was a few minutes shy of noon now. She had deliberately put herself under a time restraint so that her time with him wouldn't drag out any longer than it needed to. He was meeting her in his hour lunch break anyway.

Sienna pulled into the gravel carpark of Featherstone Park and spotted his black BMW straight away. Just seeing it parked reminded her of that evening where she had witnessed him being unfaithful with the woman from the café. She had no idea where the woman came from or how he managed to develop a relationship with her, or how it even started. She didn't want to know. That's where the chicken satay came from. She had gone to personally deliver it to him one of the nights when he was "working late". It had been a good curry, too.

Mia would murder her if she knew what she was doing. But really, she was doing herself and her sister a favour by being here. After today she would have every reason to finally block his number.

And in all honesty, she wouldn't admit it to him, but she actually did want those journals. They were hers, and they formed a big part of her story.

She pulled up beside him and turned off the engine. At the same time, he stepped from the car, dangling a plastic bag in his right hand. A strange feeling washed over her as she watched him walk over to join her.

She wondered what this moment was supposed to feel like.

She shut the door behind her. He looked different. She couldn't quite put her finger on it. It wasn't the way he was dressed. He always dressed well. In fact, today he looked like he had put in some extra effort with his navy-blue shirt and brown dress shoes she hadn't seen before. It was obvious he was wearing new work attire and she had to wonder why. Wondered if he had fully revamped his wardrobe now that he was back on the market.

The reason why she questioned what this was supposed to feel like was because she felt . . . well, nothing. Even those ocean blue eyes that had once cast a spell on her, no longer had an effect.

'Hey, thanks for meeting me.' He reached in towards her for a hug. She didn't embrace it fully but closed her left hand on his upper back in a guarded way. She didn't say anything, all she could manage was a tight smile.

He didn't seem too bothered about her silence and pointed to the park seat a few metres ahead.

'Did you get here ok?' he tried again.

With her focus down at her footsteps she nodded. 'It was fine. Not much traffic at this time of the day, luckily.'

They took a seat and he placed the bag down by his feet. She wanted to take it already and get back in the car.

'That's good.' He widened his legs and started bouncing his knees almost too casually. She could see that he was trying to play it cool, but really, he was as nervous as she was. 'How's the new job going?'

She was squished to the edge of the seat, so she crossed her legs to make a little more room. He didn't seem to notice.

'Patrick.' It was all she had to say—but her tone said everything. She wasn't here for the small talk; she just wanted him to pass her the bag and say whatever it was that he so needed to say.

'Sorry.' He slapped his hands down on his knees and stared down at the bag by his feet. After a few moments he picked it up and passed it to her. 'I think that's everything.' His face held a pained expression. This was hard for him.

She wrinkled her nose. 'Thanks.' She opened the bag and stared at the journals inside, finding any reason to shift her focus off him.

'I'm sorry I read them.' She could feel him looking at her but her head was still down.

She sighed. 'It's fine, Patrick.'

What he did next surprised her. He gently placed his right hand on her thigh. Her breathing quickened. What was he doing? She flinched, signaling for him to remove it.

He obeyed and placed them back on his knees. 'I know I invaded your privacy . . .' he started. 'But what I'm most sorry about is that I stopped trying to learn about you . . . I know that now.'

Her eyes shot up. He was frowning. No, it wasn't a frown; it was more of a pleading expression. She narrowed her eyes, feeling a twinge in her heart. He was trying to open up. It was a side of him she hadn't seen in a very long time.

Maybe this, right here, was what she had hoped to see from him today.

'There is so much depth to you, S and I failed to see that.' His blue eyes began to mist over. 'I thought I knew you but really, I had no idea what was going on in there.' He pointed towards her chest on the last word. She jolted her body back before his hand had a chance to reach her. His mouth widened for a second as if he was about to say something, before he changed his mind. 'Sorry,' he said instead. 'I'm sorry for all of it.' He looked like he was about to cry and she almost felt sorry for him. She hadn't seen him so vulnerable since . . .

'I met up with Charlie's parents,' he went on.

Since his death. She hadn't seen him so vulnerable since Charlie's death.

She felt light-headed. 'You met up with them?' This was almost too much. The root of their long-standing issues birthed at the time of Charlie's passing all those years ago—his alcohol addiction, the way he would withdraw from her. Everything. He had missed Charlie's funeral. He had never properly grieved his friend's tragic death and it had destroyed them.

'It was something I needed to do. I should have done it ages ago. I wish I hadn't been so bloody stubborn.'

They fell. The tears finally fell from his eyes and Sienna didn't quite know what to do at the sight of them.

'I thought they would dismiss me. I mean, I would if I was them. But they didn't. They were so kind and I didn't deserve it. I was meant to be his friend and I let him down.' His head collapsed into his hands.

'You didn't let him down,' she said softly.

'I did,' he replied, his voice muffled. 'And I let you down. I let us down.'

The part earlier, where she didn't feel anything, that part—well, that quickly changed. Her heart was hurting all over again. He was finally acknowledging his actions. If only they had reached this moment a year ago maybe things would be different and maybe they wouldn't be meeting up like this.

But they hadn't, and a lot had happened since.

'I believe everything happens for a reason,' she said, taking hold of his hand. Not in a way that would give him the wrong message, but in a comforting sort of way. She felt like the moment needed it.

He squeezed it. 'I know I've lost you.' He looked up and let out a shaking breath. 'I just wish I could take it back. All of it.' She could tell that he was being sincere. That this wasn't a plot to win her back.

'The things we learn . . .' she started, as she paused to acknowledge the part of her that wanted to cry. 'Sometimes the learning happens after . . . when it's too late.'

They both knew that it was over. Despite her deep sadness she felt something lift. Maybe this was the closure she was looking for.

'I'm sorry we didn't work out,' she whispered.

Patrick's eyes closed briefly, then he looked at her—really

looked at her—the way he used to. 'I know. Me too.' He cleared his throat and found a half-smile. 'I wish you the world, Sienna.'

She shifted her weight and wrapped her arms around his shoulders, this time with two hands.

His arms closed over the small of her back. They stayed that way for a while on the park bench, with their arms wrapped around each other. It was time to let go of the bitter fragments in her heart and move on.

The longer they stayed that way, the more it set in that this was it—that she would never see him again.

But the beautiful thing was that this time, she had found peace.

Do you ever have those moments where you reenter a place that no longer has a part in your life, with the feeling as though you have never left?

That is how Sienna felt when she entered the reception at Kings Cross College. The students had just been dismissed for lunch and already the grounds were filled with children running around in their navy blue wide-brimmed hats. It hadn't been that long since she had left, really. She was lucky that she was able to leave with such short notice. Her position had been filled almost instantly—they were such a reputable school where expressions of interest were submitted almost daily. But in this case, the person that filled the position was a middle-aged woman by the name of Miriam; a relief teacher at the top of the call list who stepped in a couple of times a week for numerous classes at the College. The children were familiar with her and she was brilliant. Sienna felt comfort knowing that her little mates would be finishing off the year in good hands.

This afternoon's visit wasn't about them—as much as she would enjoy seeing their bright-eyed faces again. It wasn't about meeting up with her old colleagues either, though she sadly never built any real relationships with them.

It was about Nolan.

And to return her swipe card that she had forgotten to hand in amongst all the drama that had taken place just five short weeks earlier. She was a bit apprehensive to see Damian again. Even though she had left on good terms despite her sudden exit, it was hard to predict how he would be towards her.

She took a seat on the black leather couch opposite his office, managing to avoid conversation with the receptionist ladies. That was the good thing about planning a meeting at lunch time—so much was happening, it was like a zoo with wild animals on the loose, except with children instead. Already five minutes into lunch time there were students crying to reception because one kid had "bullied" them; another was after a band aid; two had forgotten their lunch and needed a sandwich made for them.

And that was all from barely a minute's observation.

She stared at the back of his door where the plaque *Damian Withers, Principal* was engraved in gold metallic writing and tried to count the number of times she had been on the other side of that door, only to be flirted with and not ever taken seriously. As she opened the door she had hoped that this encounter—perhaps their last—would be different from the others.

41

'Look who it is!' said Damian, stepping out of the door and shaking her hand. 'Welcome back, Miss Henderson.'

So far, he was the same. Maybe no circumstance nor time would change their . . . relationship.

'Thank you for making the time to meet with me,' she said, diplomatically.

He patted her shoulder. 'Of course!' He stepped to the side and gestured her inside.

She took a seat opposite his stylish glass desk.

He smiled at her, or more like grinned, and pulled his chair in tight. 'How is the new position going?'

She filled him in on the past couple of weeks and the recent news of travelling to the U.S. with a few select girls from the dance program.

'As much of a loss as it is for us, I think you made the right move.' He smiled and swiveled on his chair. 'I know I once told you that your eyes didn't light up the way they're supposed to.' He stilled the chair and leaned in towards her slightly. 'But they do now.'

Sienna clasped her hands together and nodded. 'I'm beginning to feel like myself again,' she agreed.

'How are you travelling since, eh, everything happened?' He was referring to the breakup, of course.

The last time she had seen Damian she had been in a completely different state and had even shed a few tears in front of him as she shared what had happened; Patrick, the job offer—everything. It should have been far more awkward than it was, but Damian had known for some time that she was fighting a battle—even if Sienna hadn't really disclosed her personal life to him before that. She appreciated that he was checking in on her now.

'It's finished. But I'm okay.' She squeezed her hands tighter. 'I'm looking forward to what's next.'

And she meant it.

Damian smiled, leaned back in his chair and rested with his hands behind his head. 'I'm pleased to hear you're in a much better place.'

Sienna took the swipe card from her handbag and placed it on the table between them. 'Thank you.'

'You know . . .' Damian came forward and took the card. 'If you ever find yourself back in Melbourne, just give me a call and we'll be able to work out something for you.' His smile was gone this time as he smoothed the card between his thumb and index finger.

'Thank you, I really appreciate that,' she said. And she did. Even though she hadn't had the fondest of memories at the College, she knew that if her circumstances had been different, the experience might have been better.

'How did Nolan go finishing up the term?' She had to ask and she knew that Damian was waiting for it—his face said it all. He was well aware of the bond she had with the boy. He was like no other student she had taught before: mature, inquisitive, a little bit mysterious with a depth that Sienna hadn't been able to uncover. Which was the reason why she wasn't able to leave it alone.

'His attendance was poor, as you know.' Damian scratched the nape of his neck and sighed. 'He was only here for one day in the last week of term but was sent home early with rashes all over his body.'

'Rashes?'

'Yeah, well. Kind of . . .' he sounded flustered. 'More like spots. Reddish, purply spots.'

Sienna suddenly felt the heat of the room. 'Are you sure it wasn't bruising like I told you about?'

'No, Sienna.' He lowered his voice, and positioned his eyes on her. 'I really don't think it was.'

She frowned and slouched back in her chair. 'I'm still convinced that Miranda was inflicting harm on him.'

Damian shook his head. 'This wasn't like that.'

'Well, what was it?' She knew she was coming off demanding but this was the type of relationship they had. Damian knew she was persistent. She wasn't asking too much, was she?

He ignored her question. 'You know what communication was like with Miranda.' He sighed defeatedly. 'She probably felt at the time that she didn't owe us an explanation as they were pulling him out anyway.'

At the time?

She felt hot all over. She didn't like the way he was looking at her. His eyes told her that he knew more than he was letting on.

He took out a pen and started doodling on his notepad. She studied him closer. He was avoiding her eyes. But why? Was he holding back information because legally, she no longer had a right to know now that she wasn't employed by the College anymore?

'Damian?

He dropped the pen and looked up. 'Yes?'

44

She leaned in and narrowed her eyes on his. 'Is Nolan okay?'

He took a long moment to respond, then tentatively opened his mouth. 'I'm sure he will be fine.'

But there was something in his eyes that said otherwise.

Five

Sienna missed running.

Sure, it was hardly satisfying the way dance once had been, but it was similar in the way that it served as a release. After the weight of the day and being stuck in a car for a big chunk of it, she needed that. There weren't really any running tracks near her apartment but the four streets surrounding the area were lined with thick, beautiful trees with a pavement wide enough to run freely without colliding into anyone.

After turning the first bend a sharp stitch came upon her. There was no sugar coating it—she was unfit.

How on earth did she manage to dance ten hours a day without her body falling apart the way it did now after just two minutes of jogging? She jabbed her earphones in tighter and focused on her breath.

In and out.

Her foot was killing her. The cut the other night had been

nasty and felt like it was opening up again as it rubbed on the inside of her shoe. She probably should have gotten stitches, but oh well. She took another exasperated breath. She probably looked like she was being dramatic but she literally felt like she was dying. Did people actually enjoy this?

The stretch before her was at least another eighty metres away. All she needed was a goal. Eighty metres was a pretty good goal? It was all about baby steps, making sure she didn't dent her self-confidence. She focused on her music, syncing in and out breaths with the beat.

The next corner was in sight. After this turn she would be halfway there . . . well, halfway around one lap of the block. Either way it was progress. There was a tap on her shoulder. Out of reflex she swung her arm around and knocked some guy fair and square in the face. The man hunched over, grabbing his nose with two hands and groaned.

She yanked her earphones out and stretched out her hands. 'Oh my god, I'm so sorry. Are you ok?'

The man straightened himself up with great effort. It was Daniel.

'Is that what I get for picking up your key?' He was being sarcastic, well, at least Sienna thought he was. He looked different in his running attire. Skinnier. He was dressed in a deep blue sweat top with matching Adidas shorts. His brown hair was slick to his forehead with visible beads of sweat running down into brown sideburns.

He tapped his long fingers against the bridge of his nose. 'You dropped it.'

She took the key and zipped it up inside the pocket in her

compression tights. All the way up this time. 'I'm so sorry. Do you need ice?' She tilted her head to take a better look at it but he wasn't budging.

'Nah, I'll be right.' He finally removed his hand and smiled. He had big round brown eyes. Kind eyes. Somehow, she noticed this more in the light. 'You owe me a race back though.'

She took a breath. She had barely caught her last one. 'Race? What are we? Ten?' She laughed, already beginning to speed up her pace.

Daniel grinned, raising that unusual eyebrow of his. She looked away before he noticed her staring at it. 'I don't really care how it looks.' He sped up, and with a determined focus, went ahead of her.

Sienna stuck her earphones back in and amped it up. She was competitive by nature and with some tunes, she knew she was up for the challenge. Before she knew it, they were in sync beside each other, just metres out from reaching their apartments. He finished ahead of her, but only by a little. She did it! She actually did it. She was ready to throw up now.

She rested her hand against the trunk of the tree and let the stitch subside. She turned her head to see Daniel completely composed with a funny look on his face.

'What?' She panted. 'Don't judge.' She released her hand and placed them on her hips. He stared at the tree then back at her again.

'You love that tree, don't you?'

'Huh?' She took another breath and looked at it for the first time. Or apparently, the second time. Now that her heart rate was back to normal she finally paid attention to her surroundings.

There they were, outside the front of his place. By the tree that she had been lurking behind when she had listened to him playing the piano that time. Had he seen her standing there, listening that night? How embarrassing.

'What can I say? You're an amazing pianist,' she added.

He laughed. 'Thank you. And you're an amazing stalker.'

'I wasn't stalking!' she said, suddenly defensive. He was still smiling so she relaxed a little. He didn't seem too worried about it. 'Have you always played?' she said, desperate to change the subject.

'Not always.' He scuffed his runners into the pavement. 'It's an art I guess—playing. It's best when it's inspired.'

Sienna nodded. 'I get that. I used to dance so I can relate.' She adjusted her ponytail that had loosened from the run. 'What inspires you the most?'

He stopped moving his feet and looked up. 'Emotion. Or anything that triggers emotion.' He said it so factually, as though he had thought about the question before. He pressed the bridge of his nose, making Sienna feel bad all over again.

'Are you sure your nose is ok? I do have ice if you need it?'

'No, no.' He waved his hand and smiled, showing off all of his teeth. 'I mean, you did a good job of it but I'll be fine.'

'The incident hasn't triggered enough emotion to inspire a tune?' She meant to be funny but as soon as it came out she realised how corny it sounded.

Daniel looked at her askance and didn't respond. He fell silent for a moment. 'What do you do for work, Sienna?'

She felt a pang inside. She had offended him. Should she

apologise again or would that come off as annoying? 'I'm a teacher.'

'Ah, I see. It's a tough gig being a teacher.' He wiped the sweat from his bushy brow. 'My sister is one. I've heard all the stories.'

Sienna nodded. 'There's a reason why we get so many holidays! We come pretty close to going insane by the end of the year. We need them.'

'My sister says the same thing. It seems to be so many professions in one.'

'It sure is,' she agreed. 'Psychologist.'

'Interpreter.'

'Mentor.'

'Curriculum specialist.'

'Expert planner and organiser.'

'Third parent.'

'Yessss. More than most people know. Sometimes you're the only positive role model the child is exposed to,' she said, thinking of Nolan. She couldn't stop thinking of him.

She had to change that.

'What do you do?'

He looked down. 'I used to be a care giver before I moved here. Was in Newcastle before that.' He cleared his throat, lowering his head for a second then lifting it back up. 'But now I work in hospitality.'

Something in his tone had changed. Was he embarrassed by his profession? Was it just her, or had things gone weird?

'Oh, nice!' she said, a bit too enthusiastically. He raised his eyebrow and looked at her. She kept her smile full. 'Did work bring you here?' She was trying to make conversation, to get to know a little bit more about her neighbour.

'No,' Daniel said dryly. He peered out at his mail box—the green barrel one. He took the few steps towards it, lifted the lid and took out the two or three letters inside. Sienna suddenly felt awkward. She could tell he didn't want to elaborate. Maybe it was best if she didn't try hard to make friends with him too quickly.

'Thanks for the run!' She patted the key inside her zipper pocket. 'And for saving my key!'

Daniel smiled a half smile and gave a little nod of acknowledgement.

'You did good out there.' He lowered his gaze to the ground and with her eyes, she followed it. 'Especially after the trauma your foot went through the other night.' He looked back up. 'I hope it's feeling better. Have a nice evening.' With the letters in his hand he gave her a little wave and headed inside before she had a chance to respond.

She felt strange inside as she headed back to her apartment, not being able to pinpoint why she felt the way she did. There wasn't anything that unusual about their encounter to stir such a feeling, was there? She caught herself frowning as she shut the door behind her and lowered the blinds.

Just in time to avoid another sunset.

Six

'Excuse me, Miss Henderson?'

'Hmm, yes, Isabelle?'

She was exhausted. Mondays were tough. Not just because it was a Monday—the day where she taught six classes back to back with private lessons jammed either side of them before and after school. Even though she loved it, it made for a very long day.

That's why Sienna was only half paying attention when the girl dropped the bombshell after she finished the day with her Year Tens. She knew she only had a five-minute window to get something down her throat before her next private lesson.

The girl wasn't interested in privates—or so it seemed. Sienna found that odd as she was clearly gifted—far more naturally gifted than the other students in her class. But maybe she knew that and thought she didn't need the one on one time seeing as she was performing so well already. She did have close to perfect marks in all her theory and practical work but in the grand scheme of things, that meant little. Sure, in comparison to her classmates she was amazing. But beyond the perimetres of Aringdale, out in the real world, there were kids far more talented. The sooner she knew this, the better.

That's why the Los Angeles trip would be a perfect opportunity for Isabelle; she would see fair and square what she was up against and what was required, seeing just how fiercely competitive the industry could be. This Sienna knew all about. She was excited to be her mentor. She would be tough on her, no doubt about that, but only because she had the makings of a star.

'I can't go to L.A.'

'Pardon?' Sienna stopped piling up the syllabus books and focused her attention at the girl who was eying her nervously.

'My parents won't let me go. I'm sorry.' She picked at the bracelet on her wrist—one she shouldn't be wearing but Sienna was too preoccupied to care about her having breached the uniform policy.

'I'm sorry to hear that. Did they say why?' Sienna felt a wave of disappointment. She had been her first pick.

'They just don't think it's a good idea.'

She was still fiddling with her bracelet and looked like she was about to cry.

'Do you want to talk about it?' Sienna asked gently. She was still working out the best way to talk to teens—she was used to younger kids who fearlessly spoke their mind with little prompting. She wasn't sure that a closed question was the way to go about it but she could see that Isabelle was emotional and hoped that she would open up to her, even if they didn't know each other well.

She lifted her heart-shaped face and shrugged. 'They don't like that I dance. They want me to focus more on academic subjects. This trip pulls me away from that.' She rolled her eyes and looked down at her wrist again. 'End of discussion,' she said, adopting the stern tone of her parents.

Sienna got it. More than the girl knew. It was like she was living her past again with her own parents.

'Have you asked them why they don't want you to dance?'

Isabelle frowned. 'It's like I said . . . they want me to focus on other subjects. The important ones in their mind, anyway.'

'And why isn't dance an important subject?' she challenged her.

'It's not going to help me become a doctor,' she mumbled. 'They're not my words, Miss. They're my parents.'

'That's ok.' Sienna smiled and took a cross-legged position on the floorboards. She could see that her student had arrived for her lesson and was waiting outside the studio. 'Is that what you want to be? A doctor?'

Isabelle stared at her then reluctantly placed her bag beside her as she took a seat on the floor. 'Not at all.'

'What is your dream?'

'I want to dance,' she said bluntly, without hesitation. 'But without the support from my parents, I don't see how it's possible.' She pulled her thin legs towards her chest and rested her petite head onto her knees.

Sienna glanced at the clock. It was time for her next lesson but she felt as though they needed to have this conversation. Her student could wait.

'Isabelle . . .' she started. The girl tilted her head, waiting. 'I've been there. I can relate to exactly what you're going through. My parents were the same with me when I was your age.' Sienna leaned in towards her with sympathetic eyes. 'Let's make this possible, yeah?'

The girl smiled and lowered her legs back down again.

'How?'

'You don't need to worry about that for now. I'll come up with a plan. I'll do my best to get you there.'

Isabelle took her bag and stood to her feet. 'I'm glad you're here you know. Here at Mason Grammar. You're pretty awesome.' She slid her arms through the straps. 'Thank you for wanting to help.'

Sienna felt a tingle of delight. No one had referred to her as "awesome" before. It felt good to be liked, even by a sixteen-year-old. But she meant what she said—she would help this girl in whatever way she could.

Sienna knew they were bound to run into each other again.

It was almost 6 p.m. by the time she finished up and headed to her car. She hated that her mind never gave her rest. Not only was she still thinking about Nolan, now she had another case in her hands—Isabelle. This one was close to home having faced the same issue herself. She would find a way to have a conversation with the girl's parents.

She extended her arm towards her silver Subaru and unlocked the door. She was ready to curl up on the couch with Netflix and a nice light dinner. The weather was becoming warmer at this time of the year and the idea of salmon, brown rice and a Greek salad felt pretty appealing right about now.

'First in, last out. Can't say it surprises me.'

She turned her head, using her hand to shelter her eyes against the sun as she peered over the bonnet of her car.

There he was, his Ute parked three or four spaces from her own. 'Dedicated. What can I say?' She smiled at Ethan, unable to see much with the harsh glare of the sun.

'As long as you're making time to look after you. Don't go burning yourself out.' He jiggled his keys in his hands and stepped out from the light. He didn't look like he was in a rush to go. He was looking at her in the same way as he had the other week. As if he was waiting for her to unpack her deepest thoughts and feelings the way she once had with him a thousand years ago.

'The studios are coming along so well! You're doing great work over there.' She turned her eyes back at the Performing Arts Centre.

'Dedicated. What can I say,' he replied with a grin.

Sienna laughed. 'And very efficient. I have no idea how you can work that fast.'

'So, are you?'

'Am I what?' she asked. He always had a way of being so ambiguous at times.

'Looking after yourself,' he said with thought behind his eyes.

She rested her hand down on the bonnet. 'Well, you know, I'm doing my best.' She was careful not to give too much away but realised that her words gave the impression that she was struggling.

But was she?

He took a few steps closer, closing the space between them. She scanned her eyes around. She was always cautious of her environment and remaining professional. Especially when she was still technically on school grounds. She didn't want anyone looking, even if nothing was going on.

'You left him, didn't you?' His deep brown eyes searched hers in a way that longed for the truth. For more.

She shifted her weight, feeling that awful pull of longing and sadness all mixed together. 'Yeah. I had to.' The longer she held eye contact, the more trapped she felt. He always had a way of drawing her in. 'There was more to it . . . he was cheating.'

Ethan squinted his eyes shut for a moment, then opened them again. 'For how long?'

'Well . . .' she stared at the bonnet of her car where her hand was rested. 'I really don't know.'

'I'm so sorry, S,' he said, his voice sounded pained.

She kept her eyes down, grateful that the clouds had parted and the sun was back out, giving her an opportunity to avoid his eyes. 'It wasn't entirely his fault.' It was a fair thing to say.

Because it wasn't.

They fell silent. She knew. She knew that although nothing had happened between them, they had shared something deep, emotionally. And in a way, that had been more dangerous. Years of history, fond memories and an admiration for one another had bound them together. Was that all it had been though? An admiration for one another, expanding over two decades that she had wrongly interpreted as more?

It was a fleeting thought. One that was quickly replaced with butterflies. It was more than that. How else could it explain the physical effect he clearly had on her?

'Why do you say that?'

Her eyes shot up. Was he serious?

'Come on, don't give me that. You know why,' she said with some agitation in her voice.

Was he really going to pretend there hadn't been something between them?

He scratched his head, roughing up his mop of brown thick curls. 'I'm not sure if I do.'

She felt like she had been punched in the gut. Was he really doing this? Pretending that there had been nothing between them for the sake of protecting his own ass now that he had a girlfriend? It was like high school all over again and she wasn't going to do it. It was like a switch had gone off inside her and she was filled with anger. This is what he had been doing for years. Giving her the impression that they held some sort of palpable connection then backing down before it got too real. She wouldn't do it anymore. She felt stupid for having said anything. She should have left it the way she promised herself that she would.

'Right.' She breathed out and opened the door and sat herself inside. She didn't care how it looked. She would be dismissive too. 'I'll see you around, Ethan.'

He held the door before she had a chance to shut it.

'Hey . . .' he said softly.

She lifted her eyes to him and waited. But he didn't say anything and it pissed her off even more.

'Can I sit inside for a minute?'

'No, you can't,' she shot back.

'Sienna, what is going on?' His eyes were full of confusion as he bent forward from the waist and lowered his face inside to examine hers.

'Did I just imagine it?' She rested her hands on the steering wheel and glared ahead. Her hands were quickly burning from the heat of the leather so she started the engine to get the air con going. 'That there was something between us?' She felt sick but unlike last time, didn't have any fear in asking the question. With her eyes still focused ahead she could hear his shuffling his feet on the gravel next to her.

He took a deep breath out. 'It's always been complicated with us, S.'

It sounded like a cop out. His cryptic responses suddenly annoyed the hell out of her.

'Yes or no, Ethan.' Her eyes began to glaze over, from the air conditioner or the emotion—she wasn't sure.

'Okay, yes.'

She darted her eyes back to him and felt the world around her close in.

Yes?

'But I just don't think . . .' He cleared his throat. 'That we can be having this conversation, S. I'm with Amber now.'

She should have felt excited about what he said. Hopeful even. Wasn't this what she had anticipated for over a decade? That he had in fact, always had feelings for her? He said he did. He said *yes.* After all of this time, he admitted it. She hadn't been crazy after all. She hadn't imagined it. But why was her gut still hurting?

'I'm with Amber,' he repeated.

And that was why.

Amber. The girl that obviously meant more to him than she did. Already. After such little time.

'Yeah, I know. Of course,' she said, feeling dizzy.

'We can't . . .'

'Yeah, I know' she repeated, nodding far too many times in one go. 'I get it.'

He straightened his back up and combed his hair with his fingers and she stared out again through the dashboard. What else could she say? It was done.

This too, was done.

He cleared his throat. 'I'm not sure if you know many people around here these days but you're welcome to join us for dinner or a drink or something soon.'

'Sorry, join who?' she asked, cranking up the air con.

'Amber and I.'

She fiddled around with the air vents. What was wrong with him? Why on earth would she want that? Was he that clueless on how this would make her feel after what was just said? He wasn't thinking, that was the problem. That was Ethan. The most sensitive, yet most clueless person in the world.

'Sure,' she said instead, going against her thoughts. If he was going to pretend the words hadn't been spoken then so would she.

He bent forward again and looked at her as she continued to fiddle with whatever she could find inside her car. This time it was the glove box.

'Ok . . . we'll set something up then.'

'Fantastic,' she said bluntly, not really knowing what she was agreeing to.

She took out her sunglasses and shut the glove box. She slid them on and offered him a big smile. 'Get home safe and I'll see you soon.'

He slowly took his hand off the door frame and took a step back.

'Sienna, are you . . .'

'I'll see you soon, Ethan.'

'Ok, yeah . . . take care.'

She buckled her seatbelt and put the car into reverse. She could see in the rearview mirror that he was still standing there, his shoulders slightly hunched and arms crossed. She exhaled shakily, adjusted her sunglasses and allowed the tears to spill down her face.

She didn't know why she said yes. Why would she put herself through the Ethan and Amber show when he was clearly playing games with her? That was what he was doing, wasn't it? Playing games? Wouldn't the right guy pursue her?

That was the way she always imagined it, anyway.

Seven

Hibachi Fusion.

That was the name of the Japanese restaurant she had agreed to meet them at. She wrestled with the idea of making an effort with her appearance tonight. What did people in the country wear out to dinner anyway? She forgot how differently people dressed in the city. She had grown accustomed to a style that would probably be considered flashy here in Aringdale, where everyone wore jeans and Cons without a second thought. So, she had settled on a pair of jeans and a white linen shirt, but instead of the Cons she had worn a low-wedged shoe. It was a good compromise.

Amber was apparently still making frequent trips from Lilydale to see him. She was a petite, olive skinned brunette beauty who worked as a physiotherapist in the heart of Melbourne. Whether or not Sienna admitted it, she was jealous. But what made it worse was that she liked the woman. She had been blindsided when Ethan rocked up at a mutual friend's wedding with Amber hanging off his arm. That single moment probably hurt more than all the others combined.

She had reconnected with Ethan two months prior when she returned to Aringdale after years of absence. The wreckage of her dysfunctional relationship had sparked the return, where she reconnected with her family after shutting herself off from them during an extended season where she had lost sight of who she was. Before then, she hadn't seen Ethan pretty much since high school. Yet, a couple of days back in her hometown had rekindled feelings that they had both failed to confront during the many years they had been close friends.

They had grown up together, having once shared their deepest thoughts and desires through a series of letters right up until Sienna made the move to Melbourne to pursue her dream of becoming a dancer. From that point, the letters stopped and so did their communication as they slowly grew apart. But when they reunited years later she realised that those feelings hadn't gone anywhere. They had both felt it. It was why she had mustered up the courage to write one final letter, sharing the depths of heart, confessing her love for him once and for all. But when she saw the two of them together at the wedding she quickly changed her mind. She kept the letter close, folded tight until it dropped from her purse that night. He had spotted the letter with his name on it as he helped collect her things but she had snatched it from his hands before he had the chance to read it. By the end of the night she had destroyed it. It never saw the light of day.

And maybe neither would the love she *knew* they once shared. Love doesn't work like that, does it? It doesn't just disappear. If so, where does it go? Maybe it does disappear if it's not strong enough to hold its grip. Maybe love was a complex thing with many levels and layers. Maybe it was different with each person; what one thinks is love later turns out to be false, after they've experienced the real thing with someone else. Maybe what Ethan shared with Amber was deeper than the love he had ever felt for her. And that made sense. If it had surpassed every level and penetrated every layer then she would be the girl Ethan pursued. But she wasn't. After everything, she wasn't.

And that said everything.

But if Amber was the woman he was meant to love, then she would accept it. She would be happy for him. Really, she would. She was done holding on. She was done being bitter and trying to control things that were out of her control. That was her past life and got her nowhere.

She pushed open the little green door and stepped inside. It smelt good inside—very, very good. The last time she had eaten Japanese was months ago when she had booked a table at a restaurant her and Patrick used to go to for their anniversary. He had stood her up that night and well, everything had spiraled downwards pretty fast after that.

The place was packed, which surprised Sienna, but then even though Aringdale had its own culture it still had a way of keeping up with trends of Melbourne. She spotted him at the back, sandwiched between two little black tables on the far back wall. Amber wasn't there yet—probably still on the road and would be arriving any minute.

She remembered the last time she had met up with him like this. It had been at *Mr Sogo*—an Italian restaurant that had been their favourite growing up. It was during that period, a few months back when everything was falling apart, when she had returned to Aringdale to watch the local dance competitions that she had once been part of, all those years ago. He had been at the same theatre, watching his niece dance when they had locked eyes. He had suggested they go out for dinner and she had agreed. The night had stirred all sorts of feelings inside her, closing the divide of every year that had once separated them. He had a way of unlocking her heart, bringing the girl she once knew out again. Maybe that was what she had been holding onto for so long; his ability to help her break free from the façade she had created for herself. Maybe it was never about them, whether she was in love with him or not. Instead, maybe she loved what he *had done* for her. The change that had happened in her. How he had helped her break free—not just from Patrick, but from the chains she had shackled herself with.

So, this time, walking up to him felt different. She felt different. There's a saying that the truth will set you free. Maybe her little moment of revelation this evening was in fact, the truth. Maybe she was invited here tonight to solidify that.

Just maybe, everything did happen for a reason.

It was a hard place to find tucked away in a small lane, with a narrow staircase leading to the second floor. She finally got in and took a seat opposite him, leaving a space for Amber.

Sienna took out the black laminated menu. 'This place is cute!' She felt a peace as she settled down and studied the menu.

'Aringdale is catching on!' Ethan grinned and poured her a cup of hot tea.

'Exactly what I was thinking. They're trying to be cool like Melbourne.'

He passed her the cup. 'Hey, they are cool. You're one of us now. Watch yourself.'

'Thank you.' She smiled and took a sip. 'Yeah, I should be careful what I say!' She looked at him, the way he so easily reverted back to being himself, crooked smile and all. It was though their moment in the car park yesterday afternoon had been forgotten about.

They began chatting about their days—work, friends, all the usual things that took priority in a surface-level conversation. It was then that she realised it was the first time she hadn't felt the butterflies. Even with that crooked smile of his, she felt none.

What was going on?

'Can I start you two off with anything?'

She turned her head towards the waiter to quickly notice that it was Daniel.

'Why, hellooo,' she responded, realizing her tone sounded quite theatrical. She could feel Ethan looking at her weird. Daniel must have noticed Ethan's expression and tightened his stance.

'Hello, hello,' he responded trying to match her tone but it was obvious that he felt awkward. His brown hair was styled differently—slicked all the way back in a way that drew attention to his dark features.

'So, this is where you work! How funny!' she said all bubbly. "Funny" meaning "what were the chances" and "what a coincidence" but she quickly realised that he probably thought she was mocking his job, in the same way she was pretty sure she had offended him the other night on their run.

He gave her a tight smile then looked at Ethan in a way that suggested he was ready to hear their choices.

Ethan caught on. 'Oh, sorry mate, we need a bit more time with our order.'

'Daniel is my neighbour!' Sienna burst out.

Ethan extended his arm and gave Daniel's delicate hand a shake. 'Oh, no way! Nice to meet you, Daniel.'

'You too.' He was still being awkward as he took Ethan's hand, but maybe it was just him. 'I'm finishing my shift but I'll put you in the good hands of Marcel.' He pointed with his pencil towards the counter at a middle-aged man with a moustache. 'It's good to see you again.' He smiled at Sienna. 'And nice to meet you, Ethan.' He looked at him as he said his name and reached out his hand again.

The look on Ethan's face made Sienna want to laugh as he reluctantly took his hand again and gave it another, unnecessary shake. Sienna tried to keep a straight face as she watched Daniel's amused expression as he went in for a shake a second time.

Why was he so nervous?

Ethan looked at Sienna. 'That was odd.'

She took a sip of her tea. 'Yeah, it was a bit. But he is a cool guy, I like him.'

Ethan's mobile rang. It was Amber telling him that she was two minutes away. As he was on the phone she noticed Daniel finish up and slip past their table on his way out. She reached her arm out to get his attention.

'Oi!'

He looked at where her hand was resting on his forearm. 'Marcel will be with you soon.'

'Yeah, no. That's okay. Just wanted to say it was good seeing you!'

His lips curled. 'Sorry I'm not working later so I could give you two a discount.' He looked back at Ethan who was laughing at something in his conversation with Amber.

She would be here literally in two seconds but each to their own.

Daniel seemed to be so intrigued by him.

Maybe it was a little odd.

'That's okay, there's actually going to be three of—'

'She's parked. She's got no sense of direction, that one, but I think she'll manage to find the place,' interrupted Ethan as he slipped his phone away.

Sienna turned back at Daniel but he had already walked off, sending her a little wave on the way out. She focused back at Ethan but he was on his feet, waving towards Amber most likely, who would have passed Daniel on the stairs.

Ethan waited until she reached the table before he hugged her. 'Hey darlin!'

Sienna sat in her chair and watched them greet one another; their embrace seemed to be quite . . . well, full on. He nuzzled his face into her silky dark hair that sat perfectly below her shoulders in a gorgeous wave. She was dressed up which made Sienna feel better about her own personal shoe choice. She wore a high waist black silk skirt that fell just below her knees but hugged her figure a little too perfectly. It probably took a lot of self-control for Ethan not to grab that perky little bum of hers, while their hug went on a little longer than she felt comfortable with. Amber noticed Sienna and broke free.

'Sienna!' She reached down and gave her a little hug around the neck. 'So good to see you again. Thanks for joining us tonight.'

Sienna hugged the woman back. She even smelt amazing.

'It's lovely to see you too. Here,' she said, pulling out the seat.

Amber smiled and sat down. 'I'm sorry I'm late guys, thanks for waiting.' She tucked her hair behind her ears and studied the menu. Sienna tried her best not to stare. Anyone would think she had a girl crush the way she was admiring her. She was that damn beautiful.

'What do you all feel like? I'm happy with anything. Let's get this out of the way so I can hear about your days.' She looked up from the menu and gave her a big smile. 'You're first, Sienna.'

She wanted to hear all about her day?

She barely knew this woman and she was making such an effort with her. Even though Sienna could see that Ethan was finding ways to touch her, obviously being completely besotted by her—Amber was making a conscious effort not to be too affectionate in front of her. Sienna appreciated that. It showed maturity and an awareness of not only her surroundings but of Sienna's feelings, even if Amber wasn't aware of how she felt about Ethan.

She wondered if the woman knew there had been something between her and Ethan. She once believed that she would have. But now she wasn't so sure. What was there to share, really— they had never dated. There was no evidence of there ever being more.

She looked at Ethan, the way his eyes lit up like a boy at a candy store in Amber's presence. There was nothing subtle about his feelings for her, no question about it from what she could see. Their love was as clear as night and day. His body language hid nothing and his eyes expressed a longing she had never seen before.

She took out a cup and filled it with tea for Amber, listening in to their joyful banter. They were in love. A love that had the potential of having a depth that surpassed every level and penetrated every layer. Maybe Amber was that person for Ethan. If she was, she would be happy for them.

One day it would be her turn.

Eight

Sunday afternoons had quickly become Sienna's favorite part of her week. It wasn't just because she was given containers of delicious food to take home—whether it was batches of meals made for the week ahead, or leftovers from the day's get-together—but because it was the day her family came together. It had been that way for years, but she was only just catching on with the tradition. Not that she could catch up on the many Sundays she had missed over the years—but she would be present now. Nothing was more important than family—life had taught her that.

She loved that the weather was getting warmer. It meant that lunch was moved to their outdoor setting on the new patio her father had recently built. Now that he was retired he somehow managed to keep himself just as busy with all his little projects. Last week it was finishing off the patio, and a few weeks before that was the installation of the swing set and trampoline for her two-year-old niece Bailey. Not that she could really play on it yet. But he was planning ahead. Honestly, it was beautiful.

Her mum had gone all out today: zucchini quiche, grilled salt and pepper calamari, cured meats, smoked salmon, fresh mango salad with pavlova and caramel mousse for dessert. There was always too much food but that made for good leftovers. Besides, Lance, her sister Mia's husband, had the biggest appetite Sienna had ever come across so really, most of all the effort was for him.

Then there was Bailey. Always so delicate with her food, she made Lance look like a walrus. Maybe that was a bit harsh. Everyone was grateful that Lance was the big eater in the family. He always had a way of making her mum feel good about her over the top efforts, complimenting her after every mouthful. Sienna loved him. They all did. She hoped that one day she would find someone just as amazing.

A big feed almost always guaranteed a food coma. Lazy Sunday became just that as they all sat outside, sprawled out on the couches as they watched Bailey play with an endless amount of energy.

Sienna settled back into the couch next to her sister as she watched Mia eying Lance who was sitting across from them. They had been exchanging eye contact since lunch time, making her feel like she was being left out from a big secret. She had never seen Mia so on edge but no one else seemed to have noticed.

But she had noticed the minute she arrived.

They had been whispering in the corner of the living room while her parents were setting the table up outside for lunch. Sienna had been playing with Bailey at the time and she swore that she saw Mia take something out her handbag before swiftly stuffing it back inside. Something wooden maybe. Then there was the time when they were all sitting around the table passing around food as everyone served themselves. But not Mia—she had sat back as Lance took her plate and filled it with very little. She hadn't paid too much attention to it, not wanting to be too obvious. But she was eating significantly less than everyone else.

Now, sitting beside her sister on the couch sipping their homemade lemon, lime and bitters, she noticed Mia glancing at Lance on occasion without actually saying anything.

Mia stood to her feet. 'Bailey, honey, come over here'. Sienna's little niece was having too much fun with her pa, chasing each other around, picking the sunflowers that had sprung out of nowhere over the past couple of weeks. Her father took her hand as she came bounding towards them with a bunch of grass in her hand, held high to the sky. That little girl had so much joy, it was infectious.

Mia sat Bailey down on her lap and eyed Lance again. He looked at her and smiled as though there was some kind of code language between them.

What was going on?

'So . . . Bailey's got something to show everyone.' Mia kissed Bailey's forehead. 'Don't you sweet girl?' Bailey stuck her finger in her mouth and let out a cheeky smile.

Sienna's blood was pumping. Was this what all those shifty looks were about? Bailey jumped off Mia's lap and reached for her bag that Sienna hadn't realised she had brought out with her. Turns out she wasn't fully switched on, after all.

Bailey pulled out a square, wooden box with no writing or label on it. Everyone was staring at the box in anticipation, wondering what was so significant about it. She held it in her hands and looked at Mia who gave her a little nod of approval. With two hands Bailey passed it to her grandma who had a suspicious grin on her face.

'This is for everyone to open. You too, Sienna,' Lance said with a smile and swapped seats with her so she could be side by side with her parents and the mysterious wooden box. With her parents holding either side of it, Sienna stuck her nose over the top as though she was waiting for something inside it to jump out at her.

Mia grinned. 'On the count of three.'

'One, two . . .'

'Fweeeee!' sang Bailey, excitedly.

Sienna was the one to open the box and they all gasped in unison. The box was lined with blue tissue paper with a little stuffed teddy and a metallic card with the words "It's a Boy!" written on it. Sienna let out a little scream and started jumping up and down. Mia was pregnant! She was going to become an aunty again!

Her parents were equally delighted and the whole family started hugging each other. Bailey, feeding off the energy of everyone else, started dancing with her sunflowers all around them without actually knowing what was going on. According to Mia, she was learning about it for the first time, admitting that she didn't trust her daughter to keep the news a secret.

'This is the best news,' Sienna said after they all did their round of congratulations.

'It was so hard to keep the secret!' Mia rubbed her tummy and laughed. 'Morning sickness has got me bad this time around, and I'm devastated that I couldn't have a lot of that seafood for lunch.'

'I did wonder if something was going on,' said Sienna with a raise of her eyebrow. 'Really, I'm disappointed in myself that I didn't work it out a lot sooner.'

'I think I did well to keep it quiet this long. You know I'm not very subtle,' Mia replied.

'You're about as subtle as a gun.'

They both laughed.

'Have you heard any more from Patrick?'

Sienna had told her about her meet up with him as they didn't have the ability to keep anything from each other. In the beginning she was annoyed, accusing her for allowing herself to still be controlled by him. But when she had told Mia about his moment of reflection and what she believed to be a genuine display of regret, she calmed down. But just like Sienna anticipated—she hadn't heard from him again, nor had she been tempted to reach out.

It was quite miraculous, really.

'Not at all.' She poured herself another glass of the lemon, lime and bitters that was making her bloat to the size of Mia's sixteen-week pregnant stomach. Sixteen weeks; she still couldn't believe she had hidden it so well and for so long. 'And, you know what? I'm completely fine.'

And she truly believed she was.

Sienna had become reluctant to leave these kinds of afternoons.

Sure, she had settled into her own place just fine. And it wasn't about getting back in time for the sunset thing, either. She just felt like she was getting to know her parents all over again—or maybe, for the first time.

She had missed so much during the years she was with Patrick. It was almost like she had lost her ability to voice anything—her mouth had been forced closed for so long. She knew that they felt the same too by the way they would ask her more questions than usual. It was almost like they had changed their tone with her—hanging off every word she said with such attentiveness. Sienna hadn't shared the details of her breakup with her parents in the way she had with Mia. But she had an inkling that Mia probably passed it all on to them anyway—which she was fine about. She kind of liked the idea of her sister being a mediator as Sienna, by nature, was more of a private person. Now that that chapter was behind her, it made the questions these days far easier to find answers for.

But this afternoon's topic surprised them both.

'How's the planning going for this L.A. trip?' her dad asked her as they were back inside, sitting in the living room with the T.V. gently playing in the background. Her mum was on the other couch scrolling social media with her index finger with one hand, a cup of coffee in the other.

'Risk assessments are done, permission forms are still rolling in but there's one girl who I want there but says she can't go, so I'm working on that,' she said.

'Is it not a compulsory thing?' her mum chipped in, still keeping her eyes down on her screen.

'No, just an opportunity for a select few from each program. The ones we believe have the most potential.'

'Then why do you feel the need to convince this one girl to go?' Her dad had always been the analytical one.

'Because I see something special in her. She's got so much talent, it's ridiculous,' she said truthfully. And perhaps, a bit too passionately.

Her mum looked up from her phone. 'Honey, if the girl's family can't afford it then there's nothing you can do about that. It's beyond your job description to do more.'

Her mum didn't get it.

'It's not about the money, mum. The school is covering all costs. Her parents are the issue.'

'Do you think you're perhaps a little too invested in this girl?' Her dad was taking her mother's side. 'It's not your place to question her parents' decision. For whatever reason they have decided against it. You don't want to ruffle any feathers, sweetheart.'

Sienna bit down on her lip, feeling her face burn up.

'I don't intend to ruffle any feathers, dad.' She felt like a child again; they were treating her like someone who had no idea how to conduct herself professionally. 'I just think some insight as to why they're so against it, even if it's misguided, will help me help this girl more. I want to support her, seeing her parents are not.'

Her dad sighed heavily and her mum put her phone away and adjusted the incline on the couch so she was more upright.

'What's their opinion? What is the girl's surname?' asked her dad.

'Peters. Isabelle Peters.' Her mum squinted her eyes and

nodded as though she knew the surname. 'They think that dance isn't important,' Sienna went on, 'that it won't help her become a doctor.'

'Of course it won't,' her dad said curtly.

'Hun,' said her mum, shooting him a look.

'She doesn't want to be a doctor. She wants to dance.' Sienna's face was on fire. 'It sounds to me that they are more interested in the dreams they have for her, than the dreams she has for herself.'

Her mum looked down on that part. Her dad grew quiet too. They must have known—known that the reason why she was so invested in this girl, was because she could relate. Sienna saw herself in this girl and now, her parents had caught on.

'I still think it's best you let them work it out. It's between her and her family, Sienna.' Her dad's words came more carefully this time.

But she wasn't done.

She shifted her weight on the couch, not being able to still herself. Her soul felt restless. 'If I don't back her up, then no one will. She'll go off and study medicine according to her parents' wishes and be completely unhappy. Maybe even feel resentment for not pursuing the opportunity, and their relationship will be strained because of it.' She knew she was talking about herself. The school trip had nothing to do with a medicine degree. She was thinking beyond it—concerned that Isabelle wouldn't have the opportunity to train full time—not being able to forge her own path, or travel her own journey. She didn't mean for the conversation to turn so personal. Or maybe she did.

Maybe this was another knot of deep-rooted pain she needed to iron out.

It was hard not to compare the situation against her own story. When she was about Isabelle's age she had been given the opportunity to study at the prestigious National State Ballet. It hadn't exactly been her parents' wishes. While she had been supported financially, she hadn't been emotionally. Like Isabelle, her parents saw dance as a waste of time. A profession that was almost impossible to achieve anything in, with little money to boot. They weren't exactly off the mark. It was true; it was a difficult industry to break into and they worked like animals, placing their body through so much trauma for what seemed like so very little. Well, little according to those who simply had an uninformed perspective, judging the art from a spectator's point of view.

But to Sienna, it was so much more than that. It was her passion. Her identity. The one thing that made her excited in a world of so much uncertainty. She had lived and breathed dance as though it supported her very existence. When she got injured, all of that came to an abrupt stop and suddenly, she had to figure out who she was without it. No one counselled her through the heartbreak of it all, instead she was told to get on with her life. She threw herself into her studies because that was what was expected of her. But she felt numb. She would smile and laugh, pretending that she enjoyed what a normal life entailed. But she had never felt so lost. That's when she met Patrick and surrendered her soul as they worked hard to live the "model life"— filled with materialistic things they didn't even need or want. A life society classified as being successful, yet made Sienna feel so empty.

She wasn't blaming her parents for her relationship choice.

That wouldn't be fair. She just wished that they had swallowed their pride and championed the dreams inside her heart, honouring her gifts and talents when she most needed them to. Because if they had, maybe she wouldn't have felt the need to have gone down the road of pleasing everyone else, filling a void, proving that she was good enough. She might have saved herself a lot of heartache.

'Sienna, we realise how much we must have hurt you.' Her mum held her mug of coffee with two hands and looked into her eyes. 'I know this—what you're saying—is more about you, than it is about this student.'

Sienna felt a thickness in her throat. It wasn't that she really believed her parents were too proud to admit it, but she never expected this. They rarely had heart to heart moments like this. It just wasn't how they were. Their relationship never really consisted of a repertoire of deep and meaningfuls. 'Thanks, mum . . .' It was all she could manage.

Her dad cleared his throat again and interlaced his hands together. 'I'm with your mother; we could have done things differently. We don't always have to agree with your decisions but maybe we should have encouraged you more.' He stood from his chair and what happened next, surprised her.

He pulled her in for a hug.

'And we should have told you how proud we are of you, because we are.'

She hugged him tight and felt her heart ease and crumble at the same time. 'Thanks, dad. I know that can't be easy for you to say. It means a lot.'

They pulled apart, but he kept one hand on her shoulder and

held an expression that told her he had something important left to say.

'Be tactful about how you approach it . . . but do what you need to do.'

Nine

The girl was more troubled than she realised.

Sienna was beginning to believe more and more that there was no such thing as coincidences; that specific events unfold with the purpose to teach you something.

Like the particular Tuesday afternoon where the staff bathroom was closed due to a plumbing issue, leaving Sienna no other option but to use the girls' bathroom. Even with this being the only option for those sharing the amenities in the Performing Arts Building, Sienna still liked to respect the privacy of her students and had taken a detour to the staff toilets near Administration while the repairs were taking place.

But as the school day concluded and she miraculously had an earlier finish, she had skipped the detour at 4:35 p.m., assuming all students would have long gone home. There had been no private lessons scheduled for the afternoon, and to Sienna's disappointment no dance students staying back in one of the studios to practice for their end of year physical dance assessments. When she had been their age she had been tied to the studio, desperate to perfect her craft, hours after her final class each day. She even had to be kicked out on occasion. Which, when she thought about it, explained the injury she received from all the stress she put her body though. She had trained too hard, sending her muscles into overdrive with little time for recovery—before landing a diagnosis of Posterior Compartment Syndrome in her calves, marking the end of her dance career.

No, disappointment wasn't the word. She was proud of her girls and should be thankful that they weren't obsessive the way she had been. Burn out never got anyone anywhere.

She reached the bathroom, almost knocking Holly—one of the music students—out as she turned the corner.

'Sure you don't want the rest of this?' the girl called out into the bathroom, dangling a bag of what looked like was filled with chips, chocolate and other junk food. The other hand was holding the door slightly open so that whoever was inside could hear.

'Nah, you can have it,' the voice called out from inside.

Holly let the door open wider for Sienna and they gave each other a smile of acknowledgement.

'Ok, I'll meet you outside,' Holly added and let Sienna through.

The girl disappeared and Sienna took a moment to study her face in the mirror. She looked healthier these days, less gaunt. Her cheeks were fuller, holding more of a rounded shape she hadn't noticed before. It made her skin crawl thinking about how thin she had been just a few months prior. It was scary to think how someone could control you to feel as though what they were inflicting on you was warranted, justified—shooting you down to a point where you begin to believe their lies.

She had fallen victim to Patrick the moment he controlled her eating, and she had come scarily close to anorexia because of it. It had been a slow journey finding a healthy relationship with food again. But she was getting there one day at a time. The signs of life in her face were a good reminder of that.

There was a hurling sound coming from one of the cubicles. Sienna froze, realising she had entered without making it known to whoever was in there, that she wasn't alone. She had been standing so quietly in her moment of reflection that she had almost forgotten herself. She gently took a step towards the sound, noticing the cubicle at the end had its door closed. She was glad she was wearing flat shoes today so that she didn't have to worry about any clomping of her heel blowing her cover. She could see the shuffling of feet underneath the door. There was a bit of fumbling going on before the girl started to cough then gag. Sienna scrunched her face knowing all too well what that sound meant. The gagging sound came again, louder this time, followed by a frustrated groan.

This girl wanted to throw up and she was trying her best to do so.

Just then the girl's phone went off, making Sienna jump. She bit down on her lip and held her breath. It was like she was nine all over again, creeping down the hallway to claim her midnight snack without wanting to wake her parents.

'Hey, mum.'

Sienna suddenly felt bad for invading her privacy; listening to her attempts of throwing up, and now, overhearing a personal phone call.

'Yeah, I'm just at school but about to leave.'

She knew that voice. It was Isabelle's. She turned her head from the cubicle door as if by somehow doing so, it granted the girl some privacy as Sienna's feet stayed glued to the tiled floor.

'I'm happy with wherever for dinner . . . yeah, Italian sounds good.'

Sienna found herself frowning. This girl wasn't feeling ill. If she was unwell she would have said something.

But there was no denying that she was sick. This girl was intentionally throwing up her food.

'Yep, I will . . . yes, mum . . . okay, See you soon.'

There was a pause before she heard a zip where she must have put her phone away in her bag. There were some more shuffling sounds and Sienna wondered in that moment if she should plan her exit before someone else walked in and caught her standing in a freeze position, parallel to the back of the toilet door. Or worse, Isabelle discovering her standing there like a silent creeper. Either way, it wouldn't be a good look.

She heard the sound of the toilet seat go up followed by the sound of nails tapping on the porcelain bowl. She could see that Isabelle was sitting on her bag. The small crack under the door gave away so much. Again, there were some more dry retching sounds, before the vomit came, making Sienna close her eyes and shudder.

Why?

She knew why. This girl wanted attention, a need of control. She could only assume it was due to her feeling as though she had none, what with her parents not wanting her to dance. But she couldn't just assume as she had no idea how long it had been going on and really, she barely knew the girl.

The toilet flushed and Sienna planned her exit. She tiptoed towards the door, her arms stretched out like horizontal beams, balancing her. Then she remembered that Holly had seen her go in. She had to at least pretend that she needed to go, which was true, and pretty badly too.

Within what had to have been a second of Isabelle opening the door, she shut herself inside a cubicle a couple of doors down and plonked herself down. She hoped Isabelle hadn't suspected anything. But the sound of the gentle hum the girl was making as she washed her hands told her that she hadn't.

'What were you doing in there? You took bloody forever.'

Sienna could hear Holly's voice as the tap turned off.

'Shut up.'

She could hear some rustling sound; a bag or something followed by some crunching.

'There's some left. Want the rest?

'Yep,' said Isabelle.

'I knew it.'

The main door shut and Sienna could hear them laughing, their voices getting fainter as they walked off. This was her opportunity to relieve that burning sensation. She released a breath as her bladder slowly returned to normal.

She was concerned for Isabelle and was in two minds about bringing it up with her, knowing how sensitive the issue of bulimia was. She wondered if Holly had mentioned that her teacher was in the bathroom at the same time that she was; but was doubtful that Holly had any idea that her friend was sticking her fingers down her throat by the way Isabelle had so casually gone in for more of whatever it was that they were eating. What about her parents? Did they know? Maybe they did, and it had impacted their decision in withholding their daughter from the L.A. trip. That to Sienna, made more sense. There was often a lot more than what meets the eye. She couldn't take everything at face value. Maybe that was why her dad was so adamant that she didn't push the trip to Isabelle's parents. With this new information that she suspected to be a secret, how could she know for sure what Isabelle had told her was the actual truth?

'You seem deep in thought!'

Sienna refocused her attention, realising she had walked back towards her office without fully being aware of doing so. Richard seemed to be on a mission but had stopped short in his tracks outside one of the music rooms. 'Are you okay?' His forehead creased with lines of wrinkles as he asked the question.

'Yeah.' She knew her thinking face had a way of looking twice as dramatic as her actual thoughts. 'Just trying to piece a few things together.'

'Anything I can help with?' Richard tucked some folders he was holding more securely under his arm.

'Isabelle Peters . . . what do you know about her?' she asked, sounding like an investigator dredging up a cold case.

'Um.' Richard scratched the nape of his neck with his spare hand, his expression blank. 'She's a good girl, bright. Doesn't get into too much mischief. Comes from a good family. Why do you ask?'

'From what I've learnt about her so far, I'd have to agree with you. She is talented too. Very talented, actually . . .'

Should she tell him what she saw?

'What's going on?' He looked concerned now.

'I'm only speculating . . .' Her eyes were drawn to the boy in the music room ahead; the one whose back was turned from her. He was sitting cross-legged facing the wall with a guitar rested in his hands.

'Sienna?'

The boy had ginger hair and a round head that looked out of proportion with the rest of his body. He plucked a few chords before turning his attention to a black folder. Every time he shifted his head she could see the profile of his face, swallowed by a pair of glasses that were way too big for him. So much so, his eyes behind the lenses appeared almost twice the size. She felt a pain take root.

'Whether she has any issues with . . . food?' She focused her eyes back at Richard, trying her best to stay present.

'Oh, look. That I'm not sure of. Diane might have more history on her than I do. But I know she was good friends with a girl who left last year due to anorexia. It was quite sad actually, the poor girl had to be hospitalised.'

She couldn't get the kid in the music room, with his uncanny resemblance, out of her mind.

'Oh, right. Well, that's helpful information. I might have to check in with Diane then,' she said, sounding far more intentional than she actually felt with one eye still on the kid.

'Right then, hopefully it's nothing to be concerned about. I'll see you in the morning, ballerina.'

Sienna laughed. 'Thanks. See you then, music man.'

He darted off in his usual pace, fixated on his destination.

She stayed still in the middle of the hallway, peering in at the boy alone in the room. He was so consumed in his music, unaware that anyone was around or watching him. She could see that he was determined to focus on whatever he was practicing, often flicking through his folder with its many sheets of music. Even in his school uniform he reminded her of Nolan and it made her insides ache.

But she still hadn't worked out why.

'What would be different, Nolan?'

Her students were seconds from entering the classroom after he had run ahead of them after their music class. His face was all smushed in his hands, his eyes holding a gaze that seemed to pierce right through her. 'What do you mean by that . . . that maybe it would be a world where we would all be okay?' She tried to sound casual, as though she wasn't dissecting his intent.

He didn't seem to shy away the way he normally did when confronted with her questions. This time, he just stayed there, the only movement being the occasional twitch of his eye—his left eye to be specific; it was after all, his weaker one.

'I don't know . . . I guess it makes you forget all the bad stuff in the world.' He wrinkled his nose. 'When you were a ballerina, did it do the same for you? Did it make you forget everything else?'

He was clever in his ability to divert attention. Maybe he didn't even know that he did it.

She stretched her arms out along the edges of the table in front of her as she pondered the question. 'It did. I believe anything that is creative has a way of doing that. It's a beautiful thing when you focus on what makes your heart happy.'

He lifted his head from his hands, leaving a crease mark on his cheeks where they had been resting. 'I think we are both creative people, Miss Henderson.'

'I think we are too, Nolan.'

By that time, all the students came spewing through the doors like a herd of animals. It didn't matter how many times she had got them to practice how to correctly enter a room, by the time lunch came around they failed almost every time. Especially after music class where their teacher, Mr Arnolds, only fed their energy levels.

As the students took out their lunches and sat down at their tables as per their normal routine, Nolan had neatly placed his lunch back into his lunch box and wandered over to the bookcase. He sat down on a cushion and flicked through the books on the shelf carefully as the children chatted with one another, their mouths full with bread and banana.

He began to hum to himself—maybe a tune from their lesson—as he studied the titles on the few books he had chosen in a pile beside him. He crossed his legs and quietly looked at each one before deciding on the one with the blue cover, and began to read.

Once the children had finished their food and were dismissed for lunch she had stayed behind to set up for their next lesson, picking up any scraps that had failed to reach the bin. Along the way she passed where Nolan had been sitting, noticing that he hadn't put his book away. It was unlike Nolan to not pack up after himself. But as soon as she read the title she knew why this particular time he hadn't.

The Lost Boy.

It was her last memory of him, just days before she finished up. Somehow it was the memory that tormented her the most. He had wanted her to find it.

He was desperate to tell her *something*.

Ten

Sienna had gotten used to seeing Ethan around.

Their paths didn't always cross as she was in and out of a number of classrooms throughout the week. But the main studios were often buzzing with sounds of drills and hammers and whatever other tools were used to turn their beautiful studios into something even more majestic. After just two weeks of renovations the studios were looking like a vision; wooden barres running along three sides, full length mirrors covering two, with blue Tarkett flooring covering two thirds of the floor.

They had been restricted to the smaller learning studios while all the work was taking place, making it quite a challenge for the girls to dance at their full capacity, but they knew it was just a matter of time until it would be finished and they would have an extra dose of motivation.

New things had a way of doing that.

She didn't have a lot of time, but had fixed him a cup of

coffee during lunch time from the staff room. She was careful to make it exactly the way he liked it—a lot of milk with two teaspoons of sugar. She assumed this was still the case anyway. On the way out, she grabbed a chocolate chip cookie in a napkin for good measure.

All she had to do was follow the noise to find him. She knocked on the glass door first before quickly realising it was pointless with all the banging that was going on in there.

'Oi!' It had become her new favourite word.

He looked up and took off his safety glasses. 'Oi back at you.' His eyes widened when he saw what was in her hand. 'Awwww is that for me?'

He was honestly like a big puppy dog the way he got so excited by food.

'It sure is. I've heard that thing on all morning, I thought you were due a snack.'

He wiped his brow and took the coffee and biscuit from her hands with a grin so big she couldn't help but smile.

'Thanks, S. Looking after me!' He settled down on a chair and lengthened his legs out, thumping the heels of his boots down onto the floor.

'Someone has to. You're just as bad as me, not breaking for a feed.'

He grinned, his teeth now lined with chocolate. 'This is seriously good.'

She laughed. He was such a big kid at heart. She liked this; the way it felt normal between them. She loved how she could grab him a cup of coffee without thinking twice of how it would be interpreted. It felt like they were teenagers again—with no ulterior motive other than two friends chatting. It felt freeing.

'I know. Richard's wife makes them. She's a legend.'

Ethan nodded as he popped the last bite of cookie into his mouth. 'I need to try and get more work here, for this reason alone.'

She laughed and leaned against the barre, giving it a tap with her palm before lowering her weight down onto it.

'It's secure,' he said, watching her.

'I should probably check these things first before I go sprawling out on your handiwork.'

'Trying to break things to keep me here longer.'

'Hey,' she pointed her finger at him. 'Just think of how many more cookies you could have if I did.'

'True that.'

She stood there, slouching against the barre precisely the way she told her students not to as she watched him inhale his coffee.

'I had fun the other night,' she said.

'We did too. Amber loves you by the way.'

She felt a warmth take over. 'She seems so genuine, Ethan.'

He tucked his legs back under him in his chair with that crooked smile of his; the one that usually made her all weak inside.

'She really is something else, that one.' His eyes bore an admiration that changed the whole shape of his smile. This girl had changed him, awakened him.

She could see that.

'Is she the one that's going to be responsible for taking you out of Aringdale?' she said in a teasing tone.

'She very well could be.'

'Lucky girl!' Sienna repositioned herself so that she was upright and their eyes made contact. She knew he hadn't read into her comment. It wasn't a comment made out of jealousy, he could see that. They may not have been connected romantically, but he understood her.

'You'd be open to moving to the city?'

'We've talked about it, but it's still early days. She's actually warming up to the idea of potentially moving here.'

'Sounds like things are getting serious.'

'I think they are!' He stood and tossed his paper cup in the bin. 'We're growing up, aren't we, S?'

Her mind flickered with memories—years of them, flashing forward at a similar speed to a flip book. It only felt like yesterday where they neglected their friends at lunch time, walking laps of the school oval together as they shared their deepest secrets and desires. Now here they were, over a decade later, all grown up. Even though life had found them on a journey different from the one they had predicted as kids, she was grateful. If they had travelled a different one, they wouldn't have shared this moment of standing on the very school grounds that had moulded their friendship. A moment of clarity confirming that, perhaps, being friends was their limit and was all they had the capacity to be.

She nodded her head and a smile filled her face. 'We really are.'

Sienna had arranged for the phone call with Isabelle's parents to take place that same afternoon. Ideally, she would have liked to meet them in the flesh but she thought that a call was a good way to sus out if a deeper conversation needed to be had. She wasn't good at confrontation—at least she didn't think she was. Sure, she had a way of sounding confident when she needed to be— thanking the performer inside herself for that—but more times than not she was shaking in her boots. Unfortunately, teaching was one of those professions where confrontation was near impossible to avoid.

She dialed Leila Peters' number on the phone in her office and settled into her white leather swivel chair. Her heart was pounding in anticipation of how this would go down. She only hoped that this woman was easier to handle than Nolan's mother Miranda had been. That had been an unexpected nightmare—the lack of empathy and love she had for her sweet, intelligent son still haunted her.

'Hello, Leila speaking.'

Sienna stopped spinning on her chair and snapped into professional mode. 'Good afternoon Leila, this is Sienna Henderson— Isabelle's dance teacher from Mason Grammar.'

There was a pause on the other end of the phone and Sienna prepared herself for the worst.

'Well isn't this funny timing! How are you, Sienna? It's lovely to meet you over the phone.'

Funny timing? What was she missing here?

'Uh. It's lovely to meet you too.' She was fumbling. 'I wanted to touch base with you regarding an opportunity with the College that I believe will benefit Isabelle's development—'

'Oh, yes. Is this about the dance workshop excursion in L.A.?' she cut in, all hurried in her speech. 'I was so pleased to see that Isabelle was put forward for that.'

Sienna was confused. 'Yes, that is what I'm calling about, actually. I'm glad to hear that you're pleased she's been selected. But honestly, Mrs. Peters, it wasn't a hard choice to make as your daughter is very talented.'

This was the moment where Leila was going to say thank you but no thank you. She could feel it.

'That's very kind of you to say, thank you Sienna. I apologise that we haven't handed the permission form in, I know that that was due a few days ago now. We have been encouraging Isabelle to go but unfortunately she doesn't seem very interested.'

This was news to Sienna's ears. What did the woman mean that she didn't want to go? Hadn't Isabelle told her that her parents were against dancing and that it stood in her way of becoming a doctor?

'Oh, is that so? Sorry, I didn't realise that that was the case. Isabelle and I had a brief chat last week and she expressed her desires to attend.' She was careful how she relayed the information, not wanting to share what Isabelle had said about her parents' disapproval with dance as a whole.

There was a silence on the other end of the line.

'I have to say, this comes as a bit of a surprise.' Leila's words came slow. 'I will be honest, Sienna, in saying that she has been quite adamant about not going. She loves dancing, don't get me wrong. Between you and me, I think she is a bit intimidated and anxious about the prospect of going as the competition over there is pretty fierce. Social media and all these dance reality T.V. shows have solidified that for her.'

This had Sienna stumped. The girl had looked genuinely upset that afternoon where she had approached Sienna about the trip. Had Isabelle lied in order to cover up her insecurity of not being good enough? She did often hide at the back of the class, so that part made sense. But what about the issue of her vomiting up her food, assuming that her speculations were true. Were her parents aware of that too, or was this another thing Isabelle was hiding? It was too premature to say.

'I'm just as surprised as you are, Mrs. Peters. I was led to believe that Isabelle really wanted to go. However, if that is her wish then we can't push her as it isn't a compulsory event.'

She probably sounded more convincing than she felt. She wished that Isabelle had just told her the truth that she was scared. Period.

'You're more than welcome to keep encouraging her. If anyone can change her mind, it's you. I know for a fact that she is thoroughly enjoying her classes with you.'

This woman was nothing like Miranda. Sienna liked her and could tell that she was authentic and real.

'Thank you, I appreciate that, I'm enjoying having Isabelle in my class and look forward to extending her further. She has a huge amount of potential.'

'That's very kind of you to say. Can I just clarify what I said earlier where I referred to "funny timing"? I ran into your mother earlier today. I haven't seen her since high school I don't think! I completely forgot that she had a daughter around the same age as my eldest son. I didn't even think to put the names together in my head.'

'Oh, well there you go! Small world!' Sienna laughed, feeling their conversation take a more casual turn.

'It is indeed! We were able to work out that you were the Sienna Henderson that was teaching my daughter. I just thought I'd share that with you!'

'I'm glad you did! I'm learning quickly that everyone is connected in some sort of way in Aringdale.'

'You're not wrong there, love.'

Sienna peered at the clock. It was getting close to five thirty now and she was just about ready to switch off. 'Thank you for taking my call Mrs. Peters. I'll see what I can do to convince Isabelle to join us on this trip. I hope you have a lovely evening.'

'Thank you, darling.' The woman sounded so cheerful. 'We are about to head out for a family dinner. My eldest son, Matthew, is down from Sydney. He is a doctor and a very busy man. It's not often that we all get together but he's on leave at the moment so we'll all be enjoying that.'

Her eldest son was a doctor . . . maybe there was some truth in Isabelle's story. Yet, her mum had seemed to be so proud of her and had encouraged her to change her daughter's mind so that she could take part in this trip. Something was off here.

They said their goodbyes and hung up. It had been a good call—a very positive call actually. Yet, it left Sienna feeling rattled. She gathered her things and switched off the light.

As usual, she was one of the last ones out.

99

The car park was starting to be an eventful place.

They had been instructed to park along the back fence today as there had been an information session on, wanting to keep as many parks free as possible for those attending. Sienna had parked on the opposite side of the school on the gravel knowing that there would be lots of shade which was the deciding factor despite the longer walk, considering the weather was getting warmer. There was nothing worse than stepping into a boiling hot car and having to wait for the air con to kick in before it was safe to place your hands on the steering wheel.

Her car was sitting there, parked all alone as she walked up the hill towards it. She slid on her sunglasses to protect her eyes from the glare. The sun had more of a bite now that she was inland. She almost forgot how much warmer it was here in comparison to the city.

She saw a flicker of movement behind one of the oak trees about forty metres further along the fence line. She could tell that they were Mason Grammar girls purely by the colours of the uniform, even if she couldn't make out who they were.

She got into her car and turned on the engine, desperate to get some cool air pumping. As the air con blasted its way through the vents she stared ahead at the girls. What were they doing lurking beneath the trees after hours in this heat? She was pretty sure they were out of bounds too. Whatever they were doing she could tell that they didn't want to be seen. The girls were leaning against the tree now, fiddling with something in the girl with the brown ponytail's hands. They were careful to stay hidden behind the trunk of the tree, glued together with their rigid movement.

It wasn't until the girl with the long blonde hair's foot got tangled in something and she stepped out from the tree to shake it off, that her cover was blown. Sienna knew instantly that the girl was a dancer by the way she extended her leg, her foot flicking off whatever was on the end of it in a delicate point.

But that wasn't the concerning part.

The two girls huddled back in so tightly that their shoulders were touching and lowered their heads. The blonde girl still hadn't tucked herself back behind the tree, making it easy for Sienna to view her clearly. It wasn't until she extended her hand towards her mouth that she could identify who the girl inhaling the cigarette was. What she was smoking, she had no idea. But she did know the girl in possession of it.

Isabelle Peters.

Eleven

Sienna had begun to like running. Okay, maybe "like" wasn't the word, "tolerate" would probably be more fitting. She was getting better at it too, now that her foot was fully healed and her cardiovascular fitness was improving, even by the smallest increment. She was able to run close to a kilometre now without spluttering and wheezing for a breath.

It was serious progress.

She could see her letter box up ahead and powered along the final stretch towards it. Using landmarks was a great way to create manageable goals. She could feel her heart thumping in her ears almost as loud as the sound of her feet hitting the pavement as she sprinted the seventy metres. She reached her letter box, clutching onto it the same way Jack had desperately held onto Rose during his dying scene in *Titanic*.

She had pushed herself harder and she was proud of herself for it.

She flicked the latch, snagging the side of her finger with the metal in the process. How she managed that, she didn't know. Running was beginning to be a high-risk injury zone. She brought her finger to her mouth to catch the drop of blood that already broke its way to the surface. With her free hand, she opened the little flap door to retrieve her mail for the day. A water bill and a letter that correctly listed her address but was intended for her neighbour: Daniel Aitkens.

She glanced across into his property, not knowing if he was home or not as she couldn't see a car out front. But then again, she didn't even know if he drove one. She would take her chances and knock first. If he didn't answer she would slip it in his letter box—the quirky barrel-shaped one. As she neared the door she could hear the sweet sound of the piano humming inside.

She stood there on the porch, hovering by the front door as she got swept away by the music. It was cinematic; filled with emotion the same way it had been the other day. Although this time he seemed to be hitting the keys harder as it built up to its pivotal moment of impact, bringing passion and intent to every note. There was something about music that always transported her to a place where her heart was content. It had a way of making everything stand still. Which explained why she must have looked hypnotized the way she was just standing there, staring through the door without making it known that she was there.

The music came to an abrupt stop. She took it as her cue to curl a fist and acknowledge her presence.

The door opened before her hand even touched it.

'I thought I saw something.'

'Something? Ouch.'

'Someone. Sorry, someone.' He corrected himself, not looking as though he was in the mood for a joke.

She had no idea how to read this man.

'I'm sorry to bother you.' She held out the letter. She would keep it short. 'This landed in my mail box for some reason.'

He didn't say anything. Instead he took the envelope and leaned awkwardly against the door frame, holding it open as though he was waiting for her to invite herself into his home.

'I know you probably think I'm a liar when I tell you I'm not a stalker but I just want to say again how talented you are. I couldn't help but hear you play . . . again.'

He managed a little laugh on the word "again".

'It's okay. If it makes you feel any better I did watch your little sprint to the finishing line.'

'Finishing line?'

'Your letter box.'

She suddenly felt embarrassed and found herself staring down at her sneakers. She had always been self-conscious of her running style, the way she looked like a ballerina, pointing her toes on every stride. He would have seen her melodramatic finish, all red and puffy in the face, gasping for breath.

Oh gawd.

'I'm getting better,' she said proudly.

'That I could also tell.'

'And you say I'm the stalker.'

'I think I should've been smarter and kept my mouth shut.'

'I think so too. From now on, you should just let your music do the talking,' she said on a roll.

He went quiet after that comment and she found herself

staring at her sneakers again. The street was so damn quiet; there wasn't even a chirping bird or car zooming by to help ease the moment.

This was why she couldn't read him. He would give her the impression that he enjoyed their banter but as soon as they had a flow going she would say something that would shut him down. Was she unknowingly inconsiderate or was he just overly sensitive? Maybe they simply didn't have the same sense of humour. Or maybe she just wasn't funny.

She would cut the jokes from now on.

'You're bleeding.'

She had totally forgotten about her finger. She followed his eyes to find a sticky smudged circle of blood where she had been cut. The whole thing looked far worse than it felt. It was quite amazing how much blood could ooze from such a tiny cut.

'It was the letter box this time,' she said almost apologetically as though she was a child being scolded by an adult.

He smiled at that. 'Let's get you a band aid.' He swung open the door and already began walking down the hallway of his apartment. He was only little but his feet made quite the impact on the floorboards with each stride. Without saying anything she obediently followed him inside, trying hard not to look too attentively at the woman in the black and white photographs that covered the cream walls.

She was stunning. From the pictures it was easy to see that, like Daniel, she was petite. Even though the images were black and white she could make out that her hair was dark, yet her skin was pale. She had the biggest smile Sienna had ever seen— kind of similar to Julia Roberts. Her eyes shone with a kindness that made Sienna's lips curl. Each photo along the hall that led to the kitchen appeared to be ordered from their earliest days together to what she assumed was the present. She could tell by the change of fashion and hairstyles; long, short, long again, styled straight then curly. Daniel, on the other hand, appeared to have less hair as the years went on. But what she noticed the most was the love that was evident between them. In every photo, no matter the pose, she could tell that they were absolutely besotted by each other.

She knew she had trailed behind as she studied the photos but Daniel didn't seem to notice. He was opening and closing drawers with a serious look on his face in his pursuit of the band aid. Her finger had stopped bleeding now and would probably be fine with a rinse under the tap. But Daniel was adamant. She would have laughed, but honestly could no longer predict how he would take it. Instead, she continued to stand there like a stuffed mullet in his immaculate kitchen.

'Uh-huh!' His head popped up from behind the bench, making her to jump.

'You found one.'

'I did!'

What he did next, surprised her. He peeled off the plastic and held it out to her. She followed his command and let him curl it around her finger. There was still dried blood escaping the sides the width of the plastic failed to cover, but she didn't want to go maneuvering around his house, touching taps and tea towels.

This would do for now.

'Thank you.' She lifted her eyes, admiring how immaculate

the place was. Everything seemed to have its place and looked so clean. 'You've made a lovely home for yourself here.'

He looked up and tapered his dark eyes, sending his eyebrows down. 'Thank you.'

'Or should I be giving all the credit to your wife?' she said, taking in the pot plants, mirrors and wall art surrounding the place. The woman certainly had good taste. She wished she had the money to buy nice things. Her theme-less, mis-matched items from IKEA would be as good as it was going to get for a while.

'She sure did have an eye for detail,' he said in a small voice.

Did?

Sienna's stomach flipped. Had she put her foot in it again? She assumed the woman in the pictures was his wife. Had she interpreted the hand holding, the ring on their left hands and pressing of faces together all wrong?

Things quickly became awkward again.

She shifted her weight and puckered her lips. They were so dry. She really needed to hydrate better.

'Well, she has nailed the home décor thing. I'll let you get back to your evening. Thanks again for the band aid.'

He stared at her curiously in a way that changed the shape of his eyebrows, casting a shadow down over his eyes. She suddenly felt uncomfortable being alone in his house when really, she barely knew the guy.

'I forget they were there. Even though there are so many of them . . . I forgot that they were there.'

'Sorry,' she started, 'I'm not sure I'm following.'

'All the photo frames lining the hall. They have become like furniture. I forget that people notice these things.'

She smoothed her cracked lips together. 'I did notice them walking in, yes. They're beautiful.'

'Thank you.' There was that small voice again. It was back. 'She was very beautiful.'

Was?

Twice now he had referred to his wife, partner or whatever she was, in the past tense.

Did something happen to her?

She studied his face. He was staring down at the kitchen bench, not making eye contact with her. After a second or two he looked up and gave her a sad smile.

'Would you care for some wine?' He reached for two glasses and pulled a bottle from the cupboard, resting it between them as she stood there on the other side. He clearly didn't want her to leave. For whatever reason, this guy wanted some company. She could feel there was a lot going on in his mind that perhaps he only knew how to express through his music. Without revealing too such, she could tell that although he was in love with the woman on the walls of his apartment, she was no longer part of his life. She knew what it meant when one reached for a bottle of wine in broad daylight in the comfort of one's own home. She also knew how to read a smile that fell short of reaching the eyes.

This was a man in pain.

'Daniel . . .' She was almost certain that she was going to cross a line, but she felt prompted to. She felt as though the question she was about to ask had already been invited.

'Yes?' He played with the cap of the Shiraz bottle that was yet to be opened. He was twisting it more times than it needed to come undone.

He knew. She could tell that he knew what was coming next.

'Your wife . . . did something happen to her?'

The side of his mouth twitched. 'Yes.'

She took a breath, looked at the bottle he was fondling with, then back at him.

'I would care for some wine, thank you.'

It was amazing what a bottle of wine could do.

Sienna didn't intend to stay for more than one glass, but such was life. By the time she had finished the first she had learnt that his wife, Samantha, had passed away just eighteen months ago from breast cancer. By the second glass she had felt so bad about it that she shared with him her broken and toxic engagement with Patrick—not that it was anything near as tragic as his news but it helped him see that she had experienced pain too—even if it was in a much milder form.

By the third glass he had asked her about her relationship with Ethan and if it was heading towards marriage. The question alone was enough for her wine to slosh everywhere as she had to contain herself from laughing. She wasn't quite sure why she found the question so funny, but realised that he must have assumed they were an item when he saw them at the restaurant together that night.

By the fourth glass the whole Ethan thing suddenly wasn't so funny anymore and she felt the loss of something that had been once so perfect in her head weigh down on her, making her realise that everything she had worked through mentally had been a waste.

Maybe she wasn't as okay as she thought she was.

But as soon as Daniel spoke some encouraging words to her, she had quickly snapped out of it, feeling guilty for feeling that way when her burdens were minuscule against the scale of his.

They placed their empty glasses down on the dining room table. For the first time in hours, their mouths finally took a rest from talking, giving her a chance to realise that her head was spinning. It was almost ten o' clock and she hadn't had any dinner. Her empty stomach really didn't help the situation. She really should have been thinking about getting back considering it was a weeknight and she hadn't started getting dinner organised.

But for some reason she was reluctant to move.

She wasn't attracted to Daniel in any other way besides appreciating the quality of their conversations. They say that a problem shared is a problem halved. Even though she had shared her story before, it hadn't felt as healing as it did this time. Or maybe it had and the volume of alcohol she had consumed clouded her judgement on that.

Daniel circled his finger around the rim of his glass then clasped his hands together and rested them on the table in front of him. He had long, pianist's fingers. She didn't really know if that was a thing or not, but as she sat there observing them she couldn't help but wonder how they moved along the keys.

'I know what you're thinking; they are really gangly looking.'

'What?' She looked up at him, noticing the amused look on his face.

'You're studying my hands.'

'No, I'm not.'

He placed his hands down on the table in front of him and sprawled his fingers out wide.

She laughed. 'Fine. I was.' She pushed her glass to the side. 'But not because I think they're gangly looking. Because they're not, really. I want you to play for me.'

'Play for you?'

'Yes.'

He danced his fingers in a galloping rhythm against the wood. 'Now you're putting the pressure on.'

'How so?'

'I've had like six wines.'

'Four,' she corrected him.

'You really are a stalker.'

She slapped her hands down on top of his. 'Nah, just observant.'

He removed his hands from beneath hers and slid them so they were tucked in close to him. 'What would you like me to play?'

He must have been just as tipsy as her to have all this confidence. She loved that he was so willing like this.

'Something beautiful,' she said.

He didn't hesitate. He pushed his chair back and left the room. She followed him into the lounge room. He sat down on his leather stool and placed his hands down onto the white keys. She took a seat on the sofa and placed her hands in her lap as she waited for the magic to unfold. From the snatches she had already heard, she didn't expect anything less.

And she was right.

It was one thing to hear his music from afar—from behind a tree (as you do) or outside his front door. But sitting here, just metres apart, sharing the same air, added a whole new dimension. This time she could hear and *see* the emotion behind every note. His body swayed forward and back, responding to the melody as it built into something so powerful. It had a force that might as well have plunged towards her and pulled her heart right out, there and then. Her throat thickened as she watched a combination of pain, love and passion drive his performance.

It was, hands down, the most beautiful piece of music she had ever heard.

The music finished. His fingers rested on top of the keys where his final notes were played. She cleared her throat, not being fully aware of the tears that had splashed her cheeks. His head was down but she didn't need to see his face to know how much this particular piece had impacted him.

'That was . . . incredibly beautiful.'

He lifted his fingers slightly, curling them into fists. He smiled as he lengthened them out again, placing them on either knee.

'Thank you. It was a piece I created for Samantha . . . not long before she died,' he said with a renewed strength, as though the music had been responsible for upholding him.

Music was incredibly powerful in that way.

'Only a deep love could inspire a masterpiece like that.' Sienna quickly wiped her cheeks the same time he lifted his head and turned to face her. He noticed her tears, his eyes shining with compassion at the sight of it.

Why was he looking at her this way, all empathetic, when his pain far outweighed her own?

'Have you ever experienced a deep love, Sienna?'

A month or two ago she would have jumped at the question, answering "yes" without hesitation. But now that she had taken time to navigate through everything, she had a clarity she hadn't reached before. Even though at times it hurt like hell, as it was the one thing she had wanted more than anything in the world, she knew the revelation would be freeing.

'No, I haven't . . .' She squeezed her hands together again. 'I'm yet to experience what that feels like.'

Twelve

In just under four weeks' time Sienna would be in L.A. with sixteen students from the performing arts program whose lives were bound to be changed from the experience; especially as there were scholarships on the table.

There was only one girl who she believed was in the running for the dance scholarship from the College; Isabelle Peters. It was all looking a bit impossible at this stage, her being torn between the conflicting messages she had heard from the same family. But after what Sienna had witnessed in the car park that afternoon, along with the bathroom incident, she was beginning to think that Isabelle was deeply troubled. Actually, she was sure of it. It wasn't uncommon for teenage girls at her age to lie, so she was learning. But what didn't sit right was how convincing Isabelle had been in the studio that afternoon about not being allowed to go.

With time ticking, she knew today had to be her opportunity.

She didn't know what to say but the girl seemed to like her so was hopeful that it would naturally lead to something.

Isabelle had been particularly distant that afternoon in class. Even though she still hid herself in the back row every time they rehearsed a piece of choreography, Sienna had begun to notice more; she was more alert now after what she had seen and heard. In the past she had put the girl's lack of concentration down to a confidence issue, but now her view had changed.

She could see that Isabelle was struggling, her body bending forward, where she often rested there with her hands on her knees as though she had finished a race. Her attentiveness was pretty much shot to hell too.

Every time Sienna stopped the class to break down each step in detail, she would sway side to side and stare without really watching. While the girls followed her every correction, trying their best to imbed the movement into their muscle memory, Isabelle would mimic each step at half capacity. It was obvious that she wasn't in the headspace the way her eyes were dilating, wide like a rabbit in headlights.

Sienna wanted to bring Isabelle to the front, wanting to push her out of her comfort zone the way she did in every other lesson, but today she felt like it would be cruel to. She could see that the girl was exhausted but at the same time, was also a great actress the way she could pick and choose her moments. Although she didn't engage in conversation with her peers throughout the class, she was quick to "snap back into it'" whenever she needed to. Her physical stance changed instantly as she placed her hands on her hips, lifted her chin, widened her eyes and presented a confident smile. Her whole physiology completely changed.

But Sienna wasn't fooled.

The bell went for lunch. With sweaty faces the girls grabbed their belongings and slowly dribbled out the double doors. She had worked them hard. She honestly didn't know any other approach and thanked her former professional career for instilling that into her.

Isabelle must have been more fatigued than she realised by the way she was lagging behind, taking her time to put on her shoes. It looked like she was deliberately taking her time, wanting to be alone with Sienna. It was the perfect set up really, and she hadn't even had to work for it.

The girl was noticeably sweatier than normal, as though even with her minimal efforts today she had still somehow over-exerted herself. She took a seat on the floor where her bag was resting against the wall, took a towel and wiped her forehead. Sienna studied her; she looked sedated—as though she was in her own little world.

It only made her think of Nolan all over again. He had been similar in that way—his true self coming to light once he felt safe enough to let his guard down. Wasn't that how most introverts worked? She had been the same.

'How are you, Isabelle'? She took a sip from her drink bottle, feeling a bead of sweat work its way down her back. Even she was sweating.

Isabelle stuffed her towel back in her bag and reached for her phone. 'Yeah, good,' she said casually as her fingers tapped away on the screen.

Sienna gritted her teeth. There was a strict no phone policy at their school. Mobiles were meant to stay in lockers until the end of the day. She opened her mouth to say something but thought against it. She didn't want the girl to be against her—especially when she could sense an attitude coming on.

'Good . . .' Sienna waited for her attention, but Isabelle didn't seem to notice. 'How are you feeling about the assessment dances?'

The girls had to perform two dances for their end of year practical assessments; a group piece, choreographed by the teacher and an own choreography solo of their chosen style of dance. The group item was almost complete and Sienna had seen glimpses of what she had come up with so far. She had chosen contemporary as her genre and had so far choreographed six counts of eight that cleverly showcased her strong technical ability. They hadn't had any one-on-one time to flesh it out but it was on the schedule for the coming weeks.

'Yeah, I'm feeling pretty good about it,' she said as she stuffed her phone back in her bag and took another sip of water, as though she had needed a distraction while being spoken to.

'Great! I look forward to seeing what you come up with. I'm glad you've chosen contemporary—that was a wise move.'

Isabelle smiled but avoided eye contact. 'Thanks.'

Sienna's stomach stirred; she needed to get to the point. 'I gave your mum a call the other day.' She pulled up a chair and took a seat in front of her. She didn't know where she was going with this but she had Isabelle's attention. The chair thing probably gave off the vibe that she meant business. She cleared her throat. 'I talked to her about the Los Angeles trip like I promised I would.'

Isabelle secured the lid of her drink bottle and zipped it inside her bag. 'I know.'

'You do? Did she tell you about our conversation?'

'Yeah, of course.' She made a face as though it was obvious.

'I have to say that our chat confused me a bit.'

'Which chat?' she said quickly.

'Well, both—ours and the one with your mother. But in this case, I'm referring to the one with your mother.'

'How come?'

She *knew*. The way her eyes were darting about and not focusing on Sienna was a dead giveaway. She knew that she had been caught out in a lie.

'Well . . .' She crossed her legs, not trying to be too confrontational with her body language. 'After *our* chat it was my understanding that your parents were the ones who had made the decision for you not to attend the workshop tour in Los Angeles.' She narrowed her eyes, keeping her expression neutral. 'I of course, kept everything else that you shared confidential.'

Isabelle fixed her eyes on Sienna. 'Well, it's true. They don't want me to dance.'

Sienna ignored that comment. 'Your mother told me that she was keen for you to go. She seemed to agree with me that this could be a wonderful opportunity for you.'

The girl didn't say anything for a long moment.

'I can't go,' she said in a small voice.

'Of course you can. I want you to be there, Isabelle. I specifically chose you because of how much promise you have.'

Her face changed and suddenly she looked like she was about ten years old. 'You really think I show promise?'

It was then that it dawned on Sienna that the girl had no idea what she thought of her. Sure, she knew that Isabelle didn't think she was good enough, but how many people had told her that she was? That she had potential for greatness? Had she been judging herself too harshly against all the top dancers on Instagram around the world, who had hundreds of hours of training over her?

Of course, she wasn't sure of herself. The lying, bulimia and smoking reflected that. It was clear that the girl had little self-worth, making it easy for her to be so easily misled, falling into the trap of the more nefarious influences of the world.

'I *know* that.' She pulled her chair in slightly as if she was about to tell her a secret. 'Can I be honest with you about something?'

Isabelle looked on with a liveliness Sienna hadn't seen from her all day.

'You remind me a lot of myself when I was your age.' She cleared her throat, not really knowing where this would go. 'Dance was everything to me, my whole life. Everyone who knew me could see that, but very few encouraged it. I felt alone in my dream of "wanting to make it". I was told by my family that I was living in "la la land" and that I wouldn't beat the odds in making it.'

She felt a lump in her throat as she thought back on it. 'I was just this country girl from a small town with big dreams. I was born and bred here. Like you, I was actually a student here, although back then we didn't have the facilities or the opportunities that you have now. There were local dance competitions running and that was about it. The thought of dancing beyond the safety net of a small town was scary. Even though I didn't have the support, I was determined to do the dance thing with the little self-confidence I had. And I'm glad I did. Yes, the competition was fierce in Melbourne, especially coming from a local school. I left Aringdale at the top, but entered Melbourne at the bottom. But you know what?'

Isabelle's eyes were still glued on hers. 'What?'

'It was a humbling experience,' Sienna said with a smile, 'and made me realise how much I wanted it and how hard I needed to work for it. I was desperate to prove my parents wrong. I *had* to achieve this "impossible dream". I had no idea if it would actually happen for me, but knew that it was who I was. Nothing made my heart soar more than dance did. Unfortunately, I got injured right before a company contract but I didn't see it as failing. Not one bit. Because those experiences—that testing mental, emotional and physical journey I went on—helped shape who I am today and led me to all these other wonderful opportunities that I never would have considered if I hadn't. All of which wouldn't have been possible if I had given in to the voices around me that told me otherwise. Because Isabelle, only you know you. No one knows you better than yourself.'

Sienna took a breath, surprising herself with how passionate she was getting. It was something she had acknowledged within herself, but hadn't openly expressed.

Not like this.

'I've learned that success isn't measured by status, or your occupation. It runs much deeper than that. At the end of the day people are going to remember you for who you are, and how you impacted lives—not how much money you made.'

Isabelle was still looking at her in a way that told her that everything she was saying was healing the broken pieces inside her.

Sienna uncrossed her legs and leaned forward ever so slightly. 'You've been blessed with a precious gift and know there is so much you can achieve with that passion of yours. You're a creative, Isabelle. Don't neglect that.'

Isabelle's eyes darted about, eventually slowing to focus in on something on the other side of the studio. 'What if my parents don't give me the chance to do any of it?'

'I think they're more open to the idea of you dancing than you realise.' She looked into Isabelle's glassy eyes even though the girl's eyes were still staring out elsewhere. 'Maybe that "block" you're facing derives from your own fear of failure more than anything else.'

A tear slid down Isabelle's cheek but she didn't flinch. Sienna felt a warmth enclose her.

She was reaching this girl. She could feel it.

'Let's take this journey one step at a time, yeah? Let's start with this L.A. trip. No expectations, but see it for what it is—an amazing learning experience. A chance to practice what you love across the other side of the world. As for everything beyond it, trust that the rest will work itself out, because it always does. My goodness, when I was your age my parents were adamant that I completed year twelve before I left this place. You're already in a better position than I ever was. You have a greater natural facility than I ever had too, Isabelle. This is just the beginning for you, I promise you that.'

Maybe she shouldn't have said the last part. She really shouldn't be promising the girl anything. What the future held was out of her control. But she knew what Isabelle was capable of. She knew that this girl could do anything if she really wanted to. She was young, pretty, intelligent and talented. She had all the makings of a star no matter what route she took.

Isabelle's attention flickered back to Sienna. She wiped away the tear with the back of her hand and curled it so that it cupped the side of her face. She smiled.

That was her cue.

Sienna stood to her feet and rested her hands behind the back of the chair. She tilted her head to the side and returned the smile. 'So, can we do this together, starting with L.A.?' Her voice came strong, like a commander confronting his tribe of soldiers.

Just like that, something in Isabelle's eyes changed. 'Okay . . . I'm in. You've got me.'

She didn't need to say anything for Sienna to know.

She knew what her answer would be before the words even came out of her mouth.

Thirteen

There was one thing Sienna really missed about the city. It wasn't the shopping, the never-ending choice of restaurants or the quirky hidden bars; it was Jacqui.

The woman had been her best friend since they were semi-professional, dancing at the same ballet institution that broke both of them. It would be fair to say that their time there had been nothing short of traumatic.

Ballet was an artform steeped in tradition; their directors' dated approach injecting fear into their every decision and response. Their young minds had been polluted instead of nurtured. *Growth mindset* didn't exist in an environment where they had been constantly told that they weren't good enough. Being screamed at would be a more accurate way of describing it as they worked like dogs receiving little to no positive reinforcement or acknowledgement of their efforts. It was no wonder so many dancers had eating disorders, extreme cases of anxiety and low self-esteem, despite the face of confidence they presented on stage. Maybe that was another reason why the feeling of performing was so great; it was one of the few things you had control over in an environment where you had no choice but to be submissive to such volatile mistreatment.

Their experience may have been toxic but it made them fiercely resilient, with a work ethic that truly set them apart, making them appreciate a normal life in a way no one else could truly understand. Since leaving that world (and it was very much a world of its own) they both had taken a different direction. Jacqui had always been the nurturing girl who wanted to "fix" things so had gone off and completed her studies to become a nurse. It was not uncommon to move onto a completely different career; in fact, it was the case for eighty percent of those who graduated at the National State Ballet. The odds of securing a job were never in your favour—although many spent years trying, until they eventually discovered this harsh reality.

Jacqui always set out to make an effort with their friendship. Every Tuesday evening when her long-term partner, Josh, went off to basketball training she would give Sienna a call at eight o' clock on the dot. Even though Sienna was convinced there wasn't much going on in her life, there was always something to talk about. They easily filled an hour, entertaining each other with stories and talking through Sienna's many conflicting feelings for Ethan which thankfully—after what felt like fifty counselling sessions with Jacqui—she had finally put behind her. Having had that revelation, their conversations had taken a turn and seemed to be steered towards her getting back on the bandwagon. Jacqui was way too excited about the idea of finding her a new guy.

Her friend was adamant about setting her up on the dating sites but the thought of entertaining that idea repulsed Sienna. She wanted to find a man the old-fashioned way; the way her sister Mia and Jacqui had. She had heard too many horror stories from the apps to even contemplate it. It was such a disposable world. The thought of basing one's worth according to a swipe "left" or "right" made her stomach churn. Gone were the days where one would pursue just one person at a time. These days no one invested the time to even get to know someone properly before they were in search of "the next best thing". The whole dating thing depressed her. Maybe she was meant to be born in another era.

It was rare for her friend to get Wednesdays off. But this particular week she wasn't rostered on and had jumped at the chance to make the trip to Aringdale for a visit. It was the most excitement Sienna had had in a while as she hovered by her front door, waiting for her to arrive. She had the whole day planned out; brunch at a cute little café in one of the "posh" streets in town, followed by a spot of shopping and a walk around the lake. With the sun out and twenty-four degrees—they really couldn't have chosen a better day for it.

The sound of a car pulled up front and Sienna did a full-on victory dance.

She opened the door as soon as she saw Jacqui step from her car. One would assume that it had been years since they had seen each other even though it had just been a couple of weeks.

Is this what life had come to? Getting excited over little things like a child would? Childlike joy . . . she would take it.

'That was the straightest drive I've ever been on,' laughed Jacqui, wrapping her arms around her neck.

Sienna took hold of her wrist and pulled her in tighter. 'It's pretty direct, isn't it! Did you enjoy the cow viewing along the way?'

'And llama viewing.'

'Alpacas, you mean.'

'I've never worked out the difference.' Jacqui pulled back and grinned.

'And paddocks filled with kangaroos.'

'Well, that's just a given.'

'The things you take for granted being a country girl.' Jacqui adjusted her handbag on her shoulder and grinned. 'So, show me your new place, country girl!'

Sienna stepped to the side and ushered her friend in. 'I've only just got myself organised and found a home for everything,' she said apologetically, even though she probably should have been proud of her IKEA efforts. Her set up really didn't reflect the tight budget with which she'd achieved everything. She did need some plants though. After seeing Daniel's place all pretty with them, she had decided it was a necessity.

Jacqui was walking ahead, sticking her head in and out of every room, finishing the unguided tour in about twenty seconds.

It was a small apartment.

She was carrying an unusually happy look on her face as she darted in and out of each room. Sienna stood in the middle of the kitchen, unable to keep up with her buzzing dynamism. Jacqui was a bubbly person and often had a level of energy that was on par with a four-year-old child.

But today she had taken it up a notch.

'Ready for brunch? You'll love their eggs benedict with a twist.' Jacqui hovered back into the kitchen giving her a look a kid would give to their mother if they were withholding something.

Sienna grinned, bracing herself for what had to be some news. 'What?'

Jacqui grinned, lifting her shoulders to her neck and stretched out her hands. Sienna took them in hers, frowning. She was completely oblivious of the bulge on her left hand until Jacqui wiggled her finger forcing Sienna's attention down onto it.

'Oh my god!' She grabbed her friend's hand and held it two inches from her face to view the rock that protruded from the silver band. 'He finally did it!'

Jacqui laughed. 'Yes, he did.'

'I thought he was going to do it months ago in Thailand, to be honest.'

'So did I. I could barely breathe every time we sat down for dinner or took a walk on the beach, but that would be too predictable, wouldn't it?'

Sienna winched on the word "beach", it having been the place Patrick had proposed to her all those years ago.

'I'm sorry, I didn't mean . . .' Jacqui picked up on what she had said straight away.

'Are you kidding? Don't be ridiculous. I'm fine. You know I'm fine.' Sienna let out a little squeal. 'So how did it happen? I'm dying to know!'

'Wellllll,' Jacqui pulled a chair from the table and sat herself down. 'You know I'm not all about grand gestures and Josh isn't either. Not to say that it wasn't special, because it was!' Her eyes danced as she told the story.

He had taken her to the Dandenong Ranges Botanical Gardens the night before—the same place Josh had taken them on their first date. He brought a picnic basket filled with her favourite snacks. After setting up the picnic blanket, they had sat down where Josh encouraged her to explore inside it. He pulled out a square jewellery box that was hidden inside, and gave it to her to open. The box was too large to be a ring box, but it was small enough to be intriguing. Inside was a ring sizing tool (a key chain with little plastic rings in each size). He told her that he was going to be starting the process of getting her a ring, and wanted to make sure that he knew the right size. She was still a bit confused, but began to sort through the different sizes to find hers. To her dismay, there was no ring that fit her finger on the key chain. Josh had pretended to be confused before reaching deeper into the basket, pulling out a much smaller red jewellery box. Getting down on one knee he untied the bow on top of the box and told her to try it on. He opened the box and showed her the diamond ring he had spent months designing and then well, the rest spoke for itself.

Sienna screeched. 'Aww Josh! What a sweetheart, seriously.'

'Who would have thought?'

They both laughed.

'This is amazing. Truly. I can't wait for your wedding. I know we've been talking about it for a while.' Sienna took a look at the rock that looked quite similar to the one Patrick had given her. She squeezed her hand. 'But now it's actually happening!'

'Only if you're my bridesmaid.'

'What would Josh think about that ultimatum?'

'It's ok, he knows we come as a package deal.'

'Solid foundations!' Sienna joked, because she could. Josh was well aware of how close they were and, unlike Patrick, he supported their friendship. She had spent countless hours with the pair over the three years they had been together. Josh was a legend; so easy-going, relaxed to the point where Sienna at times had to question who was wearing the pants in the relationship with Jacqui's strong personality. But it absolutely worked.

Within minutes they were out the door. They had planned to take Sienna's car for the four-minute drive to the cute little café where newspapers in hand were more common than mobile phones.

Daniel came out of his apartment the same time they were walking to her car. In his hands he was carrying two bags, his head down as though he was deep in thought.

Sienna cupped her hands over her mouth. 'Too late buddy!'

His head jerked up and a frown appeared as though he had been shouted at by a complete stranger.

'Bins went out this morning,' she clarified.

He stood dead in his tracks and pressed his palm to his forehead. 'Noooooo. Here I was thinking it's Thursday.'

'I'll take them and dump them if you like. We're about to head into the city.'

'City!' Jacqui erupted with a laugh as she walked towards Sienna's car.

'Yes, Aringdale is technically classified as a city,' Sienna said, pretending to be offended.

'But it's all bush.'

'You're not far off the mark,' Daniel called out, agreeing with her friend.

Sienna laughed. 'Hey, I expected more from you, country boy. You're meant to be backing me up.'

With the bags still in his hands, Daniel shrugged.

'Honestly, let me take them off you.'

'Not a chance, they'll stink your car out, S.'

They had nicknames now?

He placed one by his feet and sheltered his hand over his face in their direction. 'Hi, Sienna's friend.'

He really was in a chirpy mood this morning.

'Heya, neighbour friend. I'm Jacqui,' she called from the car.

'Daniel,' he said, the bags dangling by his sides. 'Welcome to the city.'

They all laughed.

'Jacqui just got engaged!'

'Is that so?' Daniel looked at Jacqui with a big smile, even if his eyes didn't reflect it.

'It is!' Jacqui extended her hand from where she was standing to show off her ring, even though he was too far away to really see anything.

'How exciting! Congratulations!'

'Thanks, Daniel.' Jacqui beamed, pulling her hand back in and studied the rock that more than likely set Josh back over ten thousand dollars. The thing was huge.

'Honestly, I can take them,' Sienna said again, not really knowing why she was so adamant in wanting to do so.

'Honestly, where exactly are you planning to "dump" them?' he asked.

She actually had no idea. She was just trying to be nice.

Jacqui was looking at her all funny as though there was something she was missing. When Sienna thought about it, she didn't think she had brought Daniel's name up once in their many phone conversations where they were meant to tell each other everything. But really, they had only caught up a handful of times. She wouldn't call them friends . . . would she? She wasn't quite sure what they were. Acquaintances, maybe? No, that wasn't it. They had shared too many tears and vulnerable moments in their single evening of red wine to qualify for such a platonic term.

But Jacqui could see that they had some sort of relationship even if Sienna couldn't quite articulate what it was yet.

'Would you like to join us for breakfast, Daniel?'

Sienna felt the blood rush to her head. She shot her eyes at her friend, giving her a look that very much implied the words "what are you doing?", but all with a smile in case Daniel caught on. The way she asked the question too, cornering him into answering a "yes" or "no" just wasn't ideal. She knew what her friend was doing, but Sienna wasn't interested. Not in that way anyway. It was far too soon to be thinking about getting back on the bandwagon anyway. Even if she was, Daniel wasn't the type of guy she would go for. Surely Jacqui could see that he wasn't her type? But it wasn't just about the physical. This guy was more broken than she was and was probably still deeply in love with his wife.

Deeply . . .

It was something she wasn't sure she had ever experienced when it came to love. The only thing she had deeply loved that had loved her back was ballet. But even then, that fell through. This is why in a hypothetical world, she and Daniel could never work—even if she was interested. He was still in love with someone who no longer existed and she didn't know if she believed a love that deep was possible for her.

He looked down as she asked the question. 'Uhh . . .'

She could see that he was taken aback, trying to formulate a polite way to get out of it. Clearly, he was just as uncomfortable about the idea as she was. She loved her best friend, but seriously. This was just as bad as trying to get her on the dating apps.

'It's okay,' Sienna waved off the idea, wanting to save the poor guy. 'There's no pressure. Me taking those bags off you really doesn't come with a catch!'

He was still looking down, quickly reverting back to his awkward self. She took it as an opportunity to quickly flash Jacqui a look of what she was feeling. Her friend had already caught on, mouthing the words "sorry" and they were back to being on the same page. This whole non-verbal conversation was carried out within about half a second.

He looked up and smiled. This time, it filled his whole face. 'Sure, I don't see why not. I was just going to flap around the house anyway. Breakfast sounds good! Thanks for the invite.'

'Great! I mean, there is one catch,' Jacqui started. 'You'll probably be dealing with me talking about weddings for a chunk of it.'

'Uhhh k. Well, in that case I might reconsider,' Daniel joked. 'Suit yourself.'

'Give me a minute to make myself presentable and I'll be with you.'

'I'll take the bags,' Sienna said, not giving up. She walked towards him and extended her hand.

'No, you won't.' He was already making his way back inside.

They watched him go and shut the door.

'He seems nice.'

Sienna turned. 'He's lovely.'

'So lovely that you forgot to mention him?' Jacqui was grinning.

'There's nothing much to tell. We're neighbours.' Sienna paused before her tongue made its own decision. 'I guess we've been on a run together, I've punched his face, he helped me with some broken glass and a bleeding finger and we've guzzled a bottle of wine together.'

'Hang on, what?'

'Oh, and I've listened to him play the piano. He is next level.'

Jacqui's eyes widened. 'Guzzled a bottle of wine together? So, you've been on a date?'

'He's been through a lot, Jacqui.' Sienna kept her eyes on the door in case he walked out at any moment.

'You've been on a date?' she repeated.

'No, no. Nothing like that,' she lowered her voice realising how quickly it had lifted. 'He's very broken.'

'So is everyone. You've been through hell and back too, you know.'

'Yeah, but not compared to this.'

'To what?'

The door opened. 'I'll tell you later,' she whispered.

He looked ... good. She hadn't seen him in his "street" clothes before. Until that moment she had never thought to have taken a second look, as awful as that sounded. He wasn't bad looking, that was for sure. Just not the type of guy she would ever go for . . . physically. He really wasn't much taller than she was and she was pretty sure they weighed the same with his very skinny torso.

But today, none of those things seem to stand out. Maybe it was the loose fitting black linen shirt and the tan shorts that disguised everything his work out gear had highlighted. She took a peak at his legs. Had they always been so defined? She found herself staring at how toned they were. Not only that, Daniel had a style about him she didn't know existed. She returned her eyes back at him, finding herself blush for having—unintentionally—checked the guy out.

'Ready?' she asked.

Daniel slid on his sunglasses and smiled. 'I'm ready.'

This time, she didn't even notice his caterpillar eyebrows as they poked above his shades.

Fourteen

With just two weeks left until they would fly to L.A., Sienna was feeling stressed.

Losing all of that valuable class time meant that she had no choice but to get ahead with the curriculum before exams were in full swing upon their return. The whole thing seemed possible in her head back when the timeline was first put together, but dance was an art that took hours to master and simply couldn't be rushed. She managed to place the three girls that were heading on the trip in an accelerated program for the theory component. That meant extra outside work, putting added pressure on them as they had other subjects to juggle. On top of this load, she had to somehow squeeze in extra private lessons in her already full schedule to rehearse their solos before they took off. The woman who was covering Sienna hadn't given her much confidence either. She looked as though she should have retired about a decade ago if she was brutally honest.

Naomi was the woman's name. She had dropped by a couple of days earlier to talk through the dance syllabus and work planner. Even with Sienna's clear, precise notes that easily could have been mistaken for a thesis, she wasn't convinced the woman had taken in anything she had been saying. Instead, Naomi diverted the conversation back to herself, sharing how her grandson was dancing for *The Het National Ballet* in Amsterdam, landing principal roles at just nineteen years old. That was amazing and all, but had nothing to do with her own personal competency to fulfil what the girls so desperately needed so close to the exam period. Whether the woman actually had any experience in the dance profession or not, Sienna had to remember that it was just two weeks and some sort of guidance was better than nothing.

Now that the studios were all freshly refurbished and looked brand spanking new, the girls seemed to be more motivated than ever as they stared at themselves in the full-length mirrors that lined the studio walls. Teenagers really seemed to be a different breed these days, more self-absorbed or something. You could see it in the way they held their bodies in positions that showed off their best angles; puckering their lips as they extended their arm out to take a selfie; batting their fake eyelashes as they took ten or eleven attempts to get the right picture. At just fifteen and sixteen years old at least half of these girls seemed to have either lash extensions, a spray tan, whitened teeth or hair extensions— maybe even all of the above. What did these girls' parents think? But in today's society, honestly nothing surprised Sienna anymore. Half the time they enabled it. But underneath the added layers, she knew that what all these girls wanted and needed was the same today as when Sienna had been a teen; for someone to love and support them. They were desperate for someone to see their worth and help them see that who they are is "enough."

Isabelle Peters was a perfect example of this.

Today the girl was off—even more so than the other day. Sienna put it down to stress. Isabelle must have been petrified about the upcoming tour and with the way Sienna was ramming the curriculum down the girls' throats, it was an overwhelming time for everyone.

She had thought their heartfelt chat the other week had gone well. She thought she had broken down a wall by the way Isabelle had caved in and agreed to go on the tour. Now that they had cleared the air about what she believed was holding the girl back, she had hoped they had reached a position where they could move forward. One step at a time as she said. But clearly, she had thought wrong. Today was the most distant the girl had ever been. Maybe she had her all wrong. Maybe she had no idea how to relate to teens at all. The thought alone discouraged her.

She took a sip of water and slid her watch along her wrist, partly to remove the sweat under it whilst trying to free the anxiety inside her as they had just fifteen minutes left to achieve the impossible. She had given the girls a three-minute break to rejuvenate before performing their group piece a couple more times. They had spent the last thirty minutes dissecting each section before getting into partners to give each other feedback. Isabelle and another girl by the name of Sarah, who was also going on the tour, had chosen to go together.

She had watched the girls closely, wanting to see how they responded to each other's constructive criticism. From what she had observed, Sarah had been the one doing most of the talking, manipulating Isabelle's body as the girl demonstrated the movements. Although she appeared as though she was trying, Sienna noticed how agitated Isabelle was getting, flinching every time Sarah focused on a position with her for an extended period of time. She could hear their voices rise from the other side of the room as Isabelle grabbed her long blonde hair over her shoulder with two fists with an expression of aggression that Sienna hadn't seen before.

As the three-minute break was drawing to an end she could see that Isabelle had isolated herself, keeping a clear distance from Sarah who, no doubt, only had Isabelle's best interests at heart. It was strange to see her sitting on the floor alone with her head in-between her knees when the girls were such good friends, spending many classes basically joined to the hip. She could see Sarah staring at her as though she couldn't understand why Isabelle was acting so out of character. Sienna feared this girl was crippled with anxiety. That, paired together with a potential eating disorder, was enough to ruin her.

With just a minute to go until Sienna would call them in, she contemplated saying something as the sight of her hunched over position in the corner was beginning to worry her. There were only a handful of girls left in the room, the rest either filling up their drink bottles outside the studio or doing a quick bathroom run.

She walked over to Isabelle, clearing her throat to make her presence known even though the girl's head was still angled towards the ground, her legs propped up either side of her. Her fingers were digging into the crown of her head, her red nails lost beneath the mop of golden hair that hung over her head long enough to touch the floor. Sienna could see the tension in the girl's body by the way her knuckles were turning white with an unusual pool of sweat at the base of her neck that had darkened the roots of her hair.

'Isabelle? Are you okay?'

The girl began to sway side to side, her hair sweeping the floor as her body rocked from left to right.

Sienna felt her blood begin to thump. The girl wasn't even responding properly. 'Isabelle? Can you hear me?'

The rocking continued, faster this time with enough force for the soles of her feet to lift from their planted position, as though she were a three-legged chair trying to steady itself.

Still no response.

Sienna crouched down beside her and gently rested her hand on the girl's shoulder. Even through her top she could feel the heat radiating through the thin layer of fabric along with the sweat that instantly made Sienna's hand wet. The girls hadn't even been dancing for five minutes, yet Isabelle was perspiring heavily despite being positioned directly under one of the air conditioning vents.

One by one the girls started to come back in as their short break was over. Sienna began to panic. She couldn't just leave Isabelle here like this.

'Isabelle!' she tried again, this time getting on her hands and knees so that she could get low enough to Isabelle's chin and at least observe her face. Were her eyes closed? The rocking came to a stop.

Had she passed out?

She felt everyone's eyes on her as the girls looked on in

anticipation. A few whispers circulated amongst them. She gently pulled back a layer of the girl's hair so that she could get a look at her face, praying to God that she wouldn't have to do CPR. She couldn't even remember the first thing to do if she had no other choice. Was it the recovery position or something?

She couldn't even remember what that even looked like.

To her relief Isabelle began to giggle. Sienna completely ignored the fact that it was an unusual response, more relieved that the girl had finally said something.

The giggling got louder and the room went dead quiet. Sienna could feel her heart slamming away inside her chest as she took more of the girl's hair and gently placed it over her other shoulder on the opposite side. Now that she had a clear view of Isabelle's face she could see that she almost looked like she was in . . . hysterics.

'Miss, no offence but you look like my rag doll right about now.' She lifted her chin and looked at her in a way she expected Sienna to join in.

Sienna stared at her, too shocked to respond. Even though the girl was laughing, Sienna could see that she wasn't all there. Her eyes were glazed over and her words were slurred.

'Seriously, have a look in the mirror. You look like you're about to pounce from all fours.'

Sienna could barely make out her words through her fits of laughter.

'We should put that into the choreography or something.'

Sienna didn't need to look in the mirror to know that she was referring to her being on her hands and knees with her head under Isabelle's face, trying to see what was going on.

But really, it wasn't funny.

No one was laughing either which only confirmed that Isabelle was being a nutcase, even to them. Sienna could see that this was going to take a while so told the girls to practice without her so she could have more time to get to the bottom of this. They were mature enough to mind their own business and not stare on at the odd behaviour Isabelle was displaying.

'How are you feeling?' Sienna repositioned herself in a cross-legged positioned next to her. Still, the girl's legs were propped up in front of her body but at least now her head was up and she seemed somewhat "with it".

Isabelle let out a groan, followed by an unrelated chuckle. 'I'm fine. Seriously, I don't know why you seem so worried and can't have a laugh.'

What was going on? Isabelle never spoke this way with her. She hadn't heard her speak this way with anyone.

'Can't have a laugh?'

'Yeah, you looked funny checking up on me, that's all.'

'Tell me how you're feeling, Isabelle. You don't seem yourself. I'm here to help.'

'I'm finnnnnnnnne,' she said, drawing out the "n" like a toddler wanting to be left alone. Isabelle positioned her palms on either side of her head and began massaging her temples. 'I've got a headache, but I'm fine.'

She was staring ahead, watching the girls practice across the studio. Her eyes hollowed as she glared at Sarah working solo on a move they had worked on together. Her pale face frowned as though she had been betrayed for having been rehearsing without her. Just as quickly, a smile took over. She cupped her hands over her mouth as though they had a football field of distance between them. 'Looking good, Sarzy!'

Sarah stopped what she was doing and shot a look at Sienna as if to say *what the fuck* before offering Isabelle a cautious smile. 'Thanks, hun. You coming?'

The once-reserved girl scrunched her face and gave her pretty little head a fierce shake. 'Nah . . . I'm good from here.'

Sarah gave her an awkward thumbs up as everyone stared in horror.

Isabelle seemed pissed off at that and turned to face Sienna. 'What are they all looking at?'

Sienna scratched the nape of her neck as she feared the worst. This girl was high. Starving, and high. She had seen the effects of marijuana to know what she was seeing. But why? Why was this beautiful, talented girl doing this to herself?

'I think it's best you sit out the rest of the lesson.' Her voice came stern.

Isabelle's eyes dilated as a sense of panic darkened her features. 'That doesn't sound good.'

It didn't even sound like something she would say.

'We need to have a little chat.'

Isabelle tucked her legs back under her and rested her chin on her knees. She released a heavy sigh and stared out ahead once again. 'I'm just going to sit here for a while,' she said in a small voice.

It was the end of the day and the studio had cleared. The girls had left the room without even attempting to talk to Isabelle. That in itself said a lot as the girl was well-liked by everyone. It was obvious even to them, that something was wrong and perhaps they were even scared to approach her. Sienna was scared. She was scared of how quickly the changes in Isabelle had escalated, and so close to their departure too. If the executive team found out about what she feared the girl was doing, she wouldn't be flying anywhere. Not a chance. She might even be suspended from the College or, worst case scenario, expelled.

There was no way Sienna was going to let it get to that. She may not have been able to save Nolan, but she wasn't about to give up with Isabelle.

Whatever she was on before, she seemed to be more "with it" now. Her body wasn't contorted in any tight position and her face had shifted from a ghostly complexion, to one of colour. She pulled in a chair, ignoring the niggling feeling about the fact that they were back here again, and so soon.

Isabelle was becoming more work than she had anticipated.

She wanted to do this sensitively but at the same time she knew what she was dealing with was beyond a friendly chat. This was serious. If she wasn't able to reach the girl this time then she would be out of her hands.

'What's going on, Isabelle, talk to me.' She had pulled in a chair like last time, yet was praying for a different outcome.

'I'm so embarrassed,' she mumbled.

'It's ok. You're in a safe environment. No one is judging.'

Isabelle smoothed her hair from her face and sighed. 'I was so out of it,' she whispered.

Sienna leaned forward in her chair. The girl was trying to admit to something without really saying anything. But Sienna knew. Maybe Isabelle even knew that she knew.

Sienna looked at her closely. The girl's focus was drawn between a piece of material on the ground and Sienna's eyes that had no intention of moving from hers.

'I'm concerned that you're not looking after yourself, Isabelle.'

The girl shrugged casually but she looked close to tears. 'There's nothing to worry about.'

'Hmmm.' Sienna clasped her hands together and looked deep into her eyes. 'But that's the thing . . . I think that there is.'

Isabelle's top lip began to quiver as fear paled her face a second time that afternoon. 'How much do you know?'

'More than you realise,' said Sienna, her words coming quickly.

'What do you mean?'

'I have seen the side effects before.'

Isabelle's eyes widened. 'What side effects?'

'You know what I'm talking about, Isabelle,' she said gently, hoping she hadn't jumped to the wrong conclusion. But she was sure. She knew what she had seen and the symptoms were all there.

Isabelle's face reddened. It was the most colour she had seen in her face for some time. 'How much do you know?' she repeated again.

'Enough for it to be serious enough to take it higher.'

'No!' her eyes bulged as she shot up her head. 'It would ruin me.'

'What you're doing will ruin you,' Sienna said, her heart breaking at the sight of the girl's distress. She had a duty of care to report what she knew but like Nolan, she felt as though she could somehow reach her rather than place her into a position where there would, without doubt, be an immediate consequence.

'Please don't say anything.' Isabelle sounded terrified as a desperate plea escaped her lips.

Sienna sighed heavily. She didn't mean to let it out the way she did, but if she withheld what Isabelle had indirectly confirmed to be true, she could lose her job. But the girl hadn't actually confessed to doing marijuana—she actually hadn't confessed to anything. All she knew was that Sienna knew *something*.

'I have a duty of care, Isabelle. I care for you first and foremost and have a role to play in that.'

The girl nodded her head and her body began to shake. Sienna refused to fold at the girl's tears. 'But I need to tell you that what you're doing has to stop. It's not just about the trip, it affects everything beyond that. It will impact your entire future like a domino effect, Isabelle.' She paused, realising she was coming on too strong, too passionate. She cleared her throat. 'It isn't going to be easy, it's going to take work but you have people who are here for you and love you beyond measure.' She lowered her hand on the girl's bony shoulder and looked into her tear-filled eyes. 'Believe me, no one has it all together. We are all fighting our own battles, even if the outside appears all rosy.'

'Will I miss out on the trip?'

'Is that what you want?'

'No!' Isabelle's sobs came harder.

'Then let's focus on that. Because at the moment you're not strong enough. You're at risk, sweetheart.'

'I want to go . . . I . . .' she cleared her throat, trying to calm herself before she continued. 'I know I need to make a change . . . I just don't know how to anymore.'

'One step at a time, remember,' Sienna said with a smile.

Isabelle nodded and rubbed her eyes. Even with a tear-stained face, she was still so beautiful.

The words from their previous conversation must have turned on a switch as she opened her mouth and said, 'One step at a time.'

Fifteen

Sienna's run-ins with Daniel were becoming more frequent since Jacqui's little visit.

Maybe now that he was feeling more comfortable with her, he was keen for some sort of friendship. Not that they weren't friends before, but perhaps he was now more than just a neighbour she occasionally ran into.

In fact, he always seemed to be around these days. He would be at the first bend in the road on the afternoons when she was motivated enough to go for a run; he would be collecting his mail whenever she pulled up after work even though he mostly worked night shifts, having all day to make the trip to his green-barrelled letter box. The timing really wasn't a coincidence, she knew that. But she hadn't minded.

When she thought about it, she liked it.

She had never really thought much about him up until that point, as horrible as that probably sounded. But that was before they had sat down for brunch for what had been three hours in the café, not wanting it to end. She enjoyed the way Daniel so easily slipped into her and Jacqui's conversations as though he was an old friend catching up on the events in their lives. It felt nice to have made a friend in Aringdale. She had never really had a male friend before. When she was with Patrick the whole concept of befriending a man was forbidden. She felt like she was back in primary school: not knowing how to act around him; not wanting to give off the impression that she wanted more. Because she didn't. She had more healing ahead of her before she could even contemplate the idea. But even with the palpable connection they had, he simply wasn't her type.

It was bin day and unlike last time, Daniel had gotten the day right. She wondered if he sometimes waited for her as he sat by his piano that looked out into the driveway. Rather than being creeped out by it, she found it endearing the way he jumped on every opportunity to interact with her. She wasn't used to that attention and well, she wasn't quite sure how to respond to it.

'Not long to go now,' he shouted from his driveway as they placed their bins on the edge of their property at the exact same time.

'Yep, it'll be empty in the morning, thank god. This week had quite the pile up.'

He just stared blankly at her. 'What are you talking about?' he laughed.

'What are *you* talking about?' she asked, making her way over to him so the whole neighbourhood wouldn't tune in to their conversation.

'Til you head off to the big smoke,' he said, giving her a funny look. 'L.A. Three days?'

'Oh yessssss. L.A.' She released a breath she didn't realise she was holding. 'Two.'

'Not a thought I should be putting in your head after a long day?'

'I want to be excited about it, but I'm just not.' She knew she sounded negative, and hadn't realised that it was how she was feeling until now.

'Is it about that girl?'

'Yeah.' Sienna sighed again and wiped the sweat off her brow. Today was a scorcher. 'She hasn't come to class high as a kite like she did the other week but she's still really withdrawn. I'm worried.'

'Is she going to be okay to go?'

'I really don't know, it's hard to tell. She tells me she's doing better but I have no idea what she's doing behind closed doors.'

'How are her energy levels in that core-graphedy class of yours?'

Sienna burst out laughing. 'Choreography class you mean?'

'Yeah, that,' he corrected himself. Even in the direct sunlight she could tell he was embarrassed that he hadn't gotten the word right after she had introduced it in one of their previous little chats. This particular one had been a few days earlier on one of their "timely" trips to the mail box.

'She's picked up, but probably because she knows I'm watching her like a hawk. I can tell she is fatigued.'

'And how are you going? Are you looking after yourself?'

She looked at him and found herself blushing at the question, without really knowing why. 'I dunno . . . I guess so. I'm doing my best.'

He nodded, deep in thought. 'If there is anything you need, don't be afraid to give me a bell.'

She could tell that he meant it, too.

'Actually, there is something I'm craving at the moment.'

'Is that so?'

She smiled. 'It is.'

He waited for her to go on, but she knew it was only a matter of time until he read her mind.

'That incredible wine?' he guessed. 'Because I have more!'

'Nope.'

'I'm out of ideas.'

'That was a weak effort,' she teased.

He ignored that comment. 'What is your soul craving at the moment?'

'I didn't say the word "soul"' she gasped, playfully. 'But now that you mention it my soul craves your music. I want you to play the piano for me.'

'No,' he said, but he was smiling.

'Yes,' she demanded, spiritedly. 'But you knew that was going to be my request, didn't you?'

The sun had disappeared beneath the clouds, making it easier to get a glimpse of his expression. His eyes lit up like Christmas, lifting his cheeks into a full smile.

'I did.'

'You're good.'

'Not a weak effort then?' he teased her.

She laughed. 'Not at all. I take that back.' She folded her arms across her chest. 'Looks like you get me.'

He pursed his lips together and nodded thoughtfully. 'More than you know.'

'Ouch, Sez! You're totally jabbing me with your seat belt.'

'Oh! Sorry! I thought that was the bloody socket!' Sarah said, shifting her weight to the side, sticking her head down between their seats.

'Sarahhhhhh,' Tiffany wailed as Sarah's body was now in her face as she searched for the buckle.

'Seriously guys! Where is this fuckin' thing? How do you's manage?'

'Language, Sarah!' Sienna snapped.

'Sorry, Miss,' she said, as she jabbed aimlessly into the sliver of space beside her, hoping to hear a click.

It was a positive beginning. Sienna would have thought the transition from the tarmac to the aircraft would be pretty seamless. But it was not.

The flight was full. And full of, well, quite a "diverse" array of people. From a team of obnoxious teenage boys all wearing red and white basketball jerseys acting like they were the next LeBron James, to three screaming babies, and a man who was causing a scene as he argued with a flight attendant—they were all on board. And better yet, were neatly tucked away into the two rows either side of them.

Already the girls were affected by the testosterone that filled the cabin, giggling like a pack of hyenas every time the boys' eyes landed anywhere in their direction. The boys weren't exactly oblivious to their presence either; turning back to look at them enough times for it to be annoying. Sienna wanted to wipe the cheeky smug looks off their faces; she felt that protective. She only imagined how she would feel if she had a teenage daughter of her own.

A fourteen-and-a-half-hour flight really didn't sound so bad back when they had received their itinerary. But now, crammed next to each other like sardines, with enough happening on board without the in-house flight entertainment, made the prospect of a direct flight without a stopover feel almost unbearable.

With fifteen minutes until take off, her bum was already cramping up. It didn't help that she had no way to release it with Richard filling the entire seat next to her to overflow. She would have to forgo the concept of space and deal with the fact that their arms would be brushing each other for the entire flight. It was one way to get to know each other on an intimate level.

'Oh my god he's looking at you, Issy,' Sarah hissed with an exaggerated energy. She leaned forward to reach Isabelle who looked, to be honest, half-dead in her seat. The girl barely reacted other than lifting an eyebrow, curling her mouth into a dazed smile. It was obvious that Isabelle wasn't interested, keeping her eyes focused on the magazine she was reading.

She was here, she had made it. Despite the many issues this girl was facing, she had shown up. The past week had been better— as far as Sienna could tell. She wasn't naive to the fact that the girl would be cautious to do and say all the right things around her, well aware that she was being watched. Sienna hadn't reported anything about the incident and had been feeling guilty about it. What if something horrible happened and then the school found out she had been withholding this information? She could lose her job . . . maybe even her teaching license. The thought alone honestly kept her up some nights.

She wiggled her bum hoping the cramp would subside, but it didn't. It began to run down the back of her thighs, cooling as it reached her ankles. Her arm brushed against Richard's as she tried to shake it out. Nothing was working.

'Nervous flyer?' he joked.

She twisted uncomfortably in her seat. 'One hundred percent'.

Nervous would be the word but it had nothing to do with flying. She unbuckled her seat belt and half stood up out of the minuscule chair. Had the seats in Economy always been so tiny?

The cooling sensation subsided and the cramp finally released.

She didn't need to be nervous. Isabelle would be fine. She hadn't withheld anything other than her own speculation. She had to convince herself that it would be all okay so she could go into this trip with a clear mind.

With just minutes until take off, phones were out snapping more selfies than Sienna had taken in her whole life. She watched the girls take snaps with pouted lips and sultry eyes as though they were posing for *Playboy* magazine. It was safe to say it was drawing the attention of the basketball team like a pack of hungry wolves. Their voice levels skyrocketed with their thick American accents as they interacted more confidently with the girls. If only the girls realised how ridiculous they looked, not being able to respond to them without giggling. It was quite funny to watch.

She peered over the seat where Holly—the girl she had run

into at the bathroom that day—was seated. She was a year above Isabelle, but still a year too young to be casually swiping what she was swiping: *Bumble*.

It was one of the dating apps that treated humans as disposable, swiping away a face if it didn't appeal; a judgement made simply by how well one could curate their profile, even if it didn't reflect who they were inside. Or maybe it reflected who they were perfectly—fake.

The whole thing made Sienna furious. She hated how someone's worth was determined simply by image and status. She needed not to get so worked up. She was on a plane to the United States. Why couldn't she just focus on that? It was as much of an opportunity for her as it was for the girls, even if they couldn't see it yet. Another thing she despised about people these days; so many were so entitled.

As soon as she saw his photo flash across Holly's screen, her irritation dissolved into disbelief. Surely, she hadn't seen it right? The girl's thumb stayed positioned over the swipe key. She hovered there, long enough for the image to stare at Sienna's face as though it was making a mockery of her. She was tempted to grab Holly's phone and delete the app there and then, while giving her a lecture about how inappropriate it was for a seventeen-year-old girl to pretend she was of legal age. Not to mention fantasising over an image of someone over a decade older than her. Why was she searching for someone in that age bracket, anyway?

She wanted to vomit as she leaned forward to view the image closer. The blood in her body began to run thin, her mouth seizing up the same way her bum had just minutes ago. So far, this whole experience was causing a full body paralysis and they hadn't even left the fricking airport.

'You ok, ballerina?' came Richard's voice, interrupting her momentum.

She nodded her head, unable to take her eyes from the screen holding the image that grew in detail the more she stared at it. 'Yes, all good over here,' she said, feeling like she was having some out-of-body experience.

One of the girls next to Holly leant in to check out the man on the screen. They whispered something and cupped their hands over their mouths to soften their giggles. The same flirtatious giggles Sienna had heard earlier. Even though the team was comprised of teenage boys of the most basic kind, at least they were of the same age.

That was it.

Before she knew it, she had lost all sense of reason as she reached her arm to take the phone off Holly as though she was a toddler snatching a doll from another girl's hands.

'What the fuck,' said Holly the second it was out of her possession.

Sienna felt too panicked by what she was witnessing to care about the student's reaction. With the phone in her hand she was able to look at it clearly.

She had seen it right, after all.

There, staring in front of her, or should she say, in front of god knows how many girls had been exposed to his picture, was Patrick.

Her ex-fiancé claiming to be a twenty-two-year-old.

Sure, he had a baby face. But twenty-two? Her stomach churned. She felt sick.

'Miss Henderson, can I have my phone back please?' Holly's voice wavered with panic. It was clear that the girl was horrified to have been caught out. In this particular moment, Sienna didn't even care about that. She was more disgusted about the fact that her ex-fiancé, whom she had once believed to be a genuine, trustworthy guy, was positioning himself for teenagers whilst wearing the white linen top she had bought him last Christmas.

'Sienna, is everything alright?'

Now both Richard and Holly were staring at her.

She nodded her head slowly, feeling Holly's panicked eyes on her in anticipation that she would be turned in, or worse, have her phone confiscated. But Sienna wasn't angry at the girl at all. She felt protective of her. With her back still turned to Richard she cleared her throat and made eye contact with Holly. The air hostesses were beginning to get into position, ready to lead everyone through the safety procedures. She had seconds to make her message clear, yet a whole flight to stew over how disgusting he was.

Was she overreacting? No, she really didn't think she was.

'You need to delete that thing now,' Sienna hissed, eyeballing the girl in a way that scared herself. The last thing she wanted was to pass it back, but she had no choice. She held out her hand and handed the phone with the man from her past into the hands of the child.

The girl took the phone and nodded. 'Yes, Miss.' She nervously eyed her friend next to her but she had already turned to face the front, not wanting to be part of it.

'Right now. I need to see you delete it.'

Holly pressed down on the app and it removed from her home screen.

'I wasn't born yesterday, Holly. Please go into the app where you downloaded it, delete your profile then uninstall it so it's completely gone.'

The girl nodded again, submissively this time, too scared of what could happen if she didn't. She did what she was asked.

'Thank you,' Sienna said, giving her a look that sent the girl a strong message. She plonked herself back down next to Richard, feeling his eyes on her. She wanted to say something but she was fuming too much inside to open her mouth.

The timing couldn't have been better as the voice of the air hostess filled the cabin and everyone's attention diverted towards the aisle. But the thought kept playing in her mind; could you ever really truly know someone?

She was beginning to think that you couldn't.

Sixteen

Jet lag was the worst.

In just four hours they would be touring the prestigious Charlton High School with massive bags under their eyes. Well, Sienna couldn't speak on their behalf but she liked to think she wasn't the only one tossing and turning around, wide awake at four in the morning.

It didn't help that her mind wasn't at rest. At all. The image of her ex-fiancé on the seventeen-year old's phone was still burning in her retinas. It didn't help that Isabelle had eaten no more than two mouthfuls of dinner once they finally landed, having barely eaten on the plane either.

Yes, she she watching her every laboured move.

Their accommodation was nothing short of impressive; situated in the heart of Miracle Mile, just over seven miles from the school. She hadn't even thought of doing her research about the place before she left, and was glad that she hadn't. It was the pleasant surprise she needed after her most recent one.

There were sixteen of them on the trip, making it a nice little manageable group; five girls, eight boys with three staff. As Sienna was the only female teacher on the tour she had scored her own room with a king-size bed. It certainly made up for the lack of space she had on the plane as she collapsed on top of the white linen sheets, spreading her legs like a starfish. She had stayed there for a while, not being able to move until she switched on her phone, hearing the flood of emails and Facebook messages come through, backdated from the time she had boarded up to now. In just an hour the sun would be up and she hadn't had a wink of sleep. The more she focused on dozing off, the more frustrated she became. But that was usually the way, wasn't it?

It didn't help that the basketball team happened to be staying at the same hotel as them. What were the chances, honestly? Luckily, they were only staying for four nights but still. It was a distraction the girls didn't need. She had a feeling her night patrolling would have to step up a notch with the team having caused quite the stir among the girls. Surely, they wouldn't do anything dumb and test their boundaries but nothing surprised her anymore.

It was time to stop thinking, she desperately needed to get some sleep.

And eventually, she did.

The subway system was literally a dream in Los Angeles. Unlike back home, it was approaching winter and Sienna's bones could feel it. The morning air sent sharp chills down her spine making her quickly regret not packing her thermals as she was getting dressed that morning.

They had an early morning start. Schools in the region began their day at 8:00 a.m., making the morning routine a bit of a stretch. But thankfully the subway system was easy to navigate and they were on and off within twenty minutes. The school was a five-minute walk from the station, situated behind a beautiful park in an area so quiet and secluded, it didn't feel like they were in the city at all.

Sienna felt a sense of calm as they followed the path up the hill towards a traditional-looking school building identical to the ones you see in classic American films, with its amber coloured brick walls extending over two or three stories with thick cylinder pillars lining the archway out the front.

A smile spread over Sienna's face as she bit down into her donut and muffled a chuckle. She didn't know what was more blissful; the sight of the beautiful facility they would be in for the next ten days or how perfectly normal it was to eat donuts for breakfast in this country. The looks on the kids' faces proved she wasn't the only one that was impressed. How a school in the small town of Aringdale could be affiliated with a prestigious school like this one, she had no idea.

The program hadn't even technically begun yet, but she could already sense it was going to be a winner.

The students across each division of music, drama and dance would be exposed to Carlton's curriculum like an exchange program. Time would be split between the classroom and studios where they, along with the selected students from the school, would collaborate to perform a piece on their final day together. A full-scale performance had been proposed and would be viewed by members of the executive team from The Juilliard School. As soon as they had all heard the news, the students were quick to realise what a big deal this was, especially since that institution had recently lowered its age restriction for admission by two years, making it possible for students as young as sixteen to apply. Straight away the atmosphere became one of sheer focus and determination. Six scholarships to train at the prestigious and renowned performing arts school in New York were suddenly on the table. It was certainly an upgrade from what the original offer had been. It was an opportunity on top of an opportunity; an advantage that no one could take for granted. How often did one get the chance to prove their talent outside the hundreds of others standing at the barre in an audition room with a number pinned on their leotard?

The morning began with a meeting where the head of each division shared details about the curriculum, scheduling, expectations, and all of that formal stuff. Sienna's role was simply to mentor the girls, and guide their practice but the reigns were in the hands of the Charlton faculty.

Amelia was the name of the woman who would be leading Sienna's girls. She didn't expect to feel intimidated by her but she couldn't help it. Amelia was beautiful, talented, incredibly confident and had a presence about her that had a way of holding the attention of everyone in the room.

She didn't know if it was the new environment, the level

of competition or the woman herself, but Sarah, Tiffany and Isabelle's energy shifted to a place Sienna hadn't seen before. Their eyes were like sponges; hungry to absorb everything that came out of the woman's mouth. In just five minutes they were more receptive to Amelia's every word than they had been the entire term. Maybe it was part of the reason why Sienna felt so jealous. She felt like a teenager all over again, trying to win the approval of others.

The studio was stunning, which of course wasn't a surprise. They reminded her a lot of the generously sized studios at *The Australian Ballet* with its high windows allowing the sun rays to generously spill in. The way the light hit the space with a golden glow was nothing short of magical.

The day began with a contemporary class. Sienna took a seat down the front as Amelia took them through a technique class, challenging their locomotor skills. With a total of eleven girls there was much freedom to move with ease within the space. Sienna watched the Charlton girls carefully. Like Amelia, they seemed to exude confidence. It always had been something Sienna admired about American dancers; the way they could work every inch of the space with whatever choreography was thrown at them. But that wasn't to say that her girls weren't at the same level because they were; they just had different qualities.

With jet lag leaving them at a disadvantage, Sienna had thought that there would be a chance they would be struggling with adapting to a different teaching style. But the girls were killing it.

Just an hour into the class Isabelle soared with a confidence that took Sienna by surprise, even though she was aware of what the girl was capable of. She was quick to pick up choreography, performing each step with a real sense of artistry—the same way she had when Sienna first noticed her. Even though the American girls had a persona that came across as threatening, this didn't seem to affect Isabelle in the slightest. It was as though something had switched inside her and she was fully in the moment; her insecurities melting away as she danced fearlessly alongside what really was her competition. Watching her soar like that was enough for Sienna's guilt to lift. She found herself smiling in her seat as she watched the troubled girl be overcome by the power of dance that appeared to have a healing effect right in front of her. Every time Amelia's eyes landed in Isabelle's direction Sienna felt herself warm with pride.

After completing a travelling combination across the room, Amelia allowed the girls a five-minute break. There wasn't a face in the room that wasn't red and blotchy as they all staggered over to their belongings, gasping for air. Fear washed over Sienna as she watched Isabelle take a spot on the floor, half expecting her to reenact the position she had been that day when she had been high as a kite. Well, according to Sienna's analysis anyway. But instead of dropping her head between her legs, she made them long either side of her body to form a middle split, and stretched. She didn't want to stop; she wanted to keep warm.

She was completely focused.

'She has a gift, that girl of yours,' said Amelia, her eyes following Sienna's gaze.

They both watched as Isabelle extended her body over towards her right leg in a perfect split.

'I think so too. If only she knew how good she was.'

Amelia nodded as though she knew exactly what she meant and tossed her long chestnut brown ponytail over her toned shoulder. Sienna found it hard not to stare at her full fuchsia lips and green eyes with eyelashes that went on forever.

'She has something that can't be taught. Juilliard would love her.'

'You think she has a chance at the scholarship?' She had to ask.

Amelia's eyes shifted focus. She looked at Sienna with an all-knowing look. 'Come on, girl,' her Cali accent thick, 'we both know she does.'

Sienna didn't know what to say so she just laughed. It was the answer she was hoping for. She didn't want to come off arrogant in thinking that her girls had a better shot at it because honestly, they were so talented. If anything, a scholarship would be worth more for international students, so really, Amelia's girls probably had an advantage. But she wouldn't be competitive. This experience wasn't about the scholarship any more than it was about which dancer was "the best". She was cautious of maintaining a healthy environment, free from judgement or unnecessary pressure. It was the type of environment she had wished for herself when she was dancing.

Putting that aside, even if Isabelle was chosen, Sienna wasn't sure she would be in any sort of position to accept the offer.

Amelia's eyes shifted again as another teacher appeared at the door. 'I'll be right back,' she said and jogged casually over towards the man in her coordinated lululemon attire, her hips swinging.

Sienna took a moment to check her phone. No new messages. Nothing since they arrived the night before. The adrenaline she woke with was beginning to fizzle and another feeling began to fill her. Was it loneliness or a premature case of home sickness? Or was something else going on? She had always been pretty in tune with herself when it came to navigating her emotions. But this feeling had her stumped.

Amelia jogged back over to her, but her energy, unlike before, seemed to be lagging. 'Right, I need to get these girls back into it,' she said, her mind clearly elsewhere.

'Everything ok?' Sienna couldn't help but ask. It wasn't like they were friends yet, but there was something about the woman that made her feel like it was ok to check in.

Amelia tightened her ponytail and stretched her neck, gearing herself back up before she called the girls back in. 'Yeah, darl. All good.' She grinned and lowered her voice. 'Great, actually. We've been given a pretty sweet opportunity. Just working through the logistics of it all.'

Sienna smiled, not wanting to probe as it was none of her business what opportunities this fancy school was getting.

She didn't have to say anything before Amelia went on. 'It's not a secret,' she said, seeming to have read her mind. 'Juilliard wants to partner with us and use our curriculum, so students who enter at a younger age are able to complete their academics alongside their chosen vocation.'

'Wow, that's amazing,' Sienna said, genuinely blown away at even the thought of it.

'No shit.' Amelia's green eyes blinked. 'And it gets better. They want to create a mini doco to promote the new partnership.'

'Is there anything this school doesn't have?' Sienna asked, laughing. She could only imagine how wonderful it would be to work at a place like this. No wonder all the teachers looked so happy in their jobs. Their resumes would be next level.

'Well, yeah,' Amelia said thoughtfully. 'That's why Mark was in just now.'

Sienna assumed that she was referring to the guy at the door. She waited.

'The guy that's meant to be composing the music for it has pulled out so we're currently looking at a doco without music.' She looked stressed as she talked about it.

Sienna didn't know how soon it was all happening, but by the panicked expression on Amelia's face she assumed it wasn't too far off.

'I'm sure they'll find someone. I can't imagine they would have a hard time finding someone talented.'

Amelia shook her head and scattered her eyes around the room, ready to call the girls back in. 'I hope so.' She clapped her hands together three times. Before she even opened her mouth, the girls were already getting on their feet. 'You don't happen to know any composers by any chance? Any insanely talented musicians that could help us out?' She didn't wait for a response as she moved forward to acknowledge the eleven sets of eyes that were eagerly waiting for their next instruction.

The skin on Sienna's back began to prickle as a thought took form inside her head. She doubted Amelia expected her to have an answer, but she had one.

In fact, it was a thought that didn't need time to "form" at all. Immediately, she knew the perfect person for the job; the most talented pianist she knew.

Daniel Aitkens.

Seventeen

Three days in and things were well and truly underway.

It was only mid-week but already Sienna could see that the students were exhausted. Their tight schedule left very little energy by the time they took the subway back to their hotel at the end of each day. The dynamic among the students had shifted similar to a relationship; from the initial anticipation of the honeymoon stage, to one where the shine had worn off and the work had set in. She was relieved that the added focus meant that the excitement of the boys occupying the rooms at the end of the corridor had become less shiny too.

Well, it seemed to be the case for most of the girls. Out of nowhere there was one girl who had sparked an interest in one of the basketballers. If Sienna was to line the team side-by-side she would have called this guy out for being the most arrogant out of the bunch. Good girls had a way of being drawn to the bad boys. Wasn't that the way?

It seemed to be the case for Isabelle.

Even though she was killing it in the studio, the second they returned back to their accommodation she would hide behind her phone when they hung out in common room or during dinner. Sienna knew it was a boy by the way she constantly found a way to wander off from the group, her eyes searching in hope of spotting him.

Hunter was the boy's name and it described him perfectly. The boy had a way of hunting down the prettiest and—in Isabelle's case—the most vulnerable student within her care. Sienna hadn't spoken to anyone on the team and had no interest to but had noticed the way they followed the girls around as they were celebrities. She hadn't realised until now how much of a hit the Aussie accent was over here. People were always finding ways to get them to open their mouths, probably more fascinated by how "bogan" they sounded.

It was just after eight in the evening and they had gone out for dinner. Tonight's vote had been a small, privately-owned diner that made burgers as big as the ones advertised on those McDonald's ads that were, in most cases, about half the size in real life. Even though junk food appeared to be cheaper over here, by the time the tip was added its price leveled itself out. Richard on the other hand, had no problems chowing down two burgers in the same space of time it took Isabelle to pick at hers. Yes, Sienna was still watching and the girl knew it, yet both of them pretended that this wasn't the case. Every time Isabelle passed her she would smile at her sweetly, giving her a look as if to let Sienna know that there was nothing to worry about. She really wasn't that subtle about her constant monitoring, but Isabelle had little wiggle room for any of her actions to be questioned. The thing was, Sienna did worry and it didn't seem to be going away. The calm before the storm only made her worry more.

They had all retired to the common room, curled up in their track pants and oversized jumpers. Most of the crew had downloaded the game *Psych!* and were already onto their fourth or fifth round. Isabelle had joined in for the first round but then excused herself to get her phone charger. Sienna thought nothing of it even though the girl announced it loud and clear in her direction so that she wouldn't have to check her whereabouts. But twenty minutes later and with no sign of Isabelle, she was starting to get restless. She didn't want to suffocate the girl and go and check up on her. There was a good chance she was taking a call which reminded Sienna that she needed to do the same.

Soon more people began to join in the game, quickly reaching their limit with players. She took it as a sign and let someone else step in. Every staff member was entitled to thirty minutes off-duty between dinner and lights out, so she decided to take hers now. She walked upstairs to her room, closed the door behind her and flopped onto the king-size bed that had been so kind as to have given her undisturbed sleep the past two nights. Without checking to see if he was online, she went into her thread with Daniel on Facebook Messenger and pressed the call button.

'Hey, you!'

'Heyyy,' came a slurred voice on the other end.

Sienna's enthusiasm crumbled. 'Are you ok?' He sounded almost drugged.

'Hang on.' There were some shuffling sounds. 'Ok, I'm back. I'm awake.'

Sienna's eyes landed at the clock on the bedside table. She had woken him. It was after two thirty in the afternoon over there. 'You were asleep?'

'Nope' he said confidently. 'I'm awake.'

'You are not.'

'I am too.'

'Are you feeling ok? Isn't it like, day time back home?'

'Yeah, it is and I'm fine. Just catching some snoozes before work. I was up all-night playing music.'

She stifled a laugh. 'Go back to sleep, we can chat tomorrow.'

'No, no. Stay. I'm just being lazy.' He sounded more awake this time, his voice brighter.

'Are you sure?'

'Yes.'

She swore she could feel his smile from the other end of the line. 'Now, stop feeling bad.'

'Alright.'

'Good,' he said. 'Now we have that behind us, tell me about your day.'

A smile took hold as she told him all the basics before he insisted on the details. She watched the time tick over as though it had been fast forwarded. Half an hour just wasn't long enough; she needed more time. She spent too much of it harassing him to make contact with Amelia to be considered for the Juilliard documentary thing. He told her he would think about it after she had given him no option, basically forcing him into it. And why shouldn't he? It would be a waste to let his talent sit stagnant within the four walls of his house when he had a showreel ready to go. Apparently, he had even composed music for a video game that was big in Europe. It was when he had told her that he had worked with a couple of Hans Zimmer's violinists that she realised she was dealing with a star. A humble one too. It was one of the things she loved most about him.

Liked about him, she should say.

He gave in. 'Ok, fine. Only because I'm too tired to win this argument.'

'You have no idea how happy this makes me. I'll send you Amelia's details as soon as I get off the phone.' She didn't care that she was five minutes over her thirty minutes. This was bigger than that. Amelia would pass on the details and whoever reviewed his "pitch" or "expression of interest" or whatever you call it, would love it. They would love him. She knew it.

They eventually hung up forty-two minutes later. She hadn't expected to have been on the phone that long, exceeding her time by over ten minutes. She quickly sent him the information he needed, hopeful he would get onto it right away.

She was late. Not only that, she realised something else. Isabelle hadn't come upstairs to call her family, not when it was afternoon over there and would both be working. Dread took over her body. Surely not. Surely, she didn't have plans to meet up with him.

Hunter.

She scrambled off her bed in record speed and hurried back down the two flights of stairs to join the group again. Richard looked up as soon as she entered, with a startled look on his face. She must have panicked him with her somewhat dramatic entrance. But it didn't stop there as her eyes frantically scanned the room in search for Isabelle.

'Everything ok?' he asked, his eyes bulging from his round face. Her heart was thumping. She hoped she wasn't overreacting but she couldn't help it. This feeling she had didn't seem to be going away.

'Has Isabelle made it back?'

Richard's face went blank. 'I didn't know she left?'

Sienna searched the room again with her eyes. The girl definitely wasn't there. Tiffany and Sarah were both tucked away on the couch laughing at something on their phones in a secret manner which only made Sienna paranoid about the dating app all over again. They had better not be on it. But she wasn't about to snatch the girl's phone off her a second time. Now wasn't the time.

'She went upstairs about forty minutes ago. You haven't seen her?'

Richard shook his head apologetically. 'I can send a student up to her room to see if she's there?' Sweat was already beginning to bead on his forehead; she had worried him.

'It's ok, I'll go,' she said, already making her way back up the stairs as everyone stayed engrossed in their phones.

She reached Isabelle's room and gave it a firm knock. She waited for a moment, but heard nothing. She knocked again.

'Isabelle, are you there?' she asked, her tone somewhere between casual and stern.

Still nothing.

Sienna took out her phone and dialed the girl's number. Each student had to give their mobile number to the teachers at the start of the trip. She just never expected she would need to use it.

She pressed her ear against the door as she begun the call, hoping to hear the ringtone from inside the room.

There wasn't a sound.

Without thinking, she quickly sent a message to Richard to let him know she would go on a walk to try and find her. His response was instant. She walked the corridor, reaching the rooms that belonged to the cocky basketballers. There was nothing holding her back from knocking on their doors like an overprotective parent but she didn't know how successful that would be. She had no idea who she would find on the other side; they could be staff or coaches for all she knew.

When she thought about it, it was crazy to go around knocking on every door. She couldn't do that, could she? No, of course she couldn't. Maybe she could ask reception and find out, but she doubted they would be able to disclose that kind of information.

She stood at the end of the corridor not knowing what to do. Maybe she shouldn't be freaking out. The girl had been gone for less than an hour, there could be a million of explanations for that. Really.

She stared out the window and admired the way the lights lit up the sky. Everything about L.A. was truly spectacular. They were right in the heart of Miracle Mile just metres from hundreds of shops, restaurants and live entertainment. Everyone was looking forward to exploring what this exciting city offered beyond the diner, including the well-anticipated trip to Universal Studios.

The weekend couldn't come soon enough.

Her heart pounded in her chest. Was there a chance that she was out there getting a head start? Isabelle knew the boundaries. She knew that she couldn't go off wandering off with a guy she didn't know. Surely, she wouldn't be that stupid. But what teenager wouldn't jump at an opportunity like that? Especially in the company of someone she fancied, who probably knew all the best places to go.

She edged herself closer to the window to look out over the manicured gardens. It looked romantic enough, especially with the fairy lights that hung delicately from the garden walls. Maybe they had gone for a walk out there together? Her mind was racing with possibilities as she dialed Isabelle's number again just to get the automated response.

She would go down.

The air was fresh and she didn't have a jumper—or sweater, she should call it. She recognised a few familiar faces from the team and without thinking walked up to three of the boys who were bouncing a ball on the asphalt around the side of their wing.

'Have any of you seen Hunter?'

The boys turned and looked at her as if to wonder how she knew their friend's name. She realised as soon as she asked that they probably had no idea who she was. She didn't bother explaining herself and went ahead, and asked a second time. She didn't care how it looked as she felt her stress levels rising with every passing minute Isabelle wasn't accounted for.

Two of the boys ignored her, cursing under their breaths as they continued to pass the ball to each other. Sienna felt the muscles in her jaw tighten, not knowing what to do. She couldn't force the boys to talk. She couldn't really do anything. But the one that looked half-decent held eye contact. With pleading eyes, she stared at him, hoping that he could help her.

The boy scratched his mop of hair. He pushed his chest out. 'He went out.'

She stared at him. 'Did he say where?'

The boy made a face as though he regretted saying anything at all. 'No offence, ma'am. I don't even know you, why should I share that information with you?'

One of the boys stopped bouncing his ball and turned his head. 'It's kinda creepy that you know Hunter's name.'

'Yeah,' the third boy chipped in, casually. 'Who are you again?'

She let out a frustrated sigh. She honestly had no time for this.

'She's part of that Aussie mob, can't you tell bro?' the half-decent boy said.

She had obviously given him too much credit.

'That's right. I'm from that "Aussie mob" and I suspect that your lovely friend has gone off with one of our students.' She studied their faces. 'Do you know who he went out with?'

They looked at each other unnervingly as if they knew something and didn't want to share.

'He didn't say,' one of the idiots finally said.

'You can't help me?' She was frustrated. She really had no interest in playing this game.

They exchanged looks again.

Something in Sienna snapped. 'I don't expect you to know her name. But can one of you boys please tell me if Hunter left the premises with a pretty blonde, about five foot five . . . one of our girls?'

She didn't know if it was the desperation in her voice or whether her initial judgement was accurate about the half-decent boy, but he narrowed his eyes and let the air out of his chest.

'Yeah, I don't know where they went ma'am, but he left with a girl that fits that description, I guess.' He looked out towards the city lights. 'About half an hour ago.'

Suddenly the way they lit up the night sky didn't feel that spectacular anymore.

After calling Isabelle's phone another two times she was officially left in a panic. By now she had questioned all of their students, getting them to call her, but still nothing. Sarah, who was sharing a room with Isabelle genuinely seemed clueless as to her whereabouts which only concerned Sienna more. The girls were best friends. Weren't best friends meant to tell each other everything?

No one knew where she had gone.

By the time ten thirty came around, the common room had been cleared out and the students had hit their beds. It also happened to be the time where a woman on the staff had found Isabelle's phone wedged between two cushions on the couch. Sienna didn't know if she should have been relieved that the girl wasn't deliberately ignoring their calls, or worried that she was out there alone with a guy she didn't know, with no way of getting in contact if something went wrong.

By 12:07 a.m. there was a knock at her bedroom door.

Sienna dreaded the worst. A visitor at this hour was never a good thing, especially considering that a couple of their staff were out there somewhere, searching for the irresponsible teen.

Her heart was somewhere in her mouth. She held her breath and opened the door.

176

There, in front of her, was Isabelle.

The girl's head was down, but her eyes were lifted. She looked at Sienna intensely, with an expression resembling complete fear.

'I'm sorry I left without saying anything,' she said in a small voice.

Sienna opened the door wider and just stared at her, too angry to know what to say.

Isabelle reluctantly lifted her head, her eyes flickering, resisting hers.

She looked seriously messed up.

'What were you thinking, going off with a guy you barely know like that?'

'I didn't mean to worry you. I'm all good.' She lost her footing and slammed into the door. Sienna took a whiff of her alcohol-infused breath as the girl fell towards her.

'It won't happen again. I promise.' She tried to steady herself and widened her stance to balance.

Sienna wanted to believe her, but she couldn't; the teen no longer had Sienna's trust.

Before she could come up with a response, the girl's eyes rolled back, exposing the whites of her eyes as she lost balance and collapsed.

'Isabelle!'

There was no response as she was left holding the girl's limp body in her arms.

'Richard! Somebody, help!' she shouted as the girl's weight grew too heavy for her grip.

Doors opened and the sound of feet, she couldn't quite make out how many, quickly came into range. The thud of footsteps intensified, blending with the fierce sound of the beating inside her chest.

With the little strength she had left, she inhaled a breath deep enough to get some air into her lungs. 'Call 911!'

Eighteen

A million thoughts were whirling inside Sienna's head as she sat in the back of the ambulance. She was terrified at what this meant for Isabelle, but also for herself.

Had she taken drugs? She didn't know. Was Hunter in possession of them? If so, there would be more where that had come from. Or had she just had too much to drink? Drinking on an empty stomach could do that, couldn't it? She was probably overworked and exhausted from the demands of the program as well. Any of these things, not to mention the change of environment and jetlag, were all valid factors that could have led to her collapsing.

She convinced herself that it was the latter.

But it didn't help her feel any better about what she already knew. Maybe keeping her silence had found a way to punish her. Without question the girl's parents would have to be informed and the doctors would need to know everything leading up to this point.

The truth always has a way of coming to light. Hadn't she learnt that lesson already? She had failed Isabelle. She should have known better than to have trusted her word the first time.

She should never have bargained with a teenager. Period.

She had been so frantic in calling for attention, she had woken up pretty much everyone on their floor. Doors had opened in every direction as students stared in complete horror at the sight of Isabelle's unresponsive body hanging from her arms by her doorway. It probably looked like something out of a horror movie, the way the whites of the girl's eyes were in full view, her head tilted back far enough for her long hair to drape to the floor. Sienna thought she heard a few girls cry, but she didn't know for sure. She was too focused on getting the girl the help she needed, she completely neglected the impact the scene no doubt had on the other fifteen students in her care.

But there was no room to dwell on those things. Right now, Isabelle was her first priority. She was wide awake as they travelled the ten minutes to the nearest hospital. Ten minutes felt like ten hours as her heart raced with fear of the unknown. Thankfully, five minutes into the ride Isabelle regained consciousness as a paramedic placed an oxygen mask on her. She flinched, yanking it off her before rolling over onto her side on the stretcher and vomiting.

Sienna felt like *she* was going to pass out. Not only were Isabelle's movements convulsive as she fought against the paramedic trying to help her, the back of the van quickly filled with a growing smell as she projectile-vomited multiple times into the blue plastic bucket. Sienna only hoped that everything she had put down her throat had found its way out.

She gripped onto her phone anxiously, waiting for it to ring. She was nervous at how the Peters' would respond, especially when she was dealing with a family of doctors.

Just her luck.

Would she have to be sent home? Or would they all have to leave the country? Surely it wouldn't come to that?

And to think it could have all been prevented if she had just opened her damn mouth.

Isabelle rolled onto her back and stared vacantly at the roof of the van as her arms dangled either side of the bed. She was regaining a bit of colour now but her expression gave nothing away. Sienna inched closer and gently took hold of her clammy hand. She didn't flinch this time.

'How are you feeling?'

It was probably a stupid question considering the circumstances, but she didn't know what else to do. She felt powerless.

Isabelle flopped her head to the side and squinted her eyes to look at her. Even then she struggled to keep them open; she seemed to be less panicked now, more aware of her surroundings. If anything, she looked defeated.

'A lot better,' she managed to say more coherently than before.

Sienna smiled, acknowledging the ripple of relief move its way through her. The girl was responding, that had to be a good sign.

'You're going to be just fine,' she said with more confidence than she felt. She looked at the paramedic for validation.

The man nodded in a way that didn't promise anything, but permitted relief to filter its way through her completely.

'She will be ok'.

You see it in the movies . . . the way time stands still when a pivotal moment takes place—the way everything closes in around you. Without choosing, that single thing that draws your attention suddenly becomes magnified to the point where everything surrounding it disappears—like a picture without a background, as though your peripheral vision no longer exists. You become tunnel-focused; not just in a physical sense, but in your mind too. You can't think. Your sense of reason, time, logic or anything for that matter, is gone. Even though you're numb, you somehow feel everything. Every cell in your body catches fire and every sense is heightened to a measure you're not prepared for.

The difference with real life is that there is no dramatic music playing while all this is unfolding. All you can hear is the sound of the erratic beating of your heart as it slams uncontrollably somewhere inside your chest. But even in that moment, you pay no attention to its irregular rhythm and neglect the fact that your brain has completely shut down because you simply don't have room to think. You're acting on impulse. Or at least feel you are. While your body is operating in the fight stage, your brain has completely failed you. They call it "fight or flight" for a reason. Maybe it's possible for our bodies to experience both.

She didn't know how long they were in there, or even how they got from the ambulance into the hospital, but they made it.

Everything in between had been a complete blur. It was like an out of body experience as she watched Isabelle settle onto another bed, medical professionals hovering over her, muttering to each other after each standard routine test—or at least it appeared that's what they were doing. Maybe they weren't muttering at all and were speaking clearly.

But Sienna couldn't make any of it out.

With every passing minute Isabelle seemed to come more to life. She was sitting up now, nodding her head at whatever she was being asked. Sienna put it down to a good thing.

The next minute a needle made its way into Isabelle's arm, something was inserted in her mouth before her hand was being hooked up to a drip.

Sienna stared in horror.

Her reaction must have been obvious as a doctor approached her as she sat tucked away like she was a naughty girl sent to the corner. As soon as she was told Isabelle would be ok and it was a combination of low blood pressure and dehydration, Sienna could function again. The girl had vomited up most of what she had drunk in the ambulance. All other tests had been clear, which meant no drugs. The girl hadn't taken anything. To Sienna, that was the part that she had been most concerned about. It would have destroyed her.

Maybe even both of them.

After hydrating her body with a drip, the plan was to keep her in overnight for monitoring. Sienna could have hugged the man, it was such a relief.

The nurses began to clear and soon, it was just the two of them. There Isabelle lay, staring ahead with weary eyes as her dainty hands rested palms down over the blanket. There was a bung inserted into one hand; a drip hanging from the stand to the right. She looked about twelve years old the way fear lit her pale face, framed by her matted blonde hair. She looked at Sienna apologetically as though she was scared to repeat the words that had failed to hold their value. Tears pooled in her swollen eyes and Sienna knew that all she needed in that moment was to be comforted. She wasn't sure what the physical boundaries were in a position like this, but surely there had to be exceptions. If her error in judgment had got her this far she might as well cross the line and embrace the girl in the way she desperately needed.

Maybe this is what forgiveness felt like. After all Sienna had been through she never expected to have felt forgiveness this way, through a relationship with a rebellious teenager.

'I stuffed up big time. I'm going to be sent home, aren't I,' she said, her voice thick with emotion.

Despite everything, Sienna managed a smile. 'You're not going to be sent home, Isabelle.'

'I deserve to be.'

Sienna titled her head. 'You're probably right.'

Isabelle's eyes widened at that.

She took a seat on the edge of her bed. 'But the rest of your peers don't deserve it, and neither do I. That's why you're not going to do anything that will bring us closer to having to make this decision. This, here, right now,' she patted her hand, the one without the needle sticking out of it, 'is where those poor choices end and strong ones begin.'

Isabelle inhaled a shaky breath and let the tears fall down her face, dampening her hair on the way down. 'My parents are going to kill me.'

Sienna didn't doubt it. Now things had settled down it was time to give Richard a call to find out how accurate that comment was.

'You don't need to worry about that now,' she said. 'What's done is done. Let's focus on what we can control, hey?' She felt an intense wave of tiredness sneak up upon her as the adrenaline began to wear off.

'Starting with a coffee,' she said, thinking aloud.

'I'm so sorry,' the girl said.

Sienna stood up and rubbed her eyes. She had developed a migraine from all the stress. 'No more apologies either, young lady. Let's put those words into action.'

That only made Isabelle cry more.

They sat there for a while without saying anything.

'You should get your coffee now,' Isabelle said once the tears stopped flowing.

'Here I was, just waiting for your permission,' Sienna joked.

They both managed a laugh.

Isabelle sat her body more upright in her bed. 'Will you be staying long?' Concern shaded her features at the thought of being alone.

'I'm not going to leave you here all by yourself.' Sienna pointed to the corner she had come from. 'See that chair? We'll be camping out together.'

Isabelle wiped the tears from her face, flicking the damp strands of hair to one side. 'What about tomorrow?'

Sienna stood up and stretched. 'Tomorrow has enough

worries of its own. Try and rest now. You'll be good to go in the morning.'

The girl's body visibly loosened. 'Miss Henderson?'

'Hmm?' she said, rubbing her eyes. She was beginning to wonder if it was possible to fall asleep whilst standing up. She sure felt on the verge.

'What you're doing . . . all you've done for me,' she cleared her throat and positioned her eyes on Sienna's. 'Thank you.'

Sienna's jaw locked with emotion. 'I appreciate that.' She smiled, feeling her eyes droop with exhaustion. 'Rest up, I'll be back in a little bit.'

The common problem with hospitals was that they all looked the same inside, making it almost impossible to know what direction she was going or where she would end up. She assumed it would be a safe bet to follow the blue line that ran down the centre of the corridors, but with every turn she only seemed to bury herself further in an endless maze. They needed to have better signage up around the place. Surely, she wasn't the only one who couldn't navigate her way around. She didn't know whether to laugh or cry at her frustration. All she knew was that she would earn every mouthful of this coffee.

After turning another three corners she had convinced herself she was back where she started. But somehow, miraculously, she arrived to an open space presented with a sign she never expected would give her so much joy: *Cafeteria*.

She felt like she was sleepwalking as she floated over to the display cabinet to stare at the food. Hospital food wasn't that great but in this moment everything behind the glass looked divine.

Even though it was now close to 2:00 a.m. the place was operating as though it was day time. Patients coming in didn't adhere to a schedule in the same way the lights in Los Angeles never grew dim.

She ordered a latte and, embracing the new routine, ordered a strawberry donut and took a seat at one of the stainless-steel benches that held similar features to a medical tray. She took a couple of large gulps of coffee, ignoring the burning sensation as it slid down her throat. She was too tired and too thirsty to wait for it to cool. She pulled out her phone to find three missed calls from Richard. Anxiety began to creep in. Had he been in contact with Isabelle's parents? She took a bite of her donut, the sugar hitting her blood stream as a burst of energy fed her the courage to return his call. She held her phone to her ear.

It was then that the adrenaline in her body accelerated like a rocket being launched. She lost all function as her half-chewed donut rested soggy in her mouth as she stared at the woman taking a seat a couple of tables away.

The hair on her back brushed against her top as she studied the back of her woman's peroxide blonde hair. It was tied in a tight ponytail on the top of her head, slapping her neck as her head bobbed around. The woman's voice grew louder, more hostile the longer the conversation carried out.

Sienna stood there, unable to hit the call button on her own phone. Her breathing began to shallow, the same way it had in front of the team of doctors minutes earlier. She rubbed her eyes, annoyed that the coffee hadn't had enough time to work its magic.

Somehow from where she was seated, she heard it. The sound of the woman's nails tapping the stainless-steel table whenever there was a pause in conversation.

It had to be true—that your senses are heightened when your body is in a reactive state. Even with metres of tables between them she could hear it. Immediately she identified with the familiar voice and the red fire-engine nails that had waved the air in her classroom more times than any of her students' hands. The woman flicked her hair over her bony shoulder and tugged at the collar of her low-cut blouse. Was it the same one she had worn that day in their meeting? Sienna wasn't sure.

It was when she repositioned her chair that Sienna was able to get a good glance at her face. Her heart dropped.

How was this possible? she thought.

She lowered the phone from her ear. She had to be seeing things. Sienna swallowed in the hope of lubricating her throat but it had closed up. She felt paralyzed, her brain unable to send a vocal response. But somehow, she did it.

'Miranda? Miranda Livingston?'

Nineteen

The woman turned her head and stared squarely into Sienna's eyes. Her booming voice went silent and her body visibly stiffened.

It was too hard to make out details from where she was standing but it was obvious that Miranda had no idea what to do. She stood there frozen then murmured something into her phone before slipping it away in her purse.

Sienna felt her stomach churn and her head began to spin.

She clasped the back of her chair and steadied herself for a moment. She took her coffee in one hand, her donut in the other and walked towards the woman who once had been intimidating, but now looked as frail as a little bird.

Miranda watched blindly as she walked towards her. Before Sienna had a chance to reach her, she flopped down onto her seat and sunk her body forward.

'Sienna,' the woman said in a small, beaten voice.

'Hi Miranda,' Sienna picked up a seat from the table next to her and slid it over. 'I never thought I would . . . wow.' She took a breath, trying to articulate her thoughts. 'I never expected to see you again. This is, ah, a surprise. How are you?' she asked, forgetting her dislike of the woman.

Miranda lifted her head and wrinkled her button nose.

She looked a mess.

Her eyeliner had smudged into the creases of her eyelids and a few clumps of fake lashes rested near the bridge of her nose. Now that Sienna was closer she could see that her hair was oily and her nails were hardly manicured at all. Half of her fake nails had fallen off and the ones that remained had grown out.

Miranda rubbed her left eye as though she didn't care in the slightest that her physical appearance was frightful. 'You find a way of having a presence, don't you?'

This confused Sienna. She cleared her throat. 'I'm sorry, I'm not following—'

'To this day Nolan hasn't stopped talking about you and now you're here,' she said dryly.

'Miranda . . . I—'

'How did you know?' she interrupted, her eyes burning with hot tears.

'How did I know what?' Sienna asked, wanting to be sick. Her body was dealing with far too many emotions than she knew how to handle tonight.

The woman slumped forward again and shook her head. 'Please.'

Sienna stared at the floor, completely at a loss. Did she think she was some kind of stalker or something?

'I'm not sure what's going on, Miranda. I'm very confused right now.' She took a breath and decided that she would start from the beginning. 'I'm not at King's Cross anymore. I moved to Aringdale at the beginning of the term. We flew here for a workshop with some of our performing arts students. There was an incident with one of our girls tonight.'

Miranda's head shot up again. 'You didn't know we were here?' *We?*

'What's going on?' Sienna asked, barely hearing her voice as the words made their way into the open.

Miranda looked as though she wasn't going to say anything but then something flickered across her face and Sienna knew. She knew that whatever the woman was going to say next she would have to brace herself for.

'Nolan.' It was all she could manage before sobs took over her body.

Sienna shuffled her chair closer and lifted an arm over her shoulder. The woman didn't move, she didn't try to resist the gesture. Instead, she embraced it. She turned her head towards Sienna and nuzzled her face into her shoulder.

Never in a million years did Sienna imagine she would find herself with her arm around a woman she was convinced hated her.

But in a moment of grief there was no space for pride and anger, as the need for comfort and human connection took over.

Sienna's phone began to ring and she threw it in her bag before it interfered with this moment. Richard would understand.

'It's ok, take your time,' Sienna said, more because she hadn't quite braced herself for what was going to come next. She needed more time, too.

Miranda lifted her head from her shoulder and sighed. Her breath smelt of cigarettes. Sienna tried not to react. 'It's so aggressive. We thought we . . .' she took out a tissue from her bag and brought it to her face. 'We thought we could fight . . .'

'Fight what, Miranda?' Sienna jumped in. She was ready now. She needed to know.

Her phone continued to buzz inside her bag, fuelling her anxiety as her attention was pulled in two directions.

'Nolan's sick.' The tone of her voice said so much more than the two words could articulate.

Sienna held her breath, not wanting to miss a word as the woman swallowed down hard.

'He's sick, Sienna. He has been for quite some time. We were told we had more time, but . . .' The woman began picking at her nails. 'It's been vicious . . . unforgiving.' She pulled her silk skirt further down to cover her thighs.

'What has been unforgiving?'

'The cancer,' she whispered. 'We're looking at stage four.'

Sienna couldn't breathe. She felt like she was going to have a heart attack.

Not Nolan. Surely, not him.

'What cancer?' she asked, feeling guilty seeing how upset Miranda was getting by her need to find answers.

'Leukemia,' Miranda said, beginning to take control of her sobs. 'He has an extremely rare dual-lineage leukemia. Our poor boy has been diagnosed with both Acute Lymphoblastic Leukemia and Myeloid Leukemia.'

Sienna's face paled, grateful that she had chosen to sit down. How was she supposed to comfort this woman when she felt like she was going to break down herself?

There was a reason why she couldn't get Nolan out of her mind, out of her heart. His presence was with her in the same way hers had been with him.

They say when you die your life flashes before your eyes. Sienna wasn't dying but the pieces of the puzzle that had kept her up many nights were doing exactly that—fighting against each other as they rushed into her conscious all at once. Every action, every conversation that she expected to have been lost, forgotten about, came running back to her simultaneously.

'I don't know why that happens. I got all dizzy up there and . . . I couldn't think. Everything got all foggy.'

She didn't think much of it at the time, but of course it wasn't normal for him to feel that way—not Nolan who was always busting to share his magnificent discoveries during "Show and Tell". Had his "dizziness" been a result of social anxiety or was it a symptom of the disease that his body was deteriorating?

The bruises.

Of course, the bruises . . . she had been so convinced he was being abused but now it hit her that she had read about it before. She had read that the cancer often formed reddish, purple shades on the skin.

Isn't that what she had seen? Maybe what she had seen in the breezeway that afternoon on yard duty hadn't been a handprint at all. Maybe she had just seen what she wanted to see in order to make sense of the story in her head.

Miranda looked up at her, her eyes fighting to stay open as

if she was looking into direct sunlight. She could tell that this conversation was draining the life out of her, if she had any life left in her at all.

Maybe this woman wasn't evil at all.

But Sienna wasn't done yet—there was more. More memories were coming back, hitting her so vividly as though they were playing out right in front of her.

They had moved from the breezeway now and were back in her old classroom, waiting for the rest of the students to return after music class. Back to the scene where they were sitting at Nolan's table with his head in his hands, making a comment about how the world of music has a way of transporting a person to another place. A place where Nolan's world would look very different than the one she had now learnt she had little knowledge of, as the cancer moved through him like a silent killer.

'Everything would be different . . . Everything. And just maybe, it would be a world where we would all be okay.'

Her heart began to flutter like a moth at a porch light. His words haunted her, holding more meaning than she could ever had anticipated.

But still, there was more. There were more clues.

What was the name of the book he was reading later that day, the one where he had "forgotten" to put away when he was always so vigilant. *The Fallen Boy, The Sad Boy* . . . no.

The Lost Boy.

He had been desperate to tell her something, but why hadn't he? Why hadn't he told her the truth of his condition? Had he been sworn to secrecy? If so, why? Had anyone else known? Surely the school reception staff would have known about all past and any existing conditions. They have to record that kind of information on his student file, the same way they did with every student who enrolled at the college.

Damian.

With that thought, her mind sent her out of the classroom and positioned her into her most recent memory—his office.

Until that afternoon she had never looked at the man so attentively in the eyes before. But this time was different. His eyes were different. They hadn't reflected a playfulness towards her like they had in the past. Instead, they reflected an emotion she hadn't seen before; anguish. A look that told her that she had been right all along about something not being right with Nolan. But this . . . This was even worse than she had anticipated.

She had looked at him so carefully when she had asked if he was ok. Damian was slower than normal with his answer but when he finally opened his mouth he had told her that he was sure that Nolan would be fine.

They were his words; that is what he had said.

He must have known the truth. Maybe he knew well before she did—back when Miranda had blurted the news that they were moving to L.A.

Or maybe he knew all along.

Sienna placed her arm around the woman, feeling her body convulse with pain. She didn't dare ask where Stuart—her husband—was at a time like this. Maybe it had been him she had been shouting at on the other end of the phone. Either way, the relationship didn't appear healthy.

But there was one question she had to ask. One question she needed an answer to. A question that would break both of them.

'How much time does he have?'

Miranda inhaled sharply, covering one hand over her face before sliding it up into her hair line. She slowly ran the tip of her fingers down the base of her neck before joining it together with the hand in her lap. She sat there for a while, squeezing her hands together tight enough for them to change colour, then opened her mouth.

'Two to three weeks.'

Twenty

It had to have been the worst sleep Sienna had ever had in her life. She didn't think she slept at all, not even a wink. By the time she had returned back to her room, Isabelle had fallen asleep in the same position on her back with her hands placed delicately over her blanket, her golden hair tucked to one side like Sleeping Beauty.

Sienna was glad that the girl had drifted off. She had no idea how she would be able to pull off the calm, collected adult she needed to be when she felt like a child, desperate to be held. Now wasn't the time for a breakdown, not while she was working. She was a teacher, a role model, and she had a job to do. Never mind that her heart was wrestling with more grief than she knew how to handle. She didn't have to navigate through that now. In six more days, she would.

For now, she had to get Isabelle back where she belonged and focus on what dance had the ability to do; transport her to a place where everything would be okay.

Just like Nolan said.

She was thankful that the Peters' were understanding about the incident. Well, as understanding as they could be with an ocean of distance between them. They were calm and didn't seem overly panicked which helped the situation. Nothing had been demanded beyond reason, just a request for her hospital report and a room change back at the hotel that would place her as far away from the basketball team as possible. They had gone a step further to request for their daughter to be placed in a room closest to Sienna which made her feel somewhat trusted, even though she didn't know if she deserved to be.

By the time they had returned to the hotel it was just after ten in the morning. The rest of the group had left and were well into their classes for the day, which happened to be the day casting was going up for their upcoming performance. Sienna had cash on her so she ordered them both a taxi to Charlton. The ten-minute trip ended up being almost half an hour with all the traffic but she hadn't wanted to get a subway. She didn't want to have to think about which platform to get onto, or risk having to stand up. She just wanted to get there.

They were silent on their trip in. She was too exhausted to think about how their silence would make Isabelle feel. She was simply too tired to keep checking in on how she was, whether she was nervous about the casting or how she was feeling about facing her friends. All she could think about was Nolan who, unlike Isabelle, would never make it out of his hospital bed.

She fought against the tears in the taxi, staring out the window as her throat burned with emotion. How was she supposed to carry on like everything was normal with these kids for another week?

The thought was excruciating.

They arrived just as their technical class was finishing up. They hadn't missed the casting at all. She dropped Isabelle off in one of the main studios where the girls were practicing. She apologised for their late arrival, being careful not to share the details of what went down the night before. Amelia didn't seem too bothered by it all, mentioning that she had something to tell her later, but Sienna was already halfway out the door. Any prospect of news would normally spark an interest in Sienna but she was too desperate to set out to find Richard.

She would check in with Amelia later.

Somehow, she managed to put one foot in front of the other as she floated along the corridors in his direction. She found him in the studio, seated by the door with his laptop out, typing away.

'Richard?'

He turned his head. 'You're back. How did you go?'

'She seems to be ok. She's exhausted, but ok. I've spoken to Amelia and gave her the heads up that she'll be taking a step back today,' she said, rubbing her eyes. 'I didn't tell her what happened but she didn't seem too fussed about us being late.'

'Ok, good, good.' He closed the lid of his laptop and placed it on top of his seat. He stepped outside the studio door to join her. 'But Sienna,' he said, looking carefully into her eyes, 'how are *you*?'

That was when Sienna lost it.

They found an available room and she told him the story of the little boy who had captured her heart. She shared everything; from the details of his troubled time at school to seeing Miranda in the hospital.

She felt silly, embarrassed, humiliated all at once as she broke down in front of her colleague when she was meant to have it all together. She was meant to be stronger than this, especially when she was supposed to be leading these kids.

But Richard was so patient. If he thought she could be doing better, he didn't show it. Not once did he interrupt her incoherent babbling, only stopping to pass her a tissue. He let her talk.

Finally, after what felt like an hour, she was done. She had no more tears to wipe away, no more words to say and by the looks of it, no more tissues left in the box.

'I can't even imagine . . .' Richard began, scratching his shiny forehead and crossing one leg over the other, 'how horrible this must be for you. But Sienna, I don't believe in coincidences.'

Sienna blew her nose on her already soaked tissue. 'What do you mean?'

Richard tilted his head to the side, his eyes filling with compassion. 'I don't think it's a coincidence that you ran into Miranda last night. Not when Nolan has been in your heart for so long. I know the timing is shocking with the duties you have to fulfil here but you have to see this woman. You have to see Nolan. You won't get that opportunity again.'

'I don't have her U.S. number. I don't even know what ward or room he is in. The hospital won't give that information out to me. I'm not family.'

'Sure, okay, that may be true but I'm sure you have an email address?'

Sienna thought about that for a minute. 'She's never responded to any of my emails in the past. What are the chances that, during the midst of a tragedy, she would respond now?'

'Greater than if you didn't try at all,' he said, his tone bearing a sense of wisdom.

That filled her with a glimmer of hope.

'I guess that's all I can do.'

'Yes, it is and you'll write it now. And if she replies, you're going to trust that we have this in hand and go and visit that little boy. He needs you more than any of us do.'

She looked up at him.

'No offence,' he added.

'Richard, thank you.'

'You can thank me later', he said smiling, and stood to his feet. 'Now, go and write that email.'

It was probably the worst day to find time to put something so daunting together at the same time casting was due to go up. As soon as lunch break began there was a flood of students pattering down the carpeted corridors, anxious to see where their name was positioned on the casting sheet on the pinboard. They had just six days to unite segments from each division to create a performance that would best showcase their talents. But it was much more than just a performance—it was a chance to be considered for a once-in-a-lifetime position at Juilliard. Each student in the select program would be cast, but only a handful of students would have the opportunity to shine in the bigger roles that were up for grabs.

The atmosphere in the room quickly shifted as bodies huddled together like a swarm of bees, desperate to be the first to discover their fate.

This year's production was titled *Tech Invasion* based on the concept of technology and what the future could look like if it was to take over our being. It was a clever idea, reminding Sienna of the popular series *Black Mirror*.

Her eyes skimmed over the roles allocated to students from the Drama and Music program, landing on the heading *Dance*. There were four main roles listed. Two soloist roles and a pas de deux. Her sadness lifted slightly to see Isabelle's name listed for the pas de deux with a boy by the name of Sean Maine. She had never met the boy before and wasn't sure if Isabelle had much experience with partner work, but she could understand why she had been chosen; she had a unique artistry that would help pull off a convincing connection with her partner.

Sienna took a quick glance at Isabelle as she took out her laptop. The girl's face had lit up and she was jumping up and down with Sarah and Tiffany who seemed to be equally excited for her victory despite being cast as part of the ensemble themselves. She was happy to see that her energy was back and all seemed ok between the girls again.

It was time to lock herself away and write this email. On her way out, she passed Amelia coming from the opposite way with a stride on her as though she was on a mission. Even her walk intimidated Sienna.

'So, I need to tell you . . .' Amelia started, her voice loud enough for people's heads to turn.

'Yeah?' asked Sienna, completely forgetting that they were meant to catch up at some point.

'It's about your friend, Daniel. Anyway, he sent me a piece he composed for the documentary. Oh. My. Gawdddd,' she stopped in her tracks and waved her hands. 'It's mind bogglingly brilliant.'

Sienna's lips curled. 'It is?'

'It's *insane*. I'll catch up with you in a min. But farrrrrk. They usually like to go with creditable composers, you know, not amateurs but we'll see what happens.'

Sienna was about to tell her that Daniel was no amateur, but she had already taken off down the hall to join the chaos at the other end.

That reminded her, she needed to reply to his last message. She was pretty sure he had sent her the same email with his music but she hadn't properly checked her phone. She would listen to it and get back to him later.

Sienna stepped inside the same room her and Richard had their conversation in earlier and closed the door on the noise.

She sat down and massaged her temples with her index fingers, fighting her eyes to stay awake. The memories hadn't finished haunting her. They wouldn't leave her alone.

She was back in her old classroom again and the way it was most mornings. Nolan was in early, right by her side. He was always checking in, finding ways to help her set up for the day before he got lost in one of the many books he brought to school. Most teachers preferred their space, craving their peace and quiet in the mornings before the school day hit the ground running. It was the slither of time they had to gather their thoughts (or make a bathroom trip), but not Sienna. She enjoyed Nolan's company. She loved the way he brought out her most gentle and nurturing side. It was one of the few times where she wondered what it would be like as a parent and contemplated the type of mother she wanted to be.

He brought the best out of her.

What would I do if I didn't have you keeping me in check every morning, Nolan?'

He shrugged his shoulders, wriggling his freckled nose in a way that exposed his dimples and pushed his glasses higher up his face.

'I think we would both be in trouble.'

Tears welled in her eyes. She knew what he meant now.

If it wasn't for their mornings together, Nolan wouldn't have an escape from his silent killer. The classroom had been his safe haven—a place where he could take his mind off his terminal condition.

She positioned her laptop down on the white desk and opened a new email. With a heavy heart, she began to type.

Dear Miranda,

I can't imagine you responding to this, especially when your heart is full with grief during this difficult time. I wanted to let you know that I'm here for you, I'm here for your family, and I'm here for Nolan.

Having the rare opportunity to see you again at the hospital stirred something inside of me. I walked away from our conversation with a heavy heart, but with a desire to help in any small way that I can. I completely understand that it might not be possible to visit Nolan, although I am writing to you in hope that I may have that chance. I would love to be a presence in Nolan's life one last time, if you let me.

Sending you all my love and deepest thoughts. I will eagerly wait for your reply, whatever that looks like.

I will be in L.A. for six more days.

Sincerely,

Sienna x

Twenty-one

At nine o'clock that evening Sienna finally clicked into Daniel's email.

She was laying on her hotel bed with tears streaming down the side of her face, when she finally had the time to catch up on all her phone's notifications. She turned onto her side, feeling the moisture of her tears in her pillow cool her already-damp cheeks, and closed her eyes.

Amelia was right; his music was brilliant.

In fact, it was so good it only made her cry more.

How Daniel could compose something so compelling in a short amount of time was a true testament to how talented he was. He wasn't given any background information, brief, or a detailed instruction of what they wanted. In just twenty-four hours, in the space of his living room he somehow managed to create something so powerful, moving and eloquent.

They had all turned in earlier that night—everyone was

exhausted after the first day of rehearsals—which ended up running later than scheduled. They ended up ordering in pizza and donuts, being too tired to think about bracing the cold to fetch groceries.

Between slices Sienna would check her phone at every opportunity in anticipation that every notification that tinged in her pocket was an email from Miranda. But for every "ting" that went off she grew more anxious. She had never been one to pray before but in that moment as they stood around, holding their paper plates and cans of soda, she prayed a silent prayer, hoping for the chance to see Nolan again.

She clicked into Messenger, overwhelmed at the number of unopened conversations in bold, waiting for her attention. But due to the time difference hardly anyone was online so she didn't feel pressured to reply. She scrolled down to Daniel's name and clicked into their chat. He was online again which wasn't really a surprise. Without responding to his message, she pressed the call button with her thumb, taking the video off so he wouldn't see how completely ruined she looked.

'Hey stranger, busy day?'

'I'm sorry,' she cleared her throat and sat herself up on her bed, fluffing up the pillows behind her back. 'These past twenty-four hours have been a living hell. Sorry I haven't gotten back to you.'

'Living hell, really? What's going on?' He sounded frantic.

She sighed heavily into her phone, feeling her throat tingle with emotion. 'Before I get into it, I want you to know that I just heard what you submitted. Sorry it took me so long to let you know but Daniel . . . it's exceptional.'

'Sienna?'

'Yeah?'

'I don't care about that right now, much as I'm chuffed that you like my work. You sound a mess. What's happening?'

'Do you have wine?'

'When do I ever not have wine?'

She could hear movement at the other end of the line. 'Pour yourself a glass' she said, ignoring his question.

'Ok, I'm on it . . . that bad, hey?'

She nodded, wishing he could see her response instead of having to voice an answer. Her throat was burning with emotion; how was she going to do this? She had Isabelle in the room next to her. What if she heard her crying? It would be humiliating. She hadn't heard a sound on the other side of her wall all night which she put down as a good thing. She hoped it meant that she was fast asleep and not with that Hunter kid. But she hadn't seen the boy since before the incident. He was probably too scared to show face and so he should be.

But here she was, alone in an empty room on the other side of the world with a friend back home who was present (whether it was a coincidence or not) and was here for her. She would stop being so fearful and tell him everything. He had seen her cry before anyway; at least this time he wouldn't have to see her tears.

They talked for over an hour. Just as they were about to end the call, a notification appeared on her screen. An email from *mglivingston79*.

She straightened herself up on her bed and brought her knees in close as though it would somehow protect her from whatever she was about to read. She abruptly ended her call with Daniel and with her heart beating like a bongo drum, she opened the email.

Hi Sienna,

Thank you for your email. Life has been tough for our household lately as you can imagine. None of us have been coping very well, especially as Stuart and I have been through something similar to this when we lost our son to cancer four years ago. The odds that this is happening a second time with our foster son is nothing short of traumatising. Stuart has completely shut down. He has been out of the picture for some time, so it's just my sister Lindsey and I (who I believe you've met) trying to find a way to work through this.

If it wasn't for Lindsey's American husband setting us up with some of the finest doctors, we would have said goodbye to Nolan far earlier. Unfortunately, even with the best treatment and care we've received, the past month has been a spiral downhill, and a quick one. It has been a brutal process. Nolan has been through the wringer with treatments. We have gone through BiTE experimental treatment, bone marrow aspirate procedures as well as intravenous antibiotic infusions. More recently results have come back revealing that there is a large amount of pseudomonas in Nolan's blood and in his stool. It's also in his marrow—frankly, it's everywhere. This is the same particularly nasty bug that we hoped would be treated by IV antibiotics, although Nolan's bone marrow is unable to help fight the infection and the antibiotics cannot do the work on their own. Apparently, Nolan will become increasingly tired and his blood pressure will fall, along with his other vital signs. The bottom line is: his life-threatening pseudomonas bug is gathering momentum and our dear son can't seem to clear it. We are told that Nolan is now beyond rescue and that it's no longer a matter of the place of care, but the place of death. He will be returning home with us next week.

For so long I couldn't look at Nolan, I didn't know how to care for him. Every time I looked into his eyes all I saw was our son before he got sick. When Nolan was diagnosed earlier this year, the small part of me that wasn't broken shattered completely. Something inside of me died and I didn't know how to love anymore. Not just Nolan, but my husband too. I was bitter, angry and took it out on everyone and every-thing. The reason I'm telling you all of this is because I know you were a culprit of my behaviour. I know that I didn't treat you well. I'm sorry for that, Sienna.

And now, I have to wait. I have to wait and watch this innocent child that I hardly deserve, pass away.

But in response to your request, yes, Nolan would be thrilled to see you. He still talks about you. I truly believe you're his guardian angel. Please don't expect much out of me when you visit us. I have no words left, I have used them all up in this email, but your presence is welcome and appreciated.

Miranda

Written below were the details of where she could find them in the Hematology and Oncology ward in the Children's Hospital.

Sienna clutched the phone to her chest and squeezed her eyes closed as burning tears streamed down her face. She pulled up her duvet, rolled to the side and let the sobs take over her body.

Despite the gaping hole in her heart, her prayer had been answered.

It was yet another night of little sleep.

Sienna had woken up feeling like she had been beaten, she was that lethargic. Her head thumped something chronic. After applying her makeup, paying more attention than usual to cover the dark circles around her eyes, she decided that she would take up Richard's offer of cover and see Nolan. Once she was sure that the students would be ok with her absence for a couple of hours she would reply to Miranda's email.

She didn't even need to search for Richard downstairs at breakfast; he had spotted her straight away. As soon as he saw the sight of her, he pulled her aside.

'Take the morning off.' This time, it came as an order.

Sienna, too tired to challenge this, nodded. 'Thank you.'

Without grabbing a bite to eat she went back to her room, took out her laptop and formed a reply to Miranda.

Before catching the subway, she dropped into *Book Soup*; a complete paradise for book lovers, cluttered with shelves from floor to ceiling. It was just a block down from where they were staying, with big bay windows that had caught her attention every time they had walked by it.

Five minutes later she walked out with a Roald Dahl boxset under her arm, and hailed a taxi.

Upon arriving at administration, she was instructed to sanitise her hands before a nurse offered to lead her down to Nolan's ward. She was glad she didn't have to navigate the corridors by herself this time, especially with the heartbreaking distractions around her that were bound to take her off course. Out of curiosity, she was able to get a glimpse into the rooms she passed, feeling her heart heave at the sight of children ranging from infants to teens, almost unrecognisable the way they were hooked up to machines or with tubes sticking out of their bodies in all directions.

She wasn't ready for this. She wasn't ready to see Nolan this way.

But as they reached his door, she knew she had no choice. This was it, ready or not; she knew she had no more time to prepare herself. The nurse gave Sienna a tight smile then left, leaving her at the door to welcome herself in.

The room was small, but big enough for two armchairs to fit at either side of his bed. There was nothing beside him, no balloons or cards, just a small stack of picture books on his bedside table, his glasses folded on top. Miranda was sitting on the chair closest to the window, flicking through a magazine as Nolan rested on his back with his eyes closed.

Sienna took one step inside the room, creating enough movement for Miranda to look up. 'Hi,' she whispered and stood to her feet. 'Here, come sit.'

She looked more withered than Sienna had seen her the other night, but maybe that was because she wasn't wearing any make up. She looked thinner too. Sienna did what she was told, taking a glance at Nolan as she sat herself down. Her throat thickened at the sight of him. His mob of ginger hair was gone. It had completely slipped her mind that this would be the case with the chemotherapy, but it still came as a shock to her. He looked thinner too, the way his shoulders and collar bones protruded from his little frame having been the biggest giveaway. He just looked so fragile. Even the freckles on the bridge of his nose didn't pop out the way she remembered, yet hid camouflaged against his pale skin. She assumed he hadn't seen much sun at all. Maybe he hadn't seen daylight for weeks.

'You can talk to him, if you like,' Miranda said, watching her study him.

Sienna uncovered the books from her lap. 'I brought him something.'

'He will love those. You can take them to him,' she said, encouraging her to interact with the boy.

Sienna nodded and walked to the side of his bed where he lay. She felt hopeless watching his chest rise and fall with every laboured breath. She wished there was something she could do to help ease the enormous pain she could only imagine he was going through.

'Hi Nolan, it's Miss Henderson here'. She placed the boxset down onto his bedside table, careful not to knock his glasses as she repositioned them on top. She turned to face him again, noticing his eyes begin to flutter ever so slightly. 'I thought I would bring you something to read after you have some rest.'

She could see Miranda staring at her from across the room, but she didn't feel brave enough to make eye contact with her. She wanted to touch his hand, to let him know that she was here for him, but she didn't know the rules and didn't dare to ask. She respected that Miranda wasn't up for a "chit chat". She would make her presence known like she said she would, then she would be off.

Nolan's eyelids began to flutter some more, fighting their way open. Sienna's heart began to race. Had he heard her?

Miranda was quick to pick up on it and walked over to the opposite side of him. 'Nolan, dear, how are you feeling?'

It was strange to hear her tone so endearing when she spoke to him, being vastly different to the way Sienna had remembered. But grief has a way of doing funny things to people and she need not judge.

'My head hurts,' he slurred. With his eyes still closed he lifted his hand to his forehead.

Sienna took a step back, feeling completely out of place.

'I know, baby.' Miranda repositioned the pillow under his head and leaned in towards him. 'You have a special visitor,' she whispered in his ear.

Something inside of Nolan came to life as though the words alone, were magic.

'Hi Nolan,' Sienna repeated, taking it as her cue to jump in.

Nolan's eyes made their way open this time. His head jerked to the side and stared straight into Sienna's eyes. He frowned for a moment and then rubbed his eyes.

'Careful of the tubes,' Miranda said as they moved a fraction from under his nose. She reached in to put them back into place.

'I'm fine,' snapped Nolan, not being able to tear his eyes away from Sienna. 'Miss Henderson!' It was all he could manage before he began to cry, but only a little.

Sienna reached forward to take his hand, unsure if they were tears of happiness or sadness. Nolan's pale cold hand took hold of hers and latched on firmly. In the corner of her eye she watched Miranda place a hand to her mouth as though she was moved at the scene that was playing out.

'How are you feeling?'

She had researched things to say when visiting cancer patients and asking how they were apparently was the main one to avoid. Instead, you're supposed to say things along the lines of "I'm here for you," but her mouth got there before her brain did. Now she would have to deal with the answer.

'Much brighter now that you're here.' He honestly looked overjoyed to see her, as though she was some sort of celebrity making an unexpected visit. At least half of that was true.

The weight inside Sienna's chest began to lift. 'I feel the same way, Nolan. You've made my day.' She grinned, letting go of his hand and grabbed the boxset that was wrapped in a thin layer of plastic film. 'I came bearing gifts.'

'Miss Henderson, you shouldn't have' he said, sounding puffy. 'I just don't get it. How are you here? This is craziness!'

They all laughed.

'I took a trip for work,' she started. 'Not at your old school, or "our" old school I should say. I moved back to the town I grew up in at the beginning of the term and there was this trip they needed me on, so here I am.'

Nolan's eyes bulged even more at that. He looked different without his glasses. He looked so tired. 'Now that is crazy.'

'Completely crazy,' she agreed. 'But there's no such thing as coincidences,' she said, remembering Richard's words.

Nolan nodded and stretched out his arms and yawned. Her visit was exhausting him. She wouldn't stay long.

'Oh, I know that. I prayed for this.'

Sienna's heart pulsed. 'You prayed for what?'

Nolan pulled off the plastic film from the boxset and took out the first book, smoothing his hands over the glossy cover. 'I love his stuff, thank you so much.' He brought the books close to his nose. 'Mmmm, new book smell. The best.'

'It really is the best,' she agreed. In the corner of her eye she watched Miranda take a seat to give them some privacy. At the same time the woman's phone began to buzz and she stepped outside to take the call, leaving just the two of them alone.

'What did you pray for?' she asked again.

Nolan wrinkled his nose and gave her a knowing look. His lips were dry, cracked, but it didn't stop him from spreading them wide to give her his biggest smile. 'A miracle. I prayed that I would be able to see you again.'

Sienna swallowed hard, but she couldn't stop the tears from filling her eyes. 'You prayed for that?' she squeaked. She dragged her chair closer, trying hard to focus on anything that would stop her from breaking down.

'Yeah, of course,' he said cheerfully, oblivious to the impact his words had on her.

'That's really beautiful' she laughed, half crying at the same time. 'I did too.' She stared out the window, feeling her tears cloud her vision to the point where the view outside held no detail at all, just a block of colour. With a single blink they spilled down her cheeks. She wiped them away, ashamed that she couldn't be stronger for him.

'I think you're really beautiful, Miss Henderson,' he said. His head was down, flicking through the pages in the first book, not seeming to notice her tears. Or maybe it was just easier for him to ignore them.

It was easier for everyone.

'You're very sweet, Nolan.'

He shrugged and drew in a deep breath as he took out another book. It pained her to see just how much energy it took for him to do this. 'It's the truth though' he started, bringing the book to his nose to smell the pages again. 'I think it's important to recognise all the beauty in the world.'

'You're absolutely right, Nolan. It is. There is so much beauty around us. Every day.'

Nolan nodded. 'Yep. That's why I like to read so much, so I can be reminded of that, even during the bad times.'

She stared at him. When did he get so philosophical, so mature?

'I've done a lot of thinking, you know.' He placed the book back inside the box to join the others and placed them back on the table next to him.

'And what has your mastermind come up with?' she challenged him. She could hear the faint sound of Miranda on the phone outside the door, grateful that she had this time alone with Nolan.

'That life is more beautiful than whatever you're going through. You know . . . your *circumstance*,' he said, emphasising the last word as though it was a recent addition to his vocabulary.

Sienna could barely breathe.

'And, well,' Nolan let out a heavy sigh and waited for a moment. Whether it was to get more oxygen in his lungs or to think carefully about how he would construct his next sentence, she wasn't sure. He opened his mouth and continued. 'If God created all of it . . . all of this beauty, then there has to be beauty that comes from my circumstance too.'

Sienna nodded, feeling the tears stream down her face. Nolan was, by far, the most special little boy she had ever met.

Only now did his face change and he seemed to be affected by her tears. 'I know you're sad, Miss Henderson, but you don't have to be, because I thought about it, and . . .' He cleared his throat, trying to be brave, trying to find a way to keep it together while he finished what he had to say. 'Maybe the plans God has for me when I die . . . are more beautiful than the plans I had for myself on earth.'

There was a moment of silence before the walls lost their strength, and caved in.

Nolan slapped his hands to his face and let out a cry. Sienna pushed back her chair and wrapped her arms around him, feeling his brokenness mix together with hers as his little body heaved with pain. At some point Miranda must have returned to the room, her chipped red nails coming into view as she silently joined their embrace.

With their arms tight around each other, the three of them just stayed there. For how long, she didn't know.

All they could do was weep.

Twenty-two

It was hard to believe they had reached their final full day in Los Angeles.

Their trip to Universal Studios couldn't have come at a better time. It was exactly what Sienna needed after her visit to the hospital. It served as the perfect escape and everyone made sure of it. It was quite sweet actually, the way not only the staff but the students too, were encouraging her to go on all the rides she wouldn't usually dare to try, filling up every second possible with an overdose of adrenaline. It was a glorious yet overwhelming experience, but it was exactly what she needed to be reminded to be present.

Today was no different. If anything, it was a time where being present was needed the most. It was ok to grieve, but it was equally important to focus on what she could control, starting with her mindset. Her students deserved her full attention and she would give them that.

The show was coming along better than she had predicted, having barely a week to put together a full-scale performance. Everyone was pulling their weight, determined to leave an impression on the panel from the prestigious Juilliard School. It was evident that everyone wanted the scholarship.

Sienna couldn't have been prouder of her girls; the way they were cheering each other on, no matter how big or small their role was. The ensemble number was looking squeaky clean given how hard Amelia was working them. There wasn't a finger or hair out of place. She was that on top of the details; her commander style of teaching proving to be effective. Sienna was lucky to have had the opportunity to work alongside the guest chore-ographer who was working on Isabelle and Sean's duet. Their bodies moved seamlessly together—their on-stage connection was palpable. Like her, he was blonde and wasn't much taller than her. For someone quite thick in the legs, he moved with ease and with a strength that made every lift look effortless. She had been concerned about Isabelle, wondering how she would sustain the energy that was needed for such a demanding piece. But something inside of the girl had unlocked, changed. After all she had been through, Sienna could tell that she wasn't taking anything for granted. Her blue eyes burned with concentration as she soaked up every instruction, every piece of information like a sponge.

The costumes looked fabulous. Every dancer, musician and actor were clothed head to toe in silver. They were dressed creatively in hoops, netting, metallic lycra, plastic, lace, balloons and one-piece suits. She never expected the setup to look so effective. Charlton had a theatre with a two-tiered balcony that seated over eight hundred people. With a strong focus on the performers, they wanted to avoid any visual distractions, keeping the props to a minimum. The backdrop they had chosen extended down to the stage floor, leaving a thirty-centimetre gap for a white fluorescent beam of light to spill through. There were no wings either side, opening up the space to create what looked like a blank canvas. In this instance, less was more. The whole thing looked very professional.

As the students began putting on their costumes and applying metallic face paint and sequins to their faces, Sienna felt the nerves kick in. Amelia had disappeared from the dressing rooms to welcome the panel that had arrived. Unlike Amelia, she wasn't dressed as sharply; wearing a pair of high waisted black pants and blouse with a pair of heels to make her look more formal. Amelia didn't seem to care that her fuchsia-coloured dress would be an instant spot side stage by the audience if she happened to get too close. But at least her dress matched those pink lips of hers.

The panel was made up of three women and one man, all formally dressed. They were seated on the long narrow rectangular table that was situated on the first landing behind the orchestra pit. With headshots, programs, laptops and pens in hand, they were ready. The whole set up looked intense.

Sienna was glad those days were behind her.

After finishing her sneak peek, she let the curtain fall and turned her back towards the dressing rooms. There was no one side stage as she stood alone in darkness, hearing the faint noise from the dressing rooms find its way up. She needed to round up the dancers together to take them out the back for a warm up, throwing a motivational pep talk in there while she was at it. Not that she really needed to; the energy in the place was already at an all-time high.

Her phone lit up, reminding her to turn the brightness of her screen down. She clicked into Facebook Messenger to open her convo with Daniel. He hadn't written anything but sitting there was a video clip. She clicked into it but it came up blank. There wasn't enough reception in the theatre to view it. She slipped her phone into her pocket, making a mental note to watch it later.

But right now, she had a job to do.

After only getting one chance to get it right, they did just that. They nailed it. The audience exploded into applause at the end of what was a very successful performance.

Standing side stage Amelia grabbed Sienna by the waist and spun her around. 'They were perfect, absolutely perfect.' She puckered her lips and jumped on the spot, giddy with excitement. 'Isabelle was breathtaking. Shit, that girl is good.'

Sienna laughed, taken aback at how easily she had been thrown around in the air like that. The woman had endless energy. 'Thanks, lovely. She was. But so was everyone.'

But Amelia had already disappeared onto the stage, hugging each of them individually as the curtain lowered for the final time.

The house lights came on at the same time voices filled the auditorium as the audience began making their way out to the foyer. In just minutes the students would join them as the panel made their public verdict.

Five scholarships were to be awarded in total; two for music, two for dance and one for drama. Out of the five, one was awarded to a student by the name of Gavin Watson; a rising star in Richard's music program. The sixteen-year-old was bouncing off the walls when his name was read out, barely making it onto the platform to receive his certificate and shake the judges' hands. Sienna looked at Richard. The man looked like a proud father the way his eyes were shining with tears, as he brought two fingers to his mouth to let out a piercing whistle. If the boy accepted the offer it would mean that he would complete his senior years of schooling abroad and not under Richard's wing. But now wasn't the time to burst the man's bubble that one of his favourite students would be moving on. This was a huge achievement. Not just for Gavin and Richard but for Mason Grammar, too.

Sienna turned her head the other way, in search of Isabelle. She spotted her two rows ahead with her arms around Sarah's shoulders, their heads leaned in towards each other. She was clapping with a big smile on her face as the worthy recipients made a line for their photograph to be taken. This year's dance scholarship had been awarded to one of Amelia's fierce little dancers by the name of Savanagh Holmes. The girl was a power-house with far too much personality and zest to look past. With Isabelle's arm still around Sarah, she turned her head, locking eyes with Sienna. The girl's eyes shone with gratitude as she lowered her chin and sent a strong, intentional nod; one that showed that she wasn't disappointed, but she was grateful. Sienna smiled and returned the gesture. The girl's lips parted in a sincere smile before she turned her head back to finish congratulating the winners.

It was close to 11 p.m. by the time they bumped out of the

theatre. By now most of the adrenaline had worn off and the tiredness had set in. Other emotions were beginning to surface, as the Aussies and Americans said their farewells to each other. In just a few days, strong friendships had been formed with many mentions of Skype and FaceTime being a necessity once they touched down on Australian soil. It was hard to believe that this time tomorrow they would be on a flight back home.

'It was my pleasure, pretty girl,' Amelia said, giving Sienna a generous hug as they stepped into the cool of the night. It was the first time they had inhaled fresh air all day.

Sienna closed her hands over the woman's ripped back. 'It was such a joy to work with you. You're an amazing coach. Your kids are lucky to have you.'

'Likewise.'

Sienna smiled and they broke apart. 'Well, we have each other on the socials now. There's no excuses not to keep in touch.'

'We'll be in touch. I'll be wanting to suss out which cadets you'll be bringing with you next year.'

It completely slipped Sienna's mind that she would get to do this all over again. Suddenly saying goodbye didn't seem so bad.

'Game on.'

They both laughed.

'Take care of yourself,' Amelia said, taking her cell from the front pocket of her oversized bag as it started to ring. 'Please congratulate your friend for me.'

Sienna stared at her blankly as Amelia took the call. She pulled the phone away and gave Sienna a look back. 'Your friend, Daniel, tell him congrats,' she clarified and went back to her call.

That was when Sienna remembered the video. She opened

up her chat window with Daniel to find the green dot beside his name again. He was online. Without clicking into the video, she hit the call icon on the top right-hand side of her screen. She didn't need to watch it. She knew.

Like always, after a few rings he picked up.

'Oh my god, you got it, didn't you!' she shrieked, causing a few heads to turn in her direction. She turned from her tribe who were still saying their goodbyes and walked ahead into the night so she could have some privacy. They would carry on for another ten minutes at least.

He was laughing on the other end of the line. She had to laugh at herself too; she sounded about five years old at how excited she was getting.

'Hello to you, too.'

'Nah, who cares about the formalities,' she said cheerfully. 'You got the gig, yeah?'

'If you want to call it that, yeah. I got the "gig."'

'You're amazing! Quick turnaround, too! What happens next?'

'I'm actually not too sure! I think I have to tweak a few things but overall, they're pretty happy with what I made. So, I guess I'll wait for the pay check?'

'That's so good!' Sienna squealed. 'Who knows where this could lead. These are big connections! You're too talented to limit yourself to your lounge room. I won't allow it. You're made for so much more.' She shuffled her feet on the pavement and looked up into the night sky. '… I don't know, I just have a sense this is just the beginning for you. Change is coming. That's how I feel, anyway.'

It grew quiet on the other end for a moment.

'Thanks, S.'

'Anytime,' she said softly, matching his tone. She could tell that he felt moved by her little spiel. But she meant it. Life was too short. If anything, the last few days had taught her that.

'How are you holding up?'

How did she feel?

Sienna squeezed her eyes. 'I'm ready to come home. There's so much to do, so much to process. But today, I dunno . . . helped put my mind to rest for a bit.'

'You've had a rough trot over there, that's for sure, but you've handled it with grace. Time to be kind to yourself.'

She swallowed down hard. 'Yeah.'

'I have a Shiraz waiting when you return.'

She laughed, opening her eyes. Her throat began to ease up again. 'And a live performance of the soundtrack?'

'She's a greedy one.'

'Those are the terms and conditions.'

'Fine. I guess I can work with that.'

'Better start practicing.'

'And you better get back to your kids, I can hear them getting restless. Goodnight, twinkle toes.'

Sienna laughed. 'Goodnight, Danny.'

As she spun on her heel to round her students up for what she hoped was the last time, she realised something.

She was smiling.

Sienna had an idea.

She should have been sleeping. Though her sleep had been so erratic the past few days, considering it was their last night she guessed she had run out of chances.

Even though her body was screaming for rest, her mind fought against it—running wild with ideas of how she could be a presence in the little boy's life. She wouldn't sit back and count the days until Nolan slipped from this world to the next. Even though she was returning home, she wouldn't let distance be a factor.

Not when there was a way to overcome that.

After she had settled on a plan she closed her eyes, giving herself permission to fall into a deep sleep. She would do what Daniel said and be kind to herself.

She was up early, well before anyone had risen.

She jumped out of bed, not bothering to make it as she figured the cleaners would be pulling it apart in a matter of hours anyway. She threw on some dark denim jeans and a brown jacket, pairing it with her warmest scarf that looked a lot like a blanket.

The mornings were quickly becoming cold now with winter just weeks away for the citizens of this fine country.

The group were going to get a shock to their systems once they returned home where they would be dealing with the opposite.

After wrapping her blanket scarf twice around her neck, she took the lift down to the ground floor, ready to embrace the cold. After making a pit stop at Starbucks to grab herself a caramel latte, she found herself out the front of *Book Soup* shortly after.

She was the first one hovering out front as corporate workers dressed in business suits walked past.

The store hadn't even opened yet, so Sienna held her coffee warm in both hands as she glanced at her watch. A minute shy of eight thirty. She looked up as an old stocky man with little hair turned the *CLOSED* sign around and opened the door with great difficulty.

'Come inside. Just give me a minute to sort these lights out.' Sienna thanked the man and stepped inside the deserted shop. With the heaters not yet having a chance to warm the store, she was determined to get in and out as soon as possible. Luckily for her, she already knew what she was looking for. Her frozen legs led her to the aisle where she knew she would find it. And just as she hoped, there it was sitting on the shelf waiting for her.

Now it was time to put her idea into action.

Twenty-three

Sienna wasn't much of a baker. At all. But she simply couldn't turn up at his house empty handed.

After spending nearly her entire Saturday making up for lost sleep, she had woken up with a sudden inspiration to make a humble pumpkin pie. She had never made one before but figured it couldn't be that hard.

By 7 p.m. she was standing at Daniel's door with something that looked close enough to what she had envisioned. She had no idea if he even liked pumpkin pie but she figured something was better than nothing.

He seemed really happy to see her, giving her a hearty hug, basically cantering down the hallway as he led her into his kitchen. She assumed he was trying extra hard to cheer her up, or maybe he was genuinely happy to see her. Either way, it was sweet.

She paid no attention to the photo frames on the wall this time, as she focused on balancing the pie on its plate in a way so it stayed intact. She could see that the middle was beginning to give way, but disfigured or not, she figured it was there to be eaten rather than admired.

Daniel was thrilled to see it, his eyes lighting up like a Christmas tree. 'You can cook!' But it came out more like a question.

Sienna placed it on the bench and reached the top cupboard to take out a glass. She placed it under the tap and poured herself a drink. 'Well, we'll see.'

'Is this a cheesecake?'

Sienna almost choked on her water. She could understand why he guessed that. It was rather pale. Definitely not the rich orange colour she was going for. 'Sure, if you like it pumpkin-flavoured.'

Daniel raised his eyebrow and snorted a laugh. 'Oh!'

Sienna swallowed and rinsed out her glass. 'Look, I had a go. It's a pumpkin pie but who knows what it'll actually taste like.'

'You sure know how to sell it.'

'It's better to be pleasantly surprised than to go in with high expectations, right?'

'Oh, yeah, right.' Daniel took her glass and stacked it in the dishwasher. 'You have definitely done that. Look at you working my kitchen. I'm surprised you haven't gotten the plates out yet either.'

'It would be rude for me to force this thing down your throat,' she joked.

'It would be even ruder for me not to give this cheesecake slash pumpkin pie creation of yours a go.'

'It's not a cheesecake.'

'I'm not sure it's a pie either, look,' Daniel said, pointing at where it sat on the bench. It had now completely collapsed in the centre, having lost its shape completely. Just as Sienna turned to look at it, it sunk down further. It looked like an anaemic pile of goo. They burst out laughing. If they didn't know each other well enough she would have been offended by his comment. It was refreshing to have reached a stage where they could banter so freely without watching their words too carefully. It was the first time Sienna had heard him laugh in full force. He threw his head forward, slapping his knees as though it was the most hilarious thing in the world which only made her laugh harder.

'Would you care for some pie?' She took out two plates from the draw, surprising herself that she knew exactly where to pull them from. Daniel was right; she did know her way around his kitchen.

'Sure.' Daniel settled himself and took a seat at one of the swivel stools. 'Grab two wine glasses while you're at it.'

Sienna grinned. 'You read my mind.'

Evenings with him felt strangely familiar. They had only done this a couple of times but somehow, they had fallen into a routine of finding themselves in his living room; her sitting on the couch while he sat at the piano as instructed. She knew he didn't mind though, she could tell that he liked performing for her and she liked what she saw in him when he did.

This time, as his hands danced along the keys, she closed her eyes, picturing ways his music could extend even further than just her. She couldn't quite articulate it, but she could envision his music on a grander scale, impacting more lives than her own. The documentary for Juilliard was a good start. A great start—giving him a push towards where he belonged.

'What do you think?'

It was over? No, surely not. She wanted more.

'Do I really need to answer that?' she said, tilting her head to one side with a smirk on her face.

Daniel laughed and turned his body so he was facing her. 'I'm not fishing for compliments. But what do you think if this was to be used as . . . I don't know, an underscore for a video or something. Or for all of them?' His mouth twitched to mimic the same expression as the one her face was holding.

'An underscore for what video?' she asked, having some sort of an idea of where he was getting at. But before she assumed that this man would possibly do something this extraordinary for her, she had to be sure.

'For that special little boy who loves music just as much as we do.'

She had told him about her idea of recording herself reading a chapter each day. She had done a bit of research on what novel she would choose and decided on a chapter book titled *Better Nate Than Never*, written by Tim Federle. The story followed the journey of a boy chasing his dream to star in a Broadway theatre show in New York. Considering Nolan was a big lover of music, North America and storytelling she thought it was the perfect way she could connect with him, and he with her. Flicking through the chapters, she noticed that she could time her readings within the time frame that she had—that Nolan had. It was the only way she knew how to reach him until the end.

Sienna cupped her face with her hands, feeling her eyes well with tears of gratitude. 'You would really do that?'

'Of course,' he said, his eyes softening. 'If you let me.'

'I would love that. Nolan would love that. Daniel . . .'

'Hmmm?' He stood from his chair and took a seat on the couch beside her. She had never sat this close to him before. She didn't know if it was the wine or his beautiful offer, but being in such close proximity left her feeling a little . . . tingly. She raked her hair back with her hand, confused at the feeling that had overtaken her body. Whatever it was, she hadn't felt it around him before. Not like this.

She put it down to the wine.

'Thank you,' she said, remembering she hadn't said anything yet. She placed her wine glass down on the coffee table and placed her hands awkwardly in her lap. What was going on? She had never had to think twice about what her hands were doing in the past.

By now the sunset was streaming through the blinds, lighting the room in a way that some called "moon lighting". It was too quiet; she needed him to play again for her. He was still yet to play the piece he had submitted to Juilliard. But as she turned to face him, her stomach grew heavier with that same tingly feeling. He was watching her, as though he was intrigued by her every detail—which in this moment, happened to be her picking at her non-existent nails. As soon as she realised he was staring at her, tugging at the loose pieces of skin around them, she curled her hands and placed them either side of her thighs. She definitely didn't have nice long fingers like Daniel had. Hers took on a similar resemblance to her dancer's feet; mauled.

He made a noise—somewhere between a grunt and a nervous laugh and with his index finger brushed her arm. 'What is it?'

Sienna shook her head. 'My nails. They aren't pretty like yours.'

'Oh, come on,' Daniel said and reached in to take her arm that was planted at her side. 'Not as pretty? You do have a way with words.'

She pulled back playfully. 'No, they really aren't very elegant. I've destroyed them.'

'Well, then in that case I'm glad. It means you're not perfect after all.'

Sienna let out a snort. 'Oh, smooth. Who's the one that has a way with words?' She stopped resisting him and exposed her hands. 'See? I warned you.'

They were acting like children, the way they were both finding excuses to touch each other.

Daniel took her hand in his and pressed his lips together in attempt to stop the laugher. 'They're not bad.' He studied them and smoothed his thumb over the palm of her hand. 'They have . . . character.'

'Character!' She laughed, trying to mask the fact that she was blushing. She was actually blushing!

Since when did Daniel make her blush?

Daniel smiled at her, his kind eyes glistening. He knew the effect he was having on her. She could tell by the way he was looking at her. The moment only lasted a few seconds but that didn't stop his eyes from talking. He wasn't letting go of her hand, and to be honest, she wasn't sure if she wanted him to. Even though he had stopped playing she was still hearing melodies in her head.

She drew out a sigh, hoping that by emptying her lungs she would get her own breath back. But Daniel didn't seem to catch on. In fact, he must have sensed the opposite. He let go of her hand in a way that was polite and respectful to her wishes. But it wasn't her wish at all. She didn't want her hand back.

He had gotten it all wrong!

'I'll take your glass.' He reached forward, collecting hers with his. 'Would you like some water?'

Sienna brought her hands in together. 'Uh, yes please . . . yes, thanks.' She tucked her hair behind her ear and exhaled, lighter this time. 'That would be great,' she added, kicking herself for the way she had retreated back to being all polite. She thought they were miles past this and now she couldn't even speak properly.

Daniel gave her a funny look but didn't say anything.

He didn't need to.

Their banter may have been like every other time but the conversation they were having with their eyes tonight, said something different.

Sienna had fretted that the girls would be behind even though she had given Naomi very clear instructions on what parts of the curriculum needed to be covered in her absence. She felt guilty for thinking the woman wouldn't meet the brief, because she did. Not only that, she went above and beyond, leaving behind detailed notes for every lesson she covered. There was basically a diary full of them.

Really, she should have given the woman more credit.

The girls were keen to show off all they had achieved with the group dance, forcing Sienna and the girls who went on the trip to sit down the front against the mirrors as they took their position.

Sienna felt an enormous pressure lift as the girls got deeper into the performance. With assessments just over a week away the girls were in a good position—a great position. For some reason she thought she would be coming back to pick up the pieces but by the looks of it, the pieces were neatly put into place.

She owed Naomi a personal thank you. She would never be so quick to judge someone again.

'I have some news,' Isabelle said lingering around after the final bell went for the day.

Sienna never knew what to expect with the girl and as soon as she heard those words the bubble she had been floating in burst. After the phone conversation with her parents upon their return she was sceptical of what this "news" would entail. Maybe the terms and conditions of her being grounded had escalated and she was being pulled from the program in the new year.

She sure as hell hoped not.

Instead, she smiled and said, 'News? Do I need to sit down for this one?'

Isabelle laughed, waving it off. 'Not this time. I'm doing better, you know.'

'I know,' Sienna's tone changed. 'I'm sorry, that wasn't fair of me to joke about that.'

'No, it's fair,' the girl said thoughtfully. 'But what I'm about to tell you isn't.'

Sienna inhaled a sharp breath. Maybe she had been right. Maybe she did need to sit down.

But Isabelle looked calm, almost like she was holding back some kind of surprise—maybe even a pleasant surprise.

'So, I got an email this morning. Well, it came through around one in the morning but I read it over breakfast.' The girl smiled but it stopped short of her eyes. 'One of the dancers that had received a scholarship for Juilliard declined the offer. They told me I was the next person on the list that they were considering and well—' she twirled the ends of her long ponytail with her finger and looked at Sienna. 'They offered me a position for next year.'

'Oh gosh!' Sienna lunged forward and gave the girl a hug. 'Isabelle, that's fantastic! What did mum and dad say?'

Isabelle accepted her hug but didn't hold on as tight. She pulled away and continued to play with the ends of her ponytail. 'Um, it would have been more exciting if everything . . . you know, didn't happen.'

Sienna nodded. 'I can understand that, it's a lot to take in. You've had a bit of a rough trot. It's not something that—'

'I made a decision.'

Sienna pressed her lips together and waited. She would let the girl talk.

'I made it before we even talked about it as a family.' Isabelle flicked her ponytail back over her shoulder and looked at Sienna. Whatever she was about to say, it was clear that she had given this a lot of thought.

'In a perfect world I would have loved this. I mean, I still would but now isn't my time.' She cleared her throat. 'If it was, I would have been their first choice, not their second.' Tears welled in her eyes but she blinked them back before they could get in the way. 'Maybe I'm crazy to let something like this go, but it isn't my time. I'm not ready. I would love to think that I am, but I'm not. I've got stuff to figure out, you know?'

'You know what, Isabelle. I think you're making the right choice.'

Isabelle's face softened as a single tear slipped down her cheek. She brushed it away and widened her smile. 'I think so too. I mean, I know I am. You know why?'

Sienna smiled, her heart filling with compassion for the girl who had shown such tremendous growth in such a short space of time. 'Why?' she asked.

'My parents said they were proud of me.' She scratched the nape of her neck and looked to the floor. 'It's the first time they've told me that.'

'Of course, they're proud of you. And you know what?'

Isabelle looked up, her eyes yearning for validation.

'I'm proud of you too.'

She knew that the girl's time would come. Maybe the plans God had for her were better than the ones she had for herself.

Just like Nolan had said.

Twenty-four

Sienna smoothed the book over in her hands.

The glossy cover was beginning to lose its shine and the corners had begun to curl. She settled herself in her armchair and opened to where the bookmark rested.

She had grown accustomed to her new afternoon routine. As soon as she walked through the door she would set her video up on her Surface Pro and take out the book that now had more turned pages than unread ones. Every day she would position herself so that her white cube bookshelf and pot plant were perfectly framed in the screen.

She had given it a lot of thought too, as to what she wanted in the shot. As Nolan was a lover of books she was sure that he would appreciate her own little stash. And that pot plant, well, who didn't love a bit of greenery? Part of her had hoped she would get a comment back from him about one or two books, especially when she had *The Chronicles of Narnia* among her collection. She had read that one to his class earlier in the year, hoping that would spark some kind of response. She wasn't doing this for attention; it wasn't like that. But she had still hoped that from the six videos she had sent to Miranda so far, that she would get a reply. Just one reply. But even then, it didn't deter the motivation she had to record the next chapter the second she got home from work, before anything else had the chance to take her attention. As long as the emails made it out of her outbox she knew that he was receiving them.

She could feel it.

She set her laptop in the usual spot so that it captured her setup and set the timer for the video. She took a sip of water, trying to flush away the niggling thought that already, a week had passed.

Two to three weeks Miranda had said. That's all he had.

She placed the glass down and settled further back into her chair and waited. The more recordings she did, the more nervous she got going into each one. It wasn't that she didn't like being in front of the camera—she chose to do this, after all. It was deeper than that. She knew that every video sent brought her that much closer to her final one.

She smoothed her lips over and inhaled, ready to begin reading.

She didn't want to think about this ever coming to an end. Maybe if she kept them going for two weeks—three weeks—maybe even three months then she wouldn't have to face the truth. The agonising truth.

Sometimes it was easier to be in denial. Especially when the truth didn't make sense.

At all.

Putting it all aside, she put on her biggest smile, even though it didn't come close to warming her core. She would read this chapter and she would read it well.

Nolan deserved at least that.

After precisely nine minutes she placed the bookmark in its new position, trying not to focus on her being just days away from finishing the book.

She selected the file and copy-pasted it into the folder she created on her computer. She never looked back over any of her recordings; she hated seeing herself on camera. It wasn't the perfect video, she knew that, but she didn't care. Real life wasn't perfect.

She attached it in an email and sent it off to Daniel the way she did after each one. From his end he would attach his music underscore to the video, bringing more to the video than her animated voice. It was so incredibly decent of him, she couldn't believe that he would do this so willingly for her. It would have to be over an hour of work on his end. She felt bad every time she sent a video to him, but he told her off every time she expressed that.

She closed the lid of her laptop and made a start on dinner. Salmon tonight, with a simple sweet potato mash. By the time she finished preparing it, Daniel would have sent back the video file having added his part. He was that efficient. It was usually the last thing he did before he started his shift at the restaurant, so he had told her.

She wanted to do something nice for him as a way of saying thank you. Her pumpkin pie had been a bit of a disaster so she wasn't keen to repeat that again. She didn't have any musical ability other than her dancing. But she wasn't about to prance around in his living room as he played the piano. That would be weird.

Whatever she chose, she wanted it to be meaningful. Something that they would both enjoy. A thought popped in her mind but she pushed it aside. She wasn't ready to confront that idea, not yet anyway. Or was she?

Was it time?

She took out two sweet potatoes and gave them a rinse under the tap.

It had been years since she had been to the ballet. The last time she had been somewhat close to going had been in her university days—back when the company she had been offered a job at, were premiering one of her favourite productions: *Giselle*. She had been stubborn back then, too stricken with grief from her short-lived career to ever contemplate stepping into the theatre again. The thought of putting herself through the agony of watching what she had spent half her life dreaming about was excruciating. She had come a long way since then. She had healed a lot. Dance was part of her life again even though she had been sure back then that it would never make an appearance for a second time. But you can't run away from your passions; they always have a way of following you.

And she was glad that they had.

She turned the oven on and took out a tray. She decided that it was time. She knew that Daniel would love the live orchestra. He was just as much of a creative soul as she was. She knew he would love the ballet, too. The National Premier Ballet were in the middle of their *The Sleeping Beauty* season. Sienna had been following their Instagram and Facebook pages from the beginning of time, often stopping to glance at the many images they posted every season.

This time, the glance would turn into something more intentional.

She placed the potatoes in the oven and took out her phone and jumped on their site. She located *The Sleeping Beauty* and clicked the link; *find tickets*. There were a few good seats left, more so on the days where they performed a double show. She scrolled down to the Wednesday performances and found a matinee in three weeks' time. There were some good seats in the stalls still available. She felt a thrill of excitement, tempted to purchase them there and then on the spot. She wasn't an impulsive person, but she already knew that the time would suit them both. She didn't work Wednesdays and he didn't begin his shift until six or seven at the earliest. She checked the run time; the performance would conclude at 3:40 p.m. If Daniel happened to be working that night, they would make it back in time.

The more she thought about it, the more she realised that it didn't require so much thought. It was obvious what she should do. After all, there was no such thing as a coincidence.

Five minutes later the two tickets landed in her inbox.

The next week had been a bit of a whirlwind. Assessments came and went way too quickly in the same way food is demolished after hours of preparation leading up to it.

For her first term at Mason Grammar, Sienna really had to give herself a pat on the back. The girls did a fantastic job, scoring an average of eighty four percent across the board. Apparently, it was the highest scoring year in almost six years. Isabelle had made a great effort on her solo, performing with a strength and serenity that Sienna always knew was within her. It was hard to believe that in just over a couple of weeks' time the school year would be over. She was looking forward to seeing which students would join the program whilst getting to know the students who stayed on, on a deeper level.

It had been two weeks now and not a single email sent had received a response. It wasn't until the sun went down that she had the chance to read the final chapter. Taking a seat in her chair she read until there were no more pages to turn. Sienna stared at her bookcase where the novel stood among her collection. Every time she looked at it, she would be reminded of the boy that had been a part of her own story. It had been two days now since she had finished the book—her final video.

She took a sip of her cinnamon tea and lifted her glance. The sun was beginning to set now, filling the sky with generous strokes of colour. The street was quiet as though it too was admiring the piece of art the sky had painted.

'I think it's important to recognise all the beauty in the world.'

She smiled remembering Nolan's words the day she visited him in the hospital. The videos may have come to an end, but she still had a way of finding him, right where she was.

Watching the sunset.

She often wondered how he was spending his final days, whether he was in discomfort or sedated in a way where he felt no pain. She knew that, by now, he would be resting in the comfort of his own home where she hoped he was surrounded by his favourite books and music.

She placed her cup of tea down at the same time the colour of the sky took a turn. The colours began to blend into each other as they deepened in hue towards the horizon. What she was seeing was no different than life itself; that things were always changing—it was inevitable. But with that change, there is still beauty. What was unfolding in front of her eyes served as a reminder of that.

How was it possible that a nine-year-old boy could teach her so much through a sunset?

Her phone buzzed beside her. She placed her mug down and took out her phone. As soon as she saw the email address she froze.

mglivingston79

Her heart began to pound in her chest and instantly, she felt lightheaded. She wasn't sure she wanted to open it, she was almost too scared to. She squeezed her eyes closed and tried to slow her breathing. She knew this moment would come but it didn't mean she was anywhere near ready for it. She couldn't be alone during a time like this. She couldn't do this alone, no way. Instead of reading it she dialled Daniel's number, even though he lived right around the corner. It went straight to voicemail. For the first time ever, he didn't pick up. She took a shaky breath and returned to where the unopened mail laid resting in her inbox.

She would have to do this without him.

With her heart racing a million miles an hour, she clicked into the email that had no title.

It was blank. Nothing. She stared at it as though somehow, by looking at it long enough, words would magically spring onto the page. Using her thumb, she scrolled down to find an attachment. She frowned as she opened it, taking her chances that it wasn't a virus.

It wasn't.

Instead, what she uncovered was the most beautiful thing she had ever received. It was a video. She inhaled a sharp breath, feeling her eyes prickle with tears as soon as she saw Nolan's face fill the screen.

He was alive.

Without pressing play she could see that it had been filmed in what looked like his bedroom. He was sitting on a beanbag with a chest of drawers on one side and a bookcase on the other. She could see the Roald Dahl boxset she had given him in clear view, neatly stacked in the top shelf closest to him. That made her smile. Other than looking tired, he appeared to be brighter than she had seen him in the hospital. Maybe he looked more himself because he was wearing his glasses. She didn't expect him to look so good which filled her with hope. Or a false sense of hope, she wasn't sure.

Was it possible he could fight this?

He was holding a diary or some kind of exercise book—she couldn't tell. She hit play and he opened it up and began to read.

'I'm not very good in front of crowds and for some reason making a video made me feel that same nervous feeling I get in my tummy when I read in front of the class.'

He looked up and adjusted his glasses and at the same time

pulled an apologetic face. He looked into the camera for a long while before returning his eyes to his page.

'It is important that I get this right, Miss Henderson, so I wrote it all down. I hope you don't mind because it means that I won't make eye contact with my audience and all those things you usually want us to do when we read aloud. I hope that's ok.'

He looked at the camera and let out a little chuckle. He looked nervous. She didn't know what was coming next but whatever it was, she had a feeling that it wasn't going to be easy for him to say.

'Thank you for reading to me every day and sending me those cool videos. I loved the story very much. My favourite part of the day was waiting for your email because it meant that I would be able to find out what came next. It was a super story and you made a great choice in picking that one to read to me. You're a very kind teacher, Miss Henderson. You have changed my world; did you know that? I know I sometimes worried you at school, I could see it in your eyes, but you never said anything. That's why you're so kind. You never said anything to hurt my feelings when some of the other kids did.'

With one hand, he took off his glasses and gave his eye a long rub. He placed them back on and shifted his weight around on the beanbag.

'If I could pick one super power I would chose the one where you go in a teleport machine and zoom to any place you want to go. I would take myself back to school even though I don't like school very much. But you were the best part of my day, Miss Henderson. You and my books. I hope it's ok that I had two favourite things. You were always so happy to see me because you're kind, Miss Henderson. I know I have told you that already but it's the truth and I don't tell untruths. You're the kindest person I have ever met.'

He placed the book down on the floor next to him and

wandered over to the screen. It was hard to tell if someone was filming it or if he had set the timer, but it didn't wobble as he moved near. He got so close to the lens so that all she could see was his face. He looked deep into the camera and blinked a couple of times. He was breathing so deeply in the microphone she almost had to turn the volume down. Perhaps there had been someone behind the camera because he lifted his eyes and nodded. He took a few slow steps back. Now that his whole body was in range, she could see him properly again.

'And now it's my time to be kind back. I don't want you to be upset with me so you have to promise not to be mad, ok? Remember at the hospital when I told you about all the thinking I have done? About all the beauty in the world and how one day I will see that for myself? I know you remember what I told you because you had your concentrating face on Miss Henderson, and that means that you remember.'

He carefully sat back down on the beanbag and picked up the book again. It took a moment for him to find where he was at but once he did, he placed his finger down on the page and stared at it for a long moment.

'By the time you get this video I will already be in the beautiful place I told you about. Please don't be sad, Miss Henderson, because I know I will be happy in that beautiful place and I won't be sick anymore. You have to believe me because I don't tell untruths, remember?'

His voice started to thicken, sounding less steady than it did before. He wasn't looking as intently at the screen anymore, in fact, he was avoiding it.

'I better go now; Miranda doesn't like it when I talk too much because I get too exhausted and sleep for ages. I just wanted to say thank you and

that you're the best teacher in the world. I will see you one day again, Miss Henderson. I know I will.

Bye for now. Love from Nolan Livingston.'

He closed the book at the same time she hit pause on the video. With her heart breaking, she stared out the window. By now the sunset had well and truly gone; she was sitting in complete darkness. Despite Nolan's wishes, heaving sobs penetrated her entire body as she mourned for the little boy who would no longer see the light of day.

She knew why Miranda hadn't written anything now—and knew why this particular email had been blank. The video spoke for itself.

Nolan was gone.

Twenty-five

It wasn't until five days later when it hit the hardest.

'Hi Sienna, it's Damian. Do you have a minute?'

She was pulling into her driveway at the time of his call. She turned off the engine and the Bluetooth speaker, and held her phone to her ear. 'Hi Damian, yes I do. How are you?'

They got the formalities out of the way relatively quickly. She knew he wasn't calling for a good old friendly chat, even though he was always up for one. They still hadn't discussed the obvious. The reason for the call.

Nolan.

She took the reins and told him the story from her school trip to Los Angeles, running into Miranda, her visit and the videos she recorded for Nolan in his final weeks.

Damian was bewildered.

'That is . . . far out. What are the chances, honestly! Of you being in the same place at the same time, halfway across the world?' he said, taking more of an interest in their meeting than anything else.

'I know,' Sienna responded, not wanting to think about it more than she had to. She was struggling enough as it was.

'I'm sorry I couldn't tell you what was going on when you came to see me.'

She knew it. She knew that he had known, but she couldn't be angry. It wasn't his place to speak of something so confidential.

'You don't need to apologise. You didn't have a choice.'

'Yeah, but I didn't enjoy holding it back from you. I want you to know that.'

All she could do was nod and stare out the window. The sun was strong, even this late in the afternoon. Now that the engine was off it was starting to heat up but she wasn't ready to interrupt her phone call by opening up the door.

'Saying that, I wanted you to know that I have heard from Miranda since Nolan's passing.'

Tears sprung in Sienna's eyes but she didn't flinch. Beads of sweat were beginning to form on the back of her neck but she let them build as she kept staring.

'Are you there, Sienna?'

'I'm here, sorry.' She wiped the sweat before it dripped down the back of her shirt and began to gather her things. She couldn't stay in here; it was already turning into a sauna.

'Nolan had a wish that Miranda followed through with.'

Sienna closed her eyes, remembering the wish he had for her, the one where he told her not to be sad and to trust him; trust that he was in a beautiful place. Why couldn't he just stay there and not be dragged back into conversation, back into this world?

'Sienna?'

'I'm here.'

'Nolan wanted to donate all of his books to our College's library, so that's what she has done. She is honouring that.' His voice twinged on the last part. He cleared his throat. 'They have been shipped. All one hundred and twenty-eight of them.'

Sienna brought her hand to her lips and inhaled a sharp breath. She opened her mouth but no words came out. The silence was quickly filled.

'I wanted to share that with you. I was really moved by that.' He cleared his throat again, making it obvious that he was affected by all of this too.

The nurturing side of her wanted to say something—anything would do so it could turn into a two-way conversation again. She opened the car door—it being the only way she could break the silence without having to use words. The breeze hit her face and she felt herself come more alive.

'It's really . . . beautiful. Thanks for letting me know,' she finally choked out. 'I hope the students appreciate them.'

But she knew they wouldn't. Hardly anyone knew the boy existed; he barely had a single friend. She had no doubt that his most prized possessions would sit on the shelves collecting dust as everyone carried on with their lives.

It was what made this whole thing even sadder.

There weren't many kids like Nolan; he was a rare breed. In her experience of teaching, she knew this to be true.

A few more words were spoken and the call ended. Sienna wondered how the family were doing—terribly, she imagined. She couldn't even begin to comprehend what it would be like to lose a child, let alone two. The funeral would be brutal for them. Maybe it had already happened, she didn't know. And she wouldn't know. Nolan's departing message was the last time she had any form of correspondence with Miranda. And she knew it would be the last. Her heart bled for his family; her heart filled with compassion for the woman whom she had judged so quickly. She had been wrong about her—she had been wrong about everything.

'I have another lap in me if you want to join?'

Sienna looked up to find Daniel panting in front of her, wearing the same work out outfit he always wore. He was sweating profusely, his thin wispy dark hair slicked to the side like some kind of comb over. There wasn't much of it but still it seemed to stay put. He was jogging on the spot, clearly not done with his session.

Sienna checked her letter box to find nothing inside. 'You put me to shame, you know that?'

'Only because you've missed a few days.'

'Or weeks.'

'Or that.' He wiped his brow and grinned. 'How fast can you change? I can only jog on the spot for so long.'

'I think I'll have to pass today.'

Daniel stopped jogging. 'What's going on?' He was beginning to know her now. He knew her well enough to know that she wasn't fine. She couldn't lie to him either. She had never felt the need to hold it all together around him in the past.

'The principal from my last school just called. Nolan has donated his entire book collection to the school. I can't . . .' she wanted to hold it together, but she couldn't.

Without asking if it was ok or not, Daniel put his arms around her. She didn't care that his top was damp with perspiration and by the looks of it, neither did he. His embrace was tight and reassuring as he pulled her body in close and with one hand, held the crown of her head against his neck. She felt safe. The tingly feeling began to take form in her belly again. Instead of saying anything that might stuff the moment up, she let the feeling expand and swell. But after a few moments of little movement and a whole lot of sweating, she felt the need to fill the stillness. This was the right time to let him know.

She pulled apart and slowly, he lowered his hand from her.

'Are you doing ok?' His eyes were full of concern. It made her want to jump back into his arms again, sweaty or not. It felt nice to be cared for.

'It's been a hard week,' she admitted.

He nodded and placed his hand on her shoulder. 'I know. I'm here, yeah?'

She could tell that he wasn't done touching her either. Was it possible that something was taking root between them, or was this his way of being a good friend?

It was too hard to know.

'Yeah, I know,' she said, noticing the tingly feeling again. 'I've been meaning to tell you. I wanted to do something for you because, well, you know, you've been there for me.'

Daniel's eyes changed. With his hand still on her shoulder, he gave it a little squeeze.

Sienna stood still, avoiding any movement that would detract from this moment. 'What are your plans Wednesday afternoon, two weeks from now?'

He stepped closer to her and extended his arm so that it wrapped around her shoulder.

Everything inside her body lit on fire. She must have looked rigid, too scared to move as she stood there enjoying the feeling perhaps, a little too much.

'Oh wow, very specific,' he joked. 'Nothing comes to mind. Why? What do you have planned for us?' He gave her a mischievous smile.

It was happening. She could tell that he was catching on. They could both feel it. Right?

'Well—' she slipped her arm around his waist and bumped hips with him, trying to find a casual way of getting even closer to him. 'You can't say no because I've already organised it.'

'So, I have no choice but to keep it free then?'

'Shut up.'

Daniel let out a belly full laugh. 'You know I'm only teasing you.'

Feeling lighter, she gave him a playful frown. 'Just as well.'

With his arm still around her, he gave her shoulder another gentle squeeze. What he said next made her heart feel as warm as the sun on her back.

'I'm all yours.'

Sienna couldn't help but grin at that. She looked away, not being able to hide it.

'You're blushing.'

'Oh, come on. Leave me alone.'

He laughed again but it came out awkward this time. 'I'm sorry.'

He released his arm and she wished she hadn't said anything.

Why did he take it away? She wanted his arm back! She let her own arm drop from his waist and turned to him, not caring that her cheeks were flushed. It was a warm day, after all. How could he actually tell that she was flushed when the sun was glaring in their faces? He was probably just teasing her, like he said.

'Anyway, like I was saying, I have organised something. We are kinda going to the ballet.'

Daniel's eyes came to life. 'The ballet?'

'Yes, a professional performance of *The Sleeping Beauty*, if you must know.'

'Are you serious?'

'No, I'm lying,'

'This is big,' he said. It was an odd thing for him to say and it made Sienna's stomach twist. She had been worried that her idea might have been too full on.

Maybe it had been.

'Oh,' was all she managed to say.

Daniel shook his head. 'No, not like that. I meant, for you.'

'For me?'

'You haven't been to the ballet since your injury . . . yeah?'

Sienna felt her body relax and fill with emotion at the same time. He remembered.

'No, you're right. I haven't . . . I haven't been in years.'

Daniel's eyes glassed over and she knew why. This was a breakthrough. For her, maybe for both of them.

He brought his lips close to her neck and whispered. 'If you're ready, I'm ready.'

For the rest of the night all she could think about was if there was more behind the five words than he let on.

It had been a long time since she had looked forward to something this much. It wasn't just about having the courage to watch the ballet company that had offered her a contract before injury struck—it was the fact that it felt like a date.

Whether or not they admitted it, it had been one.

They took her car but as soon as she saw him she had kind of wished they had taken the train. How was she supposed to drive when she couldn't keep her eyes off him?

He had dressed up for the occasion, some would say he was even a little over-dressed. Before that night Sienna had assumed he didn't have much of a fashion sense. Not that the super-ficial stuff ever really meant anything to her. It was simply an observation.

When he arrived at her place and knocked on her door she had been taken back. He was wearing a navy shirt and beige chino pants that drew attention to his toned legs that often hid behind the many pairs of shapeless pants he wore. He hadn't shaved for a couple of days and had a bit of facial hair going on. For some reason this highlighted his features, making them stand out for the first time, or at least stand out to her. She no longer noticed his thick, caterpillar eyebrows. Her attention danced between his glistening dark eyes and his teeth that were all of a sudden glowing white. Had he been using whitening strips? She hadn't noticed much about his mouth before. She hadn't thought about what it would be like to kiss him. But for the first time she found herself watching his mouth every time he looked at her. And he really did look at her.

She couldn't help but stare at him. He looked tan too. Maybe it wasn't the stubble at all. It could have been his sun-kissed skin that brought out all these details. Since when had he scored a tan? It was all very confusing. She had never observed him this close before, nor had she really studied how she felt in his company either.

Whether or not she could admit it, she was attracted to this man. She wondered if she was alone in that, she thought that maybe she was. Maybe that was the problem. She was alone, maybe even lonely. Daniel was the first person that had shown her any attention; consistent, undivided attention. But as far as she was aware, the man was still grieving his dead wife.

Maybe he was still in love with her. If he was, he simply wouldn't have the capacity to explore anything beyond that.

Life was too complicated to make sense of. Luckily the ballet gave her an escape from everything.

There was non-stop conversation on the drive up. It was a trip that in the past had been tedious with no bends, peaks or troughs in the road but this time, the drive seemed to have more character. With her eyes on the road, her mind was elsewhere. She was hopeful that Daniel would take her hand as she left one on her lap when both hands would normally take the wheel. He had two hours of opportunity to take hold of it, but his hands stayed reserved in his lap, seemingly taking no hint. And perhaps, no thought. The day had been young. She figured they still had the ballet to go, and then the drive back; maybe he was pacing himself, waiting for the right moment.

She was nervous stepping back into the theatre that had, not all that long ago, been her whole world. It was strange to experience a completely different set of emotions as they wove through the crowd. She no longer felt anxious as her eyes scanned the foyer to spot other dancers who had once been in competition with her. Going to the theatre back in the day had been a stressful experience as dancers stared at each other, sizing each other up, making god knows how many awful comments about who they saw. The whole ordeal served zero purpose and benefited no one. This time was different. As she walked in with Daniel by her side, she was walking in as an outsider who had no ties to any of it, and no one. She didn't have to worry about whether she was thin enough or be anxious that she would "run into" someone who would be kind to her face then betray her minutes later. For the first time she was able to go to the ballet and enjoy it the way it should be enjoyed.

As soon as the curtains opened she shifted her eyes to Daniel, not wanting to miss his first impression of the whole set up. She knew he would be blown away by the costumes, sets and the sheer precision of the dancers and musicians. She wasn't wrong. His jaw dropped open before the biggest smile took over, which she had come to realise, was quite a cute face.

He caught her looking at him and let out a hushed laugh. 'This is unbelievable!'

She wriggled her nose and gave him a knowing smile. 'You just wait.' She turned her eyes back to the stage, but she could feel his eyes still on her. 'Watch the ballet,' she said, keeping her eyes on the dancers that were bounding in. Her heart was racing, but she pretended to be oblivious to the fact that he was admiring her.

It took over an hour until he reached over and took her hand.

Sienna had to catch her breath as his fingers interlaced with hers. They felt soft and warm, bringing more magic to where she sat in her seat than the ballet could have done alone. She kept her eyes on the dancers, without really watching them. All she could focus on was what was going on inside her; fireworks and butterflies all at once. If it wasn't for the music she swore he would have heard her heart thumping in her chest.

All too soon the ballet ended and the dancers had taken their final curtain call. Daniel kept hold of her hand as they stood to their feet and formed a line to make their way back into the foyer. He didn't seem to be as shy as her as he went on about how amazing the whole thing was. Sienna was happy for him to do all of the talking, somehow losing all ability to act normally around him. If he noticed, he didn't say anything. But really, Sienna could tell that he was just as nervous as he couldn't stop talking. She had to stifle some laughs by the way his mouth rattled off way more than usual. They were both so awkward around each other and she loved it.

Sienna spotted a grand piano by the cloak room before they reached the escalator. She pulled on his hand. 'Look,' she pointed to where it stood vacant as the crowd was filing out far quicker than they had come in. 'Play something!'

Daniel raised an eyebrow and held her hand tighter so that she wouldn't drag him over there. 'Not today,' he laughed but he was hardly convincing.

Sienna pulled a face, pretending to be disappointed. 'Come on, please? It's just sitting there waiting for you.'

He shook his head again.

'Please? For me?' She gave him pleading eyes, knowing that this would be the moment when he would cave.

And she was right.

He loosened his grip, signalling his permission to be led over to it. There was a sticker on the side with the words *play me* which was all the confirmation they needed to make this happen. As soon as he reached the black velvet stool he released her hand and sat down. He positioned his hands over the slightly yellowed keys and looked up at her.

'What do you want me to play?' he asked, his eyes dancing. She could tell that he loved this, and with a simple command, would set the keys alight with any one of her recommendations. But being useless with titles and names of songs, her mind went completely blank.

She shrugged and smiled dreamily. 'I don't know. Surprise me.'

Daniel squinted his eyes as he gave it some thought. With a nod, he set his hands down on the keys, and began. It started off slowly, tentatively, but as it began to build he became more passionate about what his hands were doing, flying over every note with familiarity and ease. He was so into what he was doing, so focused on those keys he didn't even notice a crowd of people begin to form around the piano. Sienna stood to the side, not being able to wipe the smile off her face as people looked on in awe of his talent.

She felt as proud as punch.

Every now and then he would look up and give her a soft smile as his fingers worked on autopilot, not missing a single note. She hadn't expected herself to get emotional as she watched him play—but his music was so moving, it was impossible not to. There was something in his face that made her feel like the piece was completely dedicated to her.

Maybe it was even made for her.

As soon as he reached the final note there was a round of applause from his onlookers. She could tell that he was shy as he nodded in appreciation, as though he was taken aback that he had received any attention at all. This only made Sienna's heart flutter more. He was so humble. Even with his quiet confidence, she wasn't convinced that he knew just how gifted he really was.

An old woman stepped forward. 'That was beautiful, young man.'

Daniel smiled. 'Thank you so much, that's very kind of you.' The woman smiled back, her face bunching up with a hundred lines of wrinkles. She stretched out a quivering hand, and pointed to Sienna. 'You are lucky you have a man who can play like that, dear.'

Sienna's face grew warm. She didn't know what to say so she let out an embarrassed laugh in agreement. She didn't have the guts to look at Daniel, she was that embarrassed, but as soon as the crowd cleared it was evident that he wasn't done watching her squirm.

'I think she was jealous of you.'

Sienna let out a grunt. 'Oh, come on. Here I was thinking you didn't have an arrogant bone inside of you.'

Daniel stood from the stool and took her hand again. Just like that, the delightful combination of fireworks and butterflies began all over again.

'What was that piece?' she asked, trying to act completely calm with all of this going on inside her. 'Ólafur Arnalds?'

Daniel widened his eyes and pretended to look surprised. 'Oooooh, she knows her composers!'.

'I suppose I do listen to you every now and then.'

Daniel led her outside, exposing them to yet another glorious afternoon. There were a lot of people around, enjoying the sunshine at the surrounding restaurants, bars and cafes. She was looking forward to showing him around Southbank before they would join Jacqui and her fiancé for a dinner by the river. As soon as Jacqui heard that they would be making the trip she was adamant that they did something, considering that they had met, and she liked him. She promised she wouldn't make it weird and Daniel hadn't shown any hesitation when she asked him. In fact, he was completely up for it.

'So, was it?' Sienna pointed to a green patch of grass by the river. They walked over to it and sat down. 'Was it an Ólafur Arnolds piece?

Daniel folded up his legs, leaning back on his hands as he stared out ahead at the water. There was a mischievous smile on his face. 'No, it wasn't,' he said, still smiling.

Sienna waited for him to go on, but he didn't. 'Okkkkk,' she finally responded, knowing she wasn't going to get an answer.

Daniel looked at her and smoothed his lips together like he was withholding something. He seemed to be enjoying that she was getting frustrated with his cryptic response.

'What was it then?' she demanded.

Daniel laughed and gave her knee a little squeeze. He was

looking at her with the same expression he had when he was playing. Sienna's heart began to pound again.

Was he about to kiss her?

'It didn't come from anywhere. It . . .' He brought his face towards her. Sienna held her breath as her body responded and moved inwards.

'It doesn't have a name yet, but you could say it's a newly composed piece.'

'Inspired by emotion?'

'The best pieces always are.' Daniel inched his face closer to hers.

She could feel his breath on her face, the smell of his cologne under her nose.

'What inspired this piece?' she whispered, not daring to move.

With their lips hovering just inches from each other he slowly parted his mouth. 'You, Sienna.'

He gently brushed his finger along the base of her neck and without another thought, he brought his lips to hers.

'I wrote it for you.'

And just like that, she came completely undone.

Twenty-six
6 months later

'Now, that's a better pumpkin pie.'

Sienna pulled the dish from the oven and rested it on the cooling tray. She let out a little squeal. 'Babe, come here for a min. It's actually perfect!' She took a step back to take a look at the full picture. It was the right colour this time. Her eyes bulged as she squatted down low and examined it at eye level. 'It's round, completely levelled . . . and orange!'

'No wayyyyy, you're telling me that it's not sagging in the middle?' She heard Daniel's voice emerge from the lounge room. His eyes widened as he saw the pie stand upright without any support. He walked over to her and kissed the top of her head. 'Look at you, my little baker.'

Sienna beamed like a child. It certainly was an achievement. She raised an eyebrow. 'Let's hope it behaves in the car.'

Daniel leaned against the bench and studied it with a massive smile on his face. 'It really is perfect! Look at how golden that crust is!' He pulled her in close and ran his hand along her back. 'Are you going to do the cream thing or not worry about it, do you think?'

Sienna presented the piping bag like she was revealing a bunny out of a magician's hat. 'One hundred percent. When you do a job, you do it properly.'

'So domesticated you are.'

Sienna laughed. 'Don't get too excited, this could be a one off yet.'

'Either way, you look great in my kitchen.'

'Do I?' She gave him a little spin and opened and shut her fingers inside the oven mittens as though they were puppets having a chat.

He pulled the mittens off and wrapped his hands around her neck. 'I could get used to this,' he murmured and kissed her lips.

Sienna had never felt so joyful. Their relationship had been an unexpected surprise. But she had begun to realise, the best kind of surprises always were. Life was funny like that. It has a way of working things out, finding ways to fit the broken pieces together to make something beautiful in its time.

'How is your music coming along?'

Since the documentary a few months ago, work had begun to roll in from all directions. As soon as Daniel's music was out there in the open, so was his name. In no time at all he was being approached by both Juilliard and Charlton to compose more works for their marketing projects. Luckily, with his set up at home it meant that he didn't have to fly in and out to complete these projects, although Sienna wouldn't complain if it came to that. Right now, he was working on a compilation video for Juilliard's summer school. For every project he undertook, he was given access to all the footage from various dancers and musicians. Sienna loved that she got to see all the raw files of all the incredible artists, giving her a regular dose of inspiration while giving her ideas for her own classes.

Daniel pulled her in close, his face lighting up at the very mention of the word. 'Goooood. I think it's almost ready to submit. I'm pretty chuffed.'

'Ha!'

Daniel gave her an eyebrow and held her tighter. 'Leave me alone. Yes, "chuffed"!'

'Well, aren't you a clever boy'.

'As are you, my dear. Look at that thing!' He took another look at the pie and picked up the piping bag. 'Do you trust me?'

Sienna laughed as she watched him bring it down to decorate the cake. 'Go for your life.'

With a steady hand he pointed it down vertically to make a perfect little swirl of cream on top. 'How did I go?'

'Do you want to take over?'

Daniel laughed. 'I wouldn't want to take credit for this masterpiece.'

'Because it all comes down to the decoration on top?'

'Exactly.'

'Pass it over then.' She took the piping bag off him and mimicked his action to create an identical shape next to his.

'When were you thinking we should leave?'

Sienna squinted as she got down at eye level with the pie and continued the pattern with the cream. 'Pretty much once this is done we can go, baby. Is twenty minutes ok?'

'Sounds good. I've nearly finished up for the day so I'll find something to put on and we can go.' He kissed her forehead again and wandered back into the lounge room. In just seconds the sweet sound of music filled the air. It often filled his house, but not once did Sienna take it for granted.

She couldn't picture the day when she would.

Like clockwork, with a pie in hand, they were ready to go exactly twenty minutes later. Like her, he was punctual and all about the details. When she thought about it, they were similar in so many ways. He was basically the guy version of her, putting aside the fact she couldn't play any instruments, and before today's baking success, unlike him, wasn't that great in the kitchen.

As she waited for him by the door while he grabbed a jacket, she glanced at the photo frames that ornamented the walls of his hallway. A lot had changed over the past few months. But time had a way of doing that. His wife would always be loved, would always be remembered. They were memories that no one could take away, nor did Sienna want to. It was Daniel's idea to replace the frames, to fill them with new memories, their own memories.

So that was what he did.

Every time they walked down the hall, the past no longer held a place in their present. Instead, their present gave them a glimpse into what their future had the potential to become.

In just six months they had shared so much together, memories exuding from the walls, forever reflecting the joy that had become the very essence of their beautiful partnership. From Jacqui's engagement party, to their ambitious hike in the Grampians, to the full makeover of Daniel's garden; the photos captured the seasons beautifully. She could barely recognise herself when she stared at them, which was often. There was something different in her eyes that stood out, even to her—different than any photo she had seen of herself in the past.

For the first time in a long time, her smile reached her eyes. Sienna stood directly underneath where they hung on the wall and studied them closer. She was wrong, it went beyond that. There was joy in every part of her body; a joy that basically leaped from the frame.

Even though the photos had been replaced, the photos of Daniel's late wife had been honoured. Sienna had compiled a scrapbook of them that now rested on his bookshelf, serving as a reminder of a love that had tragically come to an end, before a new one had been found. They were both carrying scars, burdens from their past that would take time to heal, there was no doubt about it. But they would heal together, and in time, they would be whole again. Until then, they would ride this journey together.

Daniel met her at the door and gave her a knowing smile as he followed her glance. He didn't even have to ask to know what was responsible for making her smile. He knew. She knew that he knew because she often caught him doing the same thing.

Sienna's Sunday tradition with the family had continued; only this time, there was another member added to the mix.

Actually, there were two: Daniel being the first, followed by the most recent addition to the family—Elijah James Parkes.

Just two months ago Mia had given birth to the most beautiful baby boy. Sienna couldn't get enough of him, often making a second visit throughout the week to dote over her little nephew.

Daniel adored him just as much, quickly being labelled "the horse whisperer" but the baby version. It was an ongoing joke that whenever Elijah was in his arms, he would smile and cosy into Daniel's chest as though he was sedated—calm and content. But as soon as Sienna took hold of him, Elijah would wiggle his legs ballistically before letting out a piercing cry. She was amazed his little lungs were capable of making such a traumatic sound. Now every time they went over there, Sienna would entertain Bailey as Daniel looked after Elijah. It was a good system, it worked. Her sister loved it; it was like a free pass for her. Well, for a couple of hours anyway. It didn't stop there, either. Daniel wasn't repulsed by the satay-textured poo that often sprayed halfway up the infant's back. So much so that he willingly helped Lance change him on many occasions, nailing the art of changing the never-ending diaper.

From that first visit, Daniel won them over. Mia probably appreciated him the most. She thought it was rare to find a guy that was so into all the baby stuff. Apparently, most men find it hard to connect with babies until their personalities come through months later when they're capable of more than just the "eat, poo, sleep" cycle. Her sister had been the one to give him the nickname. Daniel would humbly shrug it off, but Sienna knew he secretly loved it. She couldn't be happier that he was so warmly received by her family, not just because of how good he was with kids, but because of how good he was with her. It was obvious that they were completely smitten with each other, even though she was conscious to tone it back whenever they were in her family's company.

Mia was quick to discourage that. 'You don't have to overthink it, Sienna,' she said one Sunday afternoon. 'For too long we've watched you hold back like you were some kind of prisoner to yourself. Those days are over now.'

Sienna smiled. 'Do you think they're finally over?' It was hardly a question as they both stood in the kitchen and watched Daniel blend into their family like a piece of furniture that had always been there. With Elijah in his arms and Bailey squealing with excitement as she hung from his back, it was obvious.

'Yes,' Mia said, having kept her eyes ahead as she had watched the scene unfold. 'I think you know it, too. You're finally home, sis.'

As they took the four steps to the front door, Sienna took a moment to breathe in. It may have been a Sunday like any other, but this time, her breath signified more than just a need for oxygen.

For the first time, she breathed life.

The days were getting cooler now that winter was setting in, but it didn't diffuse the warmth inside her chest that made her feel like it was summer all year long.

Maybe that was what love felt like.

Real love. A love that had the potential of having a depth that surpassed every level and penetrated every layer.

Mia was right—she had found her home.

She turned her head to admire the man that stood firm by her side; the man who had pursued her through every season. He held the pumpkin pie in one hand, and held her close with the other. With a tender smile, he lowered his chin and planted a kiss on her forehead, the way he always did. With the wind cool on her face, and her heart growing warmer by the minute, she reached forward and gave the little silver bell a ring, remembering the words a little boy with ginger hair had once taught her.

Beauty really was everywhere.

Thank you for taking the time to read my novel!

I really appreciate all of your feedback, and
I love hearing what you have to say.
Please leave me a helpful review on Amazon and Goodreads
letting me know what you thought of this novel.
I am truly grateful!

Jessica

Acknowledgments

After receiving an overwhelming response from my readers with my debut novel *Nine Years,* I knew I had to write quickly to bring Sienna Henderson's long-winded journey to a close.

I would like to say a big thank you to my wonderful editor Dominic for your professionalism and sheer brilliance at what you do. It was such a pleasure to work with you.

Much love to my parents who watched me isolate for months on end as I locked myself up in their gazebo during my visits to finish this story. I promise to be more present the next time I come up!

I must say a special and affectionate thank you to my wonderful friends for their unwavering encouragement and support. Your belief in me has warmed my heart.

Finally, to my loyal readers – It is because of you that I dare to dream. It is because of you the pages continue to turn.

Love and light,

Jessica

About the Author

Jessica is a school teacher,
former fitness professional and dancer. She
is originally from Bendigo, Victoria. *Nine Years* and
Here I Stand form the two-part series
Beneath the Clouds.

jessleed.com
facebook.com/jessicaleedauthor
@jessicaleedauthor (Instagram)

Check out *Nine Years*, the first book of Jessica Leed's two-part series *Beneath the Clouds*.

www.ingramcontent.com/pod-product-compliance
Lightning Source LLC
Chambersburg PA
CBHW050033120726
47903CB00006B/2015